IMPERIAL LACE

'I am sorry, Miss Challis, for showing unwarranted pride, yet I do feel . . .'

'No doubt,' her Companion interrupted her, 'you will be, once properly chastised. Come, this bench will do admirably.'

'Here!' Thrift gasped. 'No, Miss Challis, you cannot!'

'To the contrary,' Miss Challis answered, seating herself, 'it is my duty.'

Thrift stayed where she was, in the middle of the path. She was burning with consternation, blushing furiously, and shaking. To go down voluntarily across her Companion's lap in the park was something she simply could not bring herself to do.

'Thrift, come now,' Miss Challis said gently, patting her lap.

'Miss . . . Miss Challis . . .' Thrift stammered. 'I beg you, no! There are Gentlemen in view!'

To Klesch, for the original concept

IMPERIAL LACE

Lady Alice McCloud

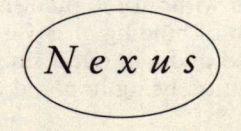

Nexus

This book is a work of fiction.
In real life, make sure you practise safe, sane and consensual sex.

First published in 2003 by
Nexus
Thames Wharf Studios
Rainville Road
London W6 9HA

Copyright © Lady Alice McCloud 2003

The right of Lady Alice McCloud to be identified as the Author of this Work has been asserted by her in accordance with the Copyright, Designs and Patents Act 1988.

www.nexus-books.co.uk

Typeset by TW Typesetting, Plymouth, Devon

Printed and bound by
Clays Ltd, St Ives PLC

ISBN 0 352 33856 3

All characters in this publication are fictitious and any resemblance to real persons, living or dead, is purely coincidental.

This book is sold subject to the condition that it shall not, by way of trade or otherwise, be lent, resold, hired out or otherwise circulated without the publisher's prior written consent in any form of binding or cover other than that in which it is published and without a similar condition including this condition being imposed on the subsequent purchaser.

You'll notice that we have introduced a set of symbols onto our book jackets, so that you can tell at a glance what fetishes each of our brand new novels contains. Here's the key – enjoy!

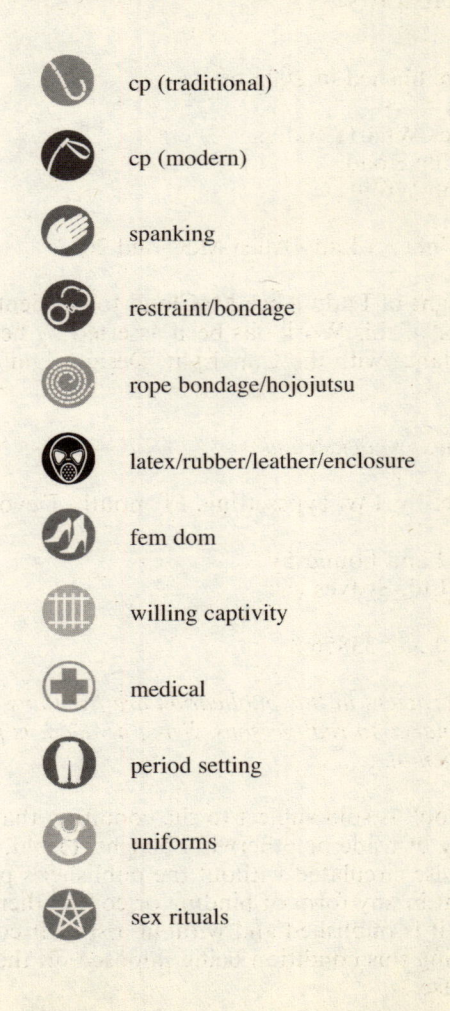

- cp (traditional)
- cp (modern)
- spanking
- restraint/bondage
- rope bondage/hojojutsu
- latex/rubber/leather/enclosure
- fem dom
- willing captivity
- medical
- period setting
- uniforms
- sex rituals

1

London, March 2004

Thrift cried out in indignant shock as she was bundled expertly across her Governess's knee. Her arm was twisted into the small of her back. Her nightie was hauled high to expose her modesty gown. Her modesty gown was hauled high to expose her pyjamas. Her pyjama seat was hauled open to expose her bottom.

It was a sequence of motions rapid, matter-of-fact and well practised, each exposure adding a new pang to her sense of embarrassment until with her bare bottom showing it had become a physical pain. Ready, she screwed her eyes up in miserable anticipation of the spanking to come. Nothing happened, save for Miss Challis's hand coming to rest lightly on her naked flesh. The Governess spoke.

'On second thoughts, perhaps not. It would hardly do to have you arrive on your first day with your face streaked with tears.'

'No, Miss Challis,' Thrift answered quickly as relief flooded through her.

'Then I shall postpone your spanking,' Miss Challis stated.

Much of Thrift's relief disappeared, to be replaced by chagrin. She made to get up, but the grip on her twisted arm did not weaken, holding her firmly in place.

'May I rise, please, Miss Challis?' she asked.

'I think not,' the Governess replied. 'You will remain exposed for a while, for the sake of your humility.'

Thrift slumped back down, red faced, her tears heavy in her eyes. Outwardly motionless, inside she was writhing in an agony of embarrassment for her position. She was, she knew, supposed to reflect on the sins that had brought her to so humiliating a state, but it was impossible. She could concentrate on nothing but the fact that her bottom was bare, while the fact that she had been bared for not leaving a small portion of her breakfast kipper on the side of her plate brought on only indignant self-pity. It just wasn't fair, a punishment out of all proportion to her crime, to have to endure the agony of physical exposure merely because she was born to a respectable station in life. Vexation was added to the jumble of her emotions as the Governess began to stroke her bottom.

'Miss Challis, please!' she protested.

'Hush, Thrift,' Miss Challis said gently and went on stroking, her hand moving gently over the contours of Thrift's bottom, to follow each ripe curve and gentle dip.

Thrift took the exploration of her bottom in stolid silence, trying to ignore the tickling sensation and the slow build-up of warmth between her thighs. Finally Miss Challis drew a deep sigh, stopped, gave a gentle pat on the crest of each buttock and spoke.

'Some day, my darling Thrift, you will make some lucky gentleman an admirable wife, at least, if you can bring yourself to bear in mind how to behave as a Lady should. Now, what should we remember?'

'Always leave one for Mr Manners,' Thrift answered sullenly, and squeaked as her bottom was slapped again, this time hard.

'Do not be ungracious!' Miss Challis snapped. 'Why, many people in the colonies never so much as see a kipper their entire lives.'

'Yes, Miss Challis, sorry, Miss Challis,' Thrift responded hastily, forcing herself to sound repentant.

'That is better,' Miss Challis went on, 'but you must learn. Rest assured that I shall continue to punish you, Thrift, until the day it becomes the responsibility of your husband. Now, up with you, and get dressed; we have a busy day.'

Her wrist released, Thrift scrambled hastily off Miss Challis's lap, at the same instant snatching back to cover her bottom, losing her balance and instead sitting down on it, hard. As Miss Challis suppressed a chuckle, Thrift found her face redder than ever. Climbing quickly to her feet, she covered herself and ran behind the dressing screen.

Everything she needed was laid out, the various brushes and pastes for her ablutions and those clothes appropriate to her age, or rather the age she had been the day before. She began to undress, her embarrassment at her body growing as she shrugged off her nightie and modesty gown, and declining only a little as she pulled on her white rubber bathing gown. It grew worse again as she wriggled out of her pyjamas and pushed them down off her feet, careful never to expose her knees or elbows. Nude beneath her bathing gown, her face was warm as always, although the embarrassment was nothing compared to the agonies of being bared for spanking.

Stepping into the broad porcelain washing trough, she pulled the rubber curtain to behind her and began to wash, leaving the awkward bits until last, her breasts, bottom and the unnamably rude bulge of split, puffy flesh between her thighs. Washing each brought her embarrassment higher, until by the time she was washing the soap from the fleshy folds and crevices of her unmentionable she was scarlet with blushes and mumbling prayers in her head. It never got any easier, and recently the impossibly improper feelings touching herself brought had been growing stronger, bringing to her the horrible conviction that she might be wilful, even wanton.

Clean, she dried herself as fast as she could without risking the exposure of her legs and arms and stepped from the trough. She applied powder and scent, then turned to her clothes. Miss Challis had selected a beautiful pair of drawers, heavy silk with six layers of lace trim, with blue Morning Glory flowers embroidered at the legs and waist and the rear panel held up with no less than a dozen ivory buttons.

As she pulled them on her embarrassment began to fade again, and further as she added her chemise, her three petticoats of cotton, flannel and taffeta, her underdress and the gown of richly embroidered forest green silk Miss Challis had selected. Stockings, gloves, boots, ladyspats completed her attire, and as she stepped from behind the screen she picked up her bonnet. Miss Challis cast a critical eye over her, then spoke.

'Yes, I think so. Indeed yes, a credit to your station, family and the Empire, or at least, you will be shortly. First I must do something about that hair, then to the establishment of Madames Cantlemere and Lucas, in Piccadilly, where your corset and bustle are to be collected.'

Miss Challis had remained on the straight-backed wooden chair in which she had sat to administer the spanking. Thrift took her prayer stool from beneath the bed and placed it at Miss Challis's feet, feeling rather childish as she knelt to have her hair done in the new style. The Governess was quick, looping Thrift's luxurious auburn curls into a soft bun, pinning it in place and slipping the jewelled net on to hold it, a task it would have taken Thrift twice as long to do half as well.

Ten minutes later, having greeted her mother in the drawing room, she was stepping out into Dover Street.

London was as ever, the morning typical of the English spring. The street sweepers, delivery men and gardeners of the night were long gone, leaving the granite of the pavements glistening wet from the light shower before dawn, the discreet shops well stocked with their produce laid out in the windows, the baskets hung from each lamppost bright with flowers.

After taking Miss Challis's arm, Thrift allowed herself to be steered down the street, to where it opened on to Piccadilly, with Green Park to the side, bright with purple and yellow crocuses against the verdant green of the grass. Few people were about, those who worked in the government departments and Imperial service offices already indoors, and the strollers and riders not yet out.

As they turned east into the main thoroughfare, a gentleman passed and tipped his hat. Thrift, recognising him, made a polite curtsey in response, but was forced to suppress a giggle as they passed on. His suit, while of respectable cut, had been brown, and, more amusing still, so had his boots, while his spats had not only been a pale tan, but patterned. Most comical of all had been his hat, a brown felt fedora. It was impossible to resist a remark as soon as they were safely out of earshot.

'How comical Mr Sullivan-Jones does look, my dear Miss Challis!'

'He is an artist,' Miss Challis replied, herself attempting to hide her amusement, 'but yes, one might wish he would dress in more conventional attire, at least within the Quality Enclave.'

They paused at the entrance to Bond Street to allow the sleek black bulk of an Austin Baron to turn noiselessly into the road, and Miss Challis spoke again as they reached the far side, in a quiet undertone.

'Naturally, my dear, within the Diplomatic Enclave you may expect to see styles of dress more unusual by far, fantastical even. The Soviets, as I understand it, actually wear trousers.'

'Why should that be thought peculiar?' Thrift asked, flushing slightly at the mention of a male garment.

'The Ladies,' Miss Challis replied.

'The Ladies wear trousers?' Thrift demanded in a disbelieving hiss.

'So I am given to understand,' Miss Challis answered her and gave Thrift a look that conveyed both disapproval and amused contempt.

Thrift shook her head, sure that her Governess was making a joke. The idea was absurd. Then again, Miss Challis never told a lie, even in jest.

They had reached the premises of Madames Cantlemere and Lucas. It was a triple-bayed shop decorated in the traditional black and gold of the Enclave, yet unusually discreet in that no trade was advertised, while the three broad windows were closed off by heavy drapes of rich, old-gold plush, each embroidered with the name of the establishment. Reaching the door, Miss Challis gave the bell a single, fastidious push. It swung open immediately, a tiny woman in black bombazine curtseying as she ushered them in. Miss Challis immediately adopted an air of haughty politeness, which Thrift struggled to imitate.

Within, the shop was no less discreet than it appeared from the street. Directly in front of them was a wide counter of brilliantly polished wood, behind which rose tier after tier of square drawers, each numbered and labelled after some cryptic system that meant nothing whatever to Thrift. A tall wooden modesty screen barred access to the rest of the shop. Another woman stood behind the counter, somewhat taller than the first, and also dressed entirely in black. She too curtseyed, greeting them.

'Good morning, Miss Challis. Good morning, Miss Moncrieff, if I may presume?'

'You may,' Miss Challis answered before Thrift could respond. 'I trust Lady Moncrieff's order is ready?'

'Indeed so, Miss,' the woman replied. 'Please step this way. Jane.'

The smaller of the two women moved quickly forward to open a panel in the screen. Miss Challis stepped through, Thrift following, to find herself in a long, high room, furnished as was the outer room, with banks of labelled drawers, also several screens which appeared to conceal alcoves. Light came in from a row of tall windows, each protected by a modesty curtain although all that could be seen beyond was the roof of the building opposite and a great deal of sky.

'May I offer you refreshment, Miss Challis?' the woman asked. 'Tea, coffee, a little Sack or laudanum?'

'Thank you, no,' Miss Challis answered. 'Miss Moncrieff and I are somewhat pressed for time.'

The woman curtseyed and went on, 'I shall fetch Madame Cantlemere directly.'

She disappeared through a door, only to return almost immediately behind a tall, stately woman and carrying two objects, both heavily wrapped in white tissue paper.

'Madame Cantlemere,' Miss Challis addressed the newcomer, making a carefully measured curtsey as she spoke. The tall woman responded in kind, then turned to Thrift.

'It is a pleasure to have your custom, Miss Moncrieff. As you no doubt know, it has been the privilege of our establishment to serve your family for five generations now, both here and in Edinburgh. Please be assured that we shall do everything in our power to provide satisfaction to the sixth.'

'Thank you, Madame Cantlemere, most gracious,' Thrift replied, pleased by the formidable woman's unctuous manner.

'Pride is unseemly in a young Lady,' Miss Challis remarked quietly as they were ushered into one of the screened alcoves.

The alcove was deep and tall, with a padded bench set against the semicircular wall. Miss Challis sat down as Madame Cantlemere took the first of the two packages from Jane, speaking as she began to unwrap it.

'If you would be so good as to disrobe, please, Miss Moncrieff.'

'Disrobe?' Thrift answered in sudden shock, the blood automatically rising to her face.

'An unfortunate necessity,' Madame Cantlemere went on, 'for the fitting of your corset, you will understand.'

'But to disrobe . . .' Thrift began.

'There is no impropriety involved, Thrift,' Miss Challis interrupted. 'You need merely slip off your gown, underdress and petticoats, no more.'

Thrift found herself blushing furiously at the mention of such intimate garments as her petticoats in front of strangers, but there was an all-too-familiar note of warning in the Governess's voice. With trembling fingers she began to unfasten the buttons at the front of her dress as all three women gave pointed attention to the series of pastoral prints that decorated the walls.

Stripped to her chemise and drawers, she found herself shaking so hard that she was forced to clasp her hands together to hide it, while she knew her face would be a rich scarlet. None of the women took any notice, Madame Cantlemere alone paying her attention, and that to run a critical eye over her figure as she held up the long satin corset. It reached from Thrift's neck down to her ankles, starting and ending in layered lace, with steel fastenings running down the length of the front at one inch intervals. It was made up of an intricate system of panels and lacing, sculpted to her body or designed to enhance it towards the fashionable ideal, with her bosom thrust out as a single full curve, her waist reduced to a wasp-like constriction and her back pulled into an elegant concavity. The original measurements had been taken by Miss Challis a fortnight before, another excruciatingly embarrassing incident.

'If you would care to step into your corset, Miss Moncrieff?' Madame Cantlemere asked.

Thrift blushed deeper still at the realisation that she had been staring dumbly at the thing and extended her arms, allowing Madame Cantlemere and Jane to slip the corset on to them and pull it tight at the front. As the two women began to close the fastenings, she found her breath forced out, although the whalebone cage encasing her breasts left them feeling oddly full and heavy, but unrestricted. It was the same with her hips, the rear bulge leaving her bottom free within, and feeling oddly exposed in comparison with her waist and thighs. Jane ducked down to complete the fastenings, which ended halfway down Thrift's calves, leaving her with no more than six inches of movement for her feet. Stepping back, Madame Cantlemere gave a satisfied nod, then spoke.

'I shall tighten the laces, Jane. Miss Challis, perhaps if you would be good enough to assist in holding Miss Moncrieff?'

The Governess nodded without speaking and rose, to take a firm grip on Thrift's shoulders. Jane ducked down, clasping Thrift's legs as Madame Cantlemere stepped around to take hold of the lacing, and tug. Thrift grunted at the sudden pressure, and was forced to pull her stomach in hard. Madame Cantlemere's fingers moved to her neck and began to walk down the lacing, tightening each cross one at a time, until she once more reached Thrift's waist, and tugged. Again Thrift grunted.

'Really!' Miss Challis exclaimed. 'Thrift, we are in company. Do attempt to show a little decorum.'

'It hurts, Miss Challis!' Thrift complained as once more Madame Cantlemere's fingers began to walk down her spine.

'Silence!' Miss Challis hissed. 'You may be a Lady now, but you are not above being taken across my knee, here and now.'

Thrift bit her lip as her face went purple with shame, determined not to speak and so give Miss Challis the excuse to dish out a spanking in front of the shopkeepers. For all the long lectures on the benefits of her exposure to her senses of humility and contrition, and on how it was unavoidable, she was sure Miss Challis actually enjoyed doing it, a thought impossible to speak aloud.

Jane rose, and a tape measure was wrapped quickly around Thrift's waist.

'Twenty and one half inches,' Madame Cantlemere remarked. 'We might, I venture to hope, aim for eighteen.'

'Seventeen,' Miss Challis answered. 'It is her mother's wish.'

'And quite the thing, I'm sure,' Madame Cantlemere hastily corrected herself.

Thrift shook her head as the laces were tied off behind her back. She was feeling a little faint and also dizzy, the room around her seeming somehow less real than it had a moment before. As Madame Cantlemere ducked down to tighten the lacing around her thighs, she was forced to reach out and steady herself on the wall, and the women's voices seemed to be coming from a great distance as they continued their conversation.

'For what is necessary,' Madame Cantlemere was saying, 'the rear panel may be released by a simple twist of these gudgeons, here and here. The panel may then be taken up and fastened to the bustle by means of these laces. Thus her drawers may be unbuttoned at leisure.'

Thrift felt her face flush hotter still as the technique was demonstrated, with the boned panel covering her bottom unfastened and lifted to expose the seat of her drawers. If anything her feelings were stronger than when she had been across Miss Challis's knee and ready for spanking, but with the Governess's next words they became abruptly worse.

'Yes, I see. Efficient, I do not doubt, for purposes of hygiene, but what of chastisement? She could be spanked, yes, but what of the efficient application of a cane?'

'You would seem to have come to the seat of the problem, Miss Challis, if I may be excused my little joke,' Madame Cantlemere replied.

Miss Challis stiffened slightly but made no reply. Madame Cantlemere continued.

'It is true that modern designs leave less scope for the application of appropriate chastisement, as the cage has an unfortunate tendency to protect the buttocks. However, there is a solution, of which you may inform the appropriate persons. Rather than stroke across the buttocks, strike down or up, standing directly behind. Alternatively, simply have Miss Moncrieff lie on her back upon a suitable table rather than adopt the customary bending position. Thus the cage lifts, allowing the bottom to protrude in such a way that the stroke of the cane in is no way incommoded. Possibly I might demonstrate?'

'No!' Thrift squealed, her manners forgotten on the instant in the face of such a terrifying and improper threat.

'Mind your manners, Thrift,' Miss Challis snapped back, 'or I might be tempted to take Madame Cantlemere up on her offer. No, Madame, I fear there is not the time, besides which, she is to take up her place at the Diplomatic School today and I would not wish her to arrive flustered. She has very little self-control.'

Madame Cantlemere responded with an understanding inclination of her head and closed the bottom panel. A sudden prickling sensation ran over Thrift's skin and she found her breathing tighter still. Sure that she was going to faint, she steadied herself against the wall and shut her eyes. The three women ignored her and when the weak spell had passed she found them inspecting the second package.

'... in this style,' Madame Cantlemere was explaining, 'which we hope to persist for the summer at least, the effect is no more protuberant than before, yet on the central line there is the merest hint of that partition which graces us all.'

'This is the fashion?' Miss Challis queried with a note of asperity in her tone.

'As advanced by the Duchess of Saxe,' Madame Cantlemere replied.

'A most daring innovation,' Miss Challis went on, her disapproval gone on the instant. 'You are privileged, Thrift.'

'Yes, Miss Challis,' Thrift answered as the bustle was pressed against her, the whalebone cage fitting snugly to her lower back and hips.

As she knew, it would flare out behind her, in a way that had always reminded her of the faintly ridiculous position in which pigeons sometimes held their tails, and would support her skirts to vastly exaggerate the size and rotundity of her bottom. It gave her body the S-shaped curve seen as the ideal of the female form, yet as it was fastened tightly around her belly and hips it was impossible to dispel the nagging thought that it would simply make her look ridiculous. She also knew that it could be inverted to provide easier access to her bottom for spanking.

With her bustle in place Jane helped her to dress once more, the large mirror on one wall allowing her to watch as she was transformed from a girl in an embarrassing state of undress to a Lady of obvious wealth and refinement. The bustle made her bottom look absolutely huge, while the depression in the whalebone made it worse, as if her gown really did conceal two monstrous buttocks. Despite that, it was impossible not to feel a certain pride, and to compare herself with Miss Challis, who might have charge over her, but was now plainly her social inferior.

Only when Miss Challis had signed for the order and they were ready to leave the shop did Thrift discover just how restrictive her new clothes were. It was impossible to walk in steps of more than six inches, forcing her to totter on her heeled boots, while even outside in the cool spring morning she quickly began to feel hot.

Not daring to remark on her discomfort, she concentrated on walking with as much grace as she could muster, speaking what was in her mind only when she was sure she was not about to fall flat on her face.

'What dreadfully vulgar people. The words that woman used, and where she put her hands! I do believe she has no sense of propriety whatsoever.'

'They are tradespeople, my dear Thrift,' Miss Challis replied, 'and besides, if they do seem to take liberties, it is only within the commission of their work. Such things must be tolerated, and are best approached with an attitude of Christian charity.'

'But to suggest I be beaten!' Thrift blurted out, unable to hold back her outrage any longer.

'I was tempted to do so,' Miss Challis answered.

'In front of them? A shopkeeper and her assistant!'

'Yes, why ever not? False pride is not becoming in a Lady, Thrift.'

'But I have done nothing to deserve it!'

'True,' Miss Challis admitted, although her tone implied that it was irrelevant, 'but I don't know why you are making such a fuss over a beating that never happened.'

Thrift pursed her lips, knowing it was true. Twice that morning she had escaped, and to argue was more likely to make sure what she dreaded happened than to soothe her ruffled feelings. Returning along Piccadilly, they had reached the entrance to Dover Street once more. After crossing the road, they made their way past the fine marble pavilion that covered the entrance to Green Park and Stratton Street Underground Railway Station. Two stolid policemen were on guard at the top of the steps as always, to watch for inappropriate people attempting to gain access to the Quality Enclave. Both nodded politely.

As they walked along the side of Green Park, she grew slowly more confident of her balance. At last she dared to look up, towards the Wellington Arch at the end of Piccadilly, and beyond that the colossal bulk of the Empire Tower, two thousand feet of black-painted steel rearing to the cupola so far above that it seemed to hang directly over her head.

Crossing Wellington Place, they made their way to the high gates of ornate iron that closed off Grosvenor Crescent and the Diplomatic Enclave. Miss Challis went to a window set low in the wall of a neighbouring building, leaving Thrift to admire the view. A sentry stood to one side, a guardsman, motionless in his scarlet jacket, his eyes never so much as moving as Thrift stole a nervous glance at the solid, muscular shape of his torso. Just to have so obviously virile a male so near sent a thrill of exquisite fear the length of her spine, but a glance from Miss Challis threatened something more frightening still and she quickly turned her eyes to the gates instead.

The black iron railings were twisted into a baroque design, the complexities of which she could remember following as a child as she and one or another of her Nannies and Governesses had waited for her father at the same gates. More fascinating still were the shields and emblems, each representing one of those countries whose embassies lay within. Even the names had always seemed magical, conjuring images of strange peoples with peculiar and barbaric customs: Liechtenstein, France, Bavaria, the Soviet Socialist Republic.

The last had one of the simplest emblems, a circular plaque with a yellow hammer and sickle crossed on a field of bright red. Vaguely she was aware that it represented government by members of the working classes, for all the obvious absurdity of the idea. Yet, if Miss Challis was to be believed, the women of the Republic wore trousers, something no less absurd. Then there was the extraordinary vulgarity of the Liechtensteiners, who, or so she had overheard her father say, discussed money openly, even the Ambassador himself, as if it were a proper subject for people of quality. By contrast, the French, with their comic eating habits, or the Bavarians, with their peculiar pointed hats, seemed quite normal.

At last the gate swung open, its bulk moved noiselessly by the agency of underground machinery, something of which Thrift was aware, as she had seen repairs being carried out, but which she also knew involved engineering and was therefore inappropriate to both her status and her sex. Miss Challis took her arm once more as they began to walk down the gentle curve of Grosvenor Crescent. A man hurried past, definitely a man, as he had long moustaches and was stark bald, yet he was wearing a dress of brilliant yellow silk with a quite fantastical dragon embroidered in vivid colours: scarlet, viridian, lapis blue.

'Do not stare, Thrift,' Miss Challis remarked. 'He is clearly foreign, and cannot be expected to have an understanding of propriety.'

'But a dress, Miss Challis?' Thrift whispered.

Miss Challis merely gave a low cough and when she spoke again it was on a different subject.

'As you are no doubt aware, Thrift, my educational responsibilities to you cease as of today. Once I have handed you over to Lady Newgate, I will no longer be your Governess. At the school you will be her responsibility, also that of Miss Evans, who I believe is to be your tutor. However, I am delighted to be able to say that your mother has chosen to offer me the post of Companion, which I have accepted.'

'I am very pleased for you, Miss Challis,' Thrift answered promptly, and immediately found herself wondering if the duties of a Companion included administering physical discipline. It was not a question that could be easily asked, and if certain things Miss Challis had said earlier suggested they did, then . . .

'Naturally this will entail certain changes,' Miss Challis went on, 'but they will not be large. I shall continue to accompany you at all times, and to see to your welfare, both moral and physical . . .'

Thrift's heart sank.

' . . . yet I would hope that you will come to think of me as a friend.'

'Absolutely, Miss Challis,' Thrift answered, struggling to keep the doubt from her voice. 'I would be honoured to consider you my friend.'

Miss Challis responded with the most friendly, open smile she had ever bestowed on Thrift, whose hopes immediately rose once more. Possibly the days of constant fear of exposure and punishment were at an end, at least outside school. There was still the school, and she had no doubt whatever that Miss Evans would give discipline. The only question was how. An Englishwoman would use the cane, a Scotswoman the tawse, but the name Evans suggested Welsh origins, which made such things less predictable.

They had reached the building, one of a row of fine four-storey mansions with colonnaded entrances that made up the north-western face of Belgrave Square. Flags adorned the buildings to either side, the diagonal blue and white diamonds of Bavaria and the white on red cross of Denmark, revealing them as embassies of minor European States, the insignia of each of which she had learned with Miss Challis until she was word perfect. By contrast the identity of the Diplomatic School was revealed only by a discreet brass plaque.

Together they climbed the steps and passed through the door as it swung open before them, a footman in black and gold livery standing motionless beside the button. The hall within was floored in black and white tiles, with a double staircase rising to the next floor and panelled walls hung with the portraits of stern men and imposing women. Thrift quickly hung her bonnet among others on a stand then paused to take it all in, only to immediately catch the sharp patter of heels on stone, indicating the arrival of a Lady of her own station. Straightening her back and composing her features, she turned to find an elderly woman approaching, tall, white haired, her figure curved into a perfect S within her steel grey dress. Miss Challis curtseyed, as did Thrift.

'Lady Newgate,' Miss Challis stated, bowing her head in deference.

The newcomer nodded in response and addressed Thrift.

'Miss Thrift Moncrieff, I presume?'

'Yes, my Lady,' Thrift answered.

'It is customary,' the woman answered, 'to arrive some half-an-hour early here at the Diplomatic School. Pray accompany me. Miss Challis, the Companion's drawing room is on the third floor, the stairs to the rear.'

She had turned even as she spoke, and began to move towards the stairs, walking so evenly that only the sharp click of her heels betrayed the fact that she was not floating on air. Thrift followed, clutching the banister on the stairs and struggling to keep up. At the landing Lady Newgate turned down a wide, high passage, brightly lit and decorated with yet more portraits, this time exclusively female.

'You father has appraised me of your abilities,' Lady Newgate stated, pausing to allow Thrift to catch up, 'and I trust you will do well with us. There will be a group of six starting this year, under the tuition of Miss Evans, who was formerly at the Priory School in Radnor, a most reputable establishment.'

They had reached a door, one of a well-spaced line, all closed and of solid, dark oak. It opened as Lady Newgate touched a button and Thrift stepped within, her companion leaving without another word. Within was a schoolroom, not so different from that where Miss Challis and others had taught her over the years at her own home. High windows looked out over Belgrave Square, bright sunlight streaming in, to show tiny dust motes dancing in the still air and reflect from the polished oak of the wall panels and furnishings. Maps, charts, genealogies and yet more portraits decorated the walls, covering almost as much panelling as was left bare. A square of Wilton covered the floor, on which rested six desks. Five were occupied.

If the room was familiar enough, the occupants were anything but, and Thrift found herself struggling not to stare. Of the six girls, she recognised only one, Decency Branksome-Brading, the daughter of her father's immediate superior. In blue, Decency's gown was if anything more elaborate than Thrift's. The bustle showed a distinct cleavage, and nothing had been spared with either embroidery or pleating. Thick, golden hair was piled high on her head, and the restraining pins and net showed tiny blue gems. She sat at the central desk of the front row, perfectly composed, her expression exactly as superior as Thrift remembered it.

To Decency's left, nearest the window, sat a slight, blonde girl in a gown of magnificent red silk, yet in a cut Thrift would have expected of the daughter of a road sweeper or gardener. There was no bustle, and evidently no corset, as her breasts were clearly outlined beneath the bodice and the front so low as to hint at a soft, pink cleavage. More shocking still, the hem ended only a short way below her knees, revealing neat calves and ankles covered only by the sheerest of stockings.

Yet more embarrassing to look at was the girl behind the small blonde. She was smaller still, tiny in fact, yet clearly a grown woman, all too clearly. Her shiny black hair was elaborately coiffed and set with jewels, her face a mask of white, red and black make-up. Her gown, if it could be called a gown, was of brilliant golden silk, lavishly embroidered with flowers, and appeared to have been painted on to her body, revealing every contour of her tiny breasts, slender hips and gently curving belly. It ended higher even than the blonde girl's, halfway down her thighs, and beneath it her legs were bare.

The girl behind Decency was little less shocking. For one thing her skin was the jet black of the African colonies, yet Thrift knew that to be at the Diplomatic School she could not possibly be a colonial. That meant one of the independent nations on the bulge of Africa; Ashanti, Leone, even Benin, where they were rumoured to wear bones in their hair and eat human flesh, also to go stark naked. Yet the girl had no bones in her hair, only a scattering of polished lapis lazuli beads, and as she greeted Thrift with a happy smile it did not reveal pointed teeth. Nor was she naked, but dressed in a conventional British gown, brilliant yellow and richly made, but many decades out of date, with the bustle worn to accentuate her hips as much as her bottom, and the corset tight to the lower slopes of large, proud breasts.

Nearest the door, to Decency's right, sat the fifth girl, whose attire was less revealing, but far more shocking. She was in trousers, and therefore presumably a Soviet, but not simply trousers. Her outfit was a military uniform, from her highly polished boots to the peaked cap of shiny black leather perched on her close-cropped blonde hair, something so implicitly male that Thrift found it hard to take in. Yet there was no questioning the girl's sex. The front of her black uniform jacket bulged with breast flesh, large and undeniably real, while the waist was neatly tailored and the tail flared to enhance her hips. The trousers left no doubt either, tight and black, with a red stripe down the outside of each, clinging to her hips, tummy and the bulge and split of her unmentionable parts. This last, unimaginably rude detail was visible from the way the girl sat, legs casually apart, one elbow on the desk as she decorated the cover of an exercise book with a hammer and sickle symbol.

Thrift took the unoccupied desk as quickly as her clothing would allow, lowering her bottom on to the backless seat with an embarrassing creak of whalebone under stress. Only then did she greet her new companions with carefully measured formality, returning the black girl's smile, bobbing to Decency and the girl in red, nodding to the others. The black-haired girl returned a shy smile and looked quickly away.

The Soviet spoke, her voice bold, her English near perfect with no more than a trace of accent. 'So, we are complete, and as fine an array of Capitalist Imperialist chattels I have yet to see. So what do they call you?'

'I am Miss Moncrieff,' Thrift answered, affronted, yet determined to maintain the formal courtesy the situation demanded.

'Comrade Tatiana Zhukov,' the Soviet girl replied, extending a hand as if she was a man.

Thrift took the girl's hand and shook it, forcing herself to suppress a giggle at the eccentric action, more suited to a comic play than a schoolroom. After withdrawing her hand, the Soviet girl thrust it inside her jacket to draw out a packet of slim black cigars, which she offered around with a casual flourish. Thrift moved back in instinctive shock, while the black girl accepted with another white-toothed grin, but the others looked away. Tatiana went on as she drew out a long black cigar holder.

'You need not be so concerned, you know. There is no true nicotine, only modified substitute and a little cannabis. We Soviets are well advanced on your science in this regard.'

'I have been given to believe,' Decency Branksome-Brading broke in, 'that talking before class is forbidden, and smoking certainly is.'

Tatiana merely shrugged and lit her cigar with a red enamelled lighter with the hammer and sickle emblem in gold, then spoke again as she offered it to the black girl.

'Pay no attention to Decency here. Her father is Chief Secretary in your Foreign Office, Baron Kessingland, one of the big pigs themselves, so she probably cannot help her behaviour.'

'I am acquainted with Miss Branksome-Brading,' Thrift answered, trying to sound as cold as Decency had but failing. 'My own father is Sir Kincardine Moncrieff, Senior Assistant Secretary in the Foreign Office and younger brother to Lord Moncrieff.'

Tatiana simply made a face, managing to suggest that the information didn't surprise her at all, took a deep draw on her cigar and went on.

'These others,' she said, gesturing with her cigar holder, 'are, in the red, Francesca Scaan, daughter of some lackey to the Liechtensteiner bankers. Behind her, another Imperialist chattel, the Chinese Xiuying Shi, and here my friend Anna Lakoussan –'

'Ana,' the black girl promptly corrected her.

'Ana then,' Tatiana went on, 'who at least has the decency to confess to the exploitation of her country's workers, unlike you, I suspect?'

'Exploitation of –' Thrift began, puzzled, and promptly broke off as the door swung wide.

Ana hastily stubbed out her cigar, grinding it beneath the heel of her boot. Tatiana didn't, but swung around in her chair to face the woman who had entered the room. Thrift did so too, and found herself looking not at a face but at the upper slopes of a colossal bosom restrained within the confines of a muted blue dress.

21

Glancing quickly up, she noted the deep green silk of the woman's scholastic collar, a broad, red face bearing a harsh, unsympathetic expression and a coil of dark red hair within a plain black net. Easily six foot in height, the woman's body was more massive than that of most men. The colossal bust hung over a waist that would have been thick had it not been for the huge hips and the sheer length of the legs beneath the voluminous skirt. More alarming still, in the woman's hand was a thick leather strap, like a tawse, but mounted on a suspiciously well-worn wooden handle.

'Good morning, Miss Evans,' Thrift chanted automatically, sure that the woman could be no other.

Decency Branksome-Brading echoed the greeting, the others joining in with less confidence, except for Tatiana, who merely nodded to the enormous woman and took another draw on her cigar. A frozen glare was turned on the Soviet girl and Miss Evans spoke, her voice deep and richly accented, also cold and threatening.

'Smoking is strictly forbidden within school premises, Miss Zhukov,' she stated. 'And as for using a cigar ... Extinguish it immediately.'

Tatiana shrugged and took a long draw on her holder, bringing the tip of her cigar up to an incandescent red ring, which moved quickly down as she sucked. With just a half-inch protruding from the holder, she flicked the tall column of ash on to the floor. Miss Evans's face had turned a rich puce, and when she spoke again Thrift found her stomach fluttering in fear and her bladder suddenly weak.

'Miss Zhukov, I am aware that you are a foreigner and –'

'Comrade Zhukov,' Tatiana interrupted.

'– and as such lack the advantages of a British upbringing,' Miss Evans went on without correcting herself. 'Nevertheless, you should be aware that while you are under my charge you will be expected to behave in at least an approximation of a ladylike manner. Otherwise –'

She stopped, but as she did so she laid the ferocious implement she was carrying on her desk with an all-too-clear implication. Thrift put her hand to her tightly laced stomach in terrified reaction, for all that the woman's anger was focused on somebody else. Tatiana merely gave another of her expressive shrugs and slid her cigar holder back into the recesses of her uniform jacket, but the Liechtensteiner, Francesca, had raised her hand.

'Yes, Miss Scaan?'

'I believe it is correct to say,' the small woman replied in heavily accented but precise English, 'that we are not subject to British law, notably as it relates to corporal punishment, this school being within the Diplomatic Enclave.'

'You are incorrect,' Miss Evans stated. 'Within this school you are subject to the laws of the British Empire, just as within each embassy you are subject to the laws of that territory, and you will abide by them. If you wish to be sure of this, you will find that each of your fathers has signed a document to the effect. These documents have been witnessed by your Ambassadors, or in Miss Zhukov's case – my pardon, Comrade Zhukov's case, by his secretary, her father being the Ambassador.'

Francesca had gone pale and was fidgeting with her fingers in her lap, but said nothing. Miss Evans extended her hand to the implement on her desk.

'This,' she stated, holding the horrible thing up for their inspection, 'is a ffolen ffrewyll or Welsh tawse. A Lady tawse, naturally, but designed for thick-skinned miners' daughters, and never for such pampered backsides as yours. Now let us be very clear on this point. I will have discipline in my class, manners and proper respect. I will be lenient, at first, allowing for your origins, but I warn you now not to try my patience. You will not speak unless spoken to by myself or by another member of staff, regardless of whether or not I am in the room. When you wish to speak, you will raise your hand. You will address me as Miss Evans, and I will address you either by your family names or by your Christian names, as appropriate, and as is only right and proper.'

'Christianity represents an outmoded belief system by which the capitalists seek to suppress their workers,' the Soviet girl stated calmly. 'I am no Christian.'

'Nor I, Miss Evans,' the Chinese girl added softly.

Miss Evans's face had gone a deep beetroot red, but by the time she replied she had gained control of herself.

'I am aware,' she said, 'that the Lord's word has not yet reached some of you, and that, sadly, others seek to deny its truths. As Divinity is not included within my educational remit, I think it best that the subject be avoided. Now, as I was saying, I will address you by your names, which I will now call out in alphabetical order so that you may confirm your presence –'

'Why?' Tatiana questioned. 'We are all six here. You know all our names, surely?'

'Indeed I do, Miss Zhukov,' Miss Evans snapped back, 'but morning roll call is part of the educational formula, and I will not see it skimped on, nor mocked. Miss Decency Branksome-Brading?'

'Present, Miss Evans,' Decency answered promptly, with Miss Evans returning a benign smile in response.

'Miss Thrift Moncrieff?'

'Present, Miss Evans,' Thrift answered.

'Miss Anna Lakoussan?'

'Ana,' the black girl corrected. 'Present.'

'Anna will do very well, I think,' Miss Evans remarked, 'for the sake of simplicity. Miss Francesca Scaan?'

'Present, Miss Evans,' Francesca answered, her fear still showing in her voice.

'Miss – X – Zi? Shoe? Really, however – Sue She?'

'Present, Miss Evans,' the Chinese girl answered in a barely audible voice.

'Miss Tatiana Zhukov?'

'I am here, as you plainly see,' Tatiana answered.

Miss Evans threw Tatiana a warning look but said nothing. Still holding the tawse, she turned to the blackboard behind her. Reaching up, she pulled out a roll of map showing the entire world marked out in its political divisions.

'The British Empire,' she stated, waving the tawse across the map to indicate the area shaded in pink. 'Our own sceptred isle, the continents of North America, Australasia and Antarctica, the Indian sub-continent, all but a tiny fraction of the continent of Africa, our Asian colonies and a proportion of Europe. All in all, well over half the land surface of the world. Given the small size of our island, I think even Miss Zhukov will admit that this is a remarkable feat?'

She had cocked one bushy eyebrow up as she turned, in a manner Thrift found highly disconcerting although it was not directed at here. Tatiana paused a moment before answering.

'Remarkable, yes. Admirable, no, unless the exploitation of your own proletariat and countless millions of native peoples is to be considered admirable.'

Miss Evans coloured but responded calmly enough.

'A curious statement from a subject of the world's second-largest empire.'

'I am a citizen, not a subject,' Tatiana corrected her. 'I owe allegiance only to the people of the Soviet Socialist Republic. Nor are we an Empire. Surely you are aware that on his election to Party Secretary Comrade Trotsky gave independence to all states held subject under the former Russian Empire?'

'This is not the matter with which we are concerned,' Miss Evans answered. 'Our subject is the origin and rise to dominance of the British Empire. Now, who can tell me the date of union between Wales and England?'

Decency's hand had shot up before Thrift could respond. Miss Evans smiled.

'Yes, Decency?'

'Twelve eighty-four, Miss Evans, Edward the First's completion of the conquest of Wales following the rebellion of Llewellyn ap Gruffydd.'

'No, Decency,' Miss Evans answered, her face still bland but her knuckles whitening on the handle of the tawse. 'Miss Moncrieff, perhaps you could tell us?'

'Yes, Miss Evans,' Thrift answered. 'England and Wales were united by the Acts of Union of fifteen thirty-six and fifteen forty-three.'

'Correct, my dear,' Miss Evans answered, and a warm, pleased flush ran through Thrift's breast, 'and it is the later date that is generally considered to mark the beginning of Imperial Britain, although with characteristic modesty the title of Emperor was not assumed until some centuries later. By then, Scotland and Ireland had also united, to form what we now know as the mother country. We had also established extensive colonies throughout Asia and the New World. Perhaps one of you foreign girls can tell me at what date the title of Emperor was, in fact, first bestowed, and upon whom?'

Francesca raised a cautious arm. Miss Evans raised an eyebrow.

'In eighteen seventy-seven, Miss Evans,' Francesca stated, 'on the abdication of Queen Victoria in favour of her husband, Albert Saxe-Coburg.'

'Excellent, Francesca,' Miss Evans responded. 'I see we have some genuinely learned young ladies among our number. Yes, eighteen seventy-seven, the date of the Proclamation of Empire, one hundred and twenty-seven glorious years ago. At the time, however, we were not the world's sole colonial power. Although the once-important Spanish and Portuguese Empires were already faded, France possessed not inconsiderable colonies in north and west Africa. There were the Dutch in the East Indies, and in Asia the Russians and the Chinese, whose territories remain. What event then gave Britain her unrivalled pre-eminence?'

'Your pre-eminence is not unrivalled,' Tatiana stated blandly. 'True power in the world belongs to the workers, to whom the Soviet –'

'Enough!' Miss Evans snapped. 'I am warning you, Miss Zhukov, that my patience is not unlimited. The British worker is a loyal subject and is proud to accept his place within the Empire and within the social order. Now, who can answer my question? You, perhaps, Miss She?'

'Yes, Miss Evans,' Xiuying Shi answered. 'The supremacy of the British Empire derives from the development of the Collins Electrical Engine, thus providing unlimited energy.'

'This is very true, Miss – er – Sue, er – Susan,' Miss Evans replied, 'yet it –'

'An invention,' Tatiana broke in, 'by which all of humanity might be liberated to a New Age were it not for the Capitalist greed –'

'Miss Zhukov!' Miss Evans roared, then continued in a milder tone as Tatiana went silent.

'Naturally you would not expect us to share the invention by which we maintain our power with rivals. How absurd! Now, while it is true that this invention has given us technological pre-eminence, I was referring to our great territorial expansion during the first half of the last century. Miss Lakoussan, perhaps? You have yet to answer a question.'

'The Great War,' Ana answered, 'after that, you just took what you wanted, by and by, 'cept Ashanti.'

'The correct answer,' Miss Evans responded, 'although I would thank you to address me properly and to be a little more respectful in your tone. As to Ashanti, it was an individual case of a complexity not appropriate to this level of your education. Yes, essentially, following the adoption of the policy of Splendid Isolation by Lord Salisbury in the late nineteenth century, a policy heartily endorsed by the Emperor, the British Empire stood aloof from rising tensions in mainland Europe. In nineteen fourteen the assassination of Archduke Ferdinand of the Austro-Hungarian Empire precipitated war, between Austria-Hungary and what was then Greater Germany on the one hand, and Russia, France and Italy on the other. The sides proved evenly matched and the most terrible of wars ensued, lasting twelve years until the final exhaustion of the combatants. Those nations which had been known as the Great Powers collapsed, Germany, Austria and Italy and into their component states, France into bucolic poverty and degeneracy, Russia into a condition of anarchy from which the Soviets emerged triumphant under the leadership of Leon Trotsky. Across the world the former colonies of these powers also collapsed, until rescued from chaos and tribal warfare by the British, or were sold to pay war debts to those nations who had remained neutral, notably Britain, Liechtenstein and Switzerland. Of the continents, only eastern Asia and South America remained untouched, and thus now, the entire world looks to us for moral leadership —'

'Hardly the entire world,' Tatiana broke in. 'If you were to investigate the facts in Africa, India, or any of those regions in which you have not actually wiped out the native population, you would discover that your much-vaunted moral system is mocked by all.'

'Silence!' Miss Evans thundered, and brought the tawse down on to the surface of her table with all her force, to create a crack that shook the windows. 'One more such interruption, Miss Zhukov and I'll tawse you until you howl!'

Tatiana shrugged but said no more. Miss Evans continued.

'Those few European States who had held themselves aloof from the struggle also benefited, to a greater or lesser degree. Not Spain perhaps, which was forced to relinquish Catalonia and the Basque territories, but Portugal, who retained her African colonies and gained somewhat in the Congo and Guinea. There was little effect on the Scandinavian countries, save those relinquished by the Russian Empire, while numerous new countries sprang up in Eastern Europe and south-west Asia. Most significant was the rise of the two great financial powers, Switzerland and Liechtenstein, whose influence remains to this day, out of all proportion to their size. Then, in nineteen twenty-seven, as Susan has so accurately informed us, came the invention of the Collins Electrical Engine by Sir Nicholas Collins –'

'Nikolai Kalinin,' Tatiana interrupted, 'a Soviet, and a traitor.'

Miss Evans had frozen, her face puce with anger, but when she finally spoke her voice was cold and level.

'So, it seems I must set an example. Miss Zhukov, you will rise and step forward to my desk, where you will bare your posteriors and adopt an appropriate position.'

Tatiana managed a shrug, but as she stood and walked to the front of the class Thrift could see that she was struggling to maintain her attitude of indifference. One egg-shaped bottom cheek was twitching within her trousers, and there was more than a little fear mixed with the defiance in her eyes as she turned to address Miss Evans.

'Does one merely strip and bend, or do your absurd moral conventions demand something more elaborate?' she asked, her voice cracking slightly on the final word.

'Your posteriors are to be naked, naturally,' Miss Evans answered, still in anger, but with an edge of malice, 'but it is not required to disrobe entirely. Such unnecessary humiliation we leave to less refined peoples.'

'There is no shame in the display of the human body,' Tatiana remarked, but her fingers were trembling as she shrugged off her uniform jacket.

As Tatiana's hands went to the front of her trousers, Thrift could only stare in horror and fascination. To see the outline of the Soviet girl's firm yet rounded buttocks within the confines of the uniform trousers was enough to send the blood rushing to her face, and as they were pushed down to expose bare flesh she found that her heart seemed to have risen into her throat.

Tatiana's skin was very pale and very smooth, her bottom cheeks two heavy eggs of flesh, well tucked under and deeply cleft, all of which was visible as she wore no proper drawers, but only a minuscule garment of bright red cotton, the rear of which covered nothing. It came down anyway, pushed low by Tatiana's thumbs, and as the Soviet girl bent forward across the desk, Thrift's mouth fell open in shock.

Those unnamed, unmentionable parts of Tatiana's body were on full, blatant display to all five of her classmates, a puckered, dun-coloured hole between the open cheeks, and twin, pouting, reddish lips between which wrinkled, fleshy folds showed. There was no hair, to Thrift's surprise, but a fine stubble showed that a razor had been applied. That was one more piece of extraordinary indecency, and compounded by the presence of a neat hammer and sickle tattoo on the plump mound of flesh above what she could only bring herself to think of as the girl's pee-pee wrinkles.

Thrift's eyes were fixed forward, her body frozen, her own belly tingling. Just to know that in the same unspeakably rude position she would look little different was raising emotions she was entirely unable to cope with. That was beside thinking of how many times Miss Challis and others had made her bend just so, that others had seen, and worst of all, that it was more than likely to happen.

Miss Evans showed only a cruel satisfaction at the sight Thrift found so hard to accept and impossible to tear her eyes away from. She was smiling now and, as she lifted the tail of Tatiana's blouse to complete the exposure of the trim young bottom, she gave a faint chuckle, then spoke.

'A round dozen, I think, my impudent young Lady, and then perhaps you will have learned a little respect for your elders and betters.'

She had picked up the tawse, and as she spoke the last word she brought it around with all the force of one massive, brawny arm. The strap hit Tatiana's bottom full across the fat of her cheeks, raising a meaty smack and leaving a broad white line that turned quickly red. Thrift had winced at the impact, but the Soviet girl had given only a low grunt as the breath was knocked from her body. Miss Evans's face set in determination as she once more lifted the tawse.

Again it came down, maybe harder than before, and again it cracked across Tatiana's bottom, to flatten her buttocks and make her flesh ripple before it all bounced quickly back into shape. Two thick, red welts now decorated the pale skin, both showing purple blotches where the edge of the tawse had caught her, but as before she only grunted.

Miss Evans stood back, giving herself more room to swing. Thrift managed to swallow the lump in her throat, but could not force herself to look away as the third blow was given, harder still and landing plum across the marks of the previous two. Thrift felt her buttocks twitch in sympathy, but once more Tatiana held back.

The fourth stroke was delivered, low, catching the girl's well-rounded cheeks under the meaty tuck, to make her buttocks bounce and leave a heavy welt. Tatiana merely shook her head.

The fifth came higher, close to the top of Tatiana's bottom, where her cleft opened out into a tiny V of flesh. Again it left a thick welt of red and purple, with the hurt flesh bulging in places and roughened in others, but still there were no screams or pleas for mercy.

The sixth was delivered lower, on unmarked flesh, the seventh also, filling in the unbeaten areas of Tatiana's bottom with red, but neither one breaking her. Thrift's stare had now become as much amazement as shock, and as the eighth blow was delivered she finally managed to steal a glance at her classmates.

All were rapt in attention. Decency, the nearest and with a view no less rude than Thrift's, was sat bolt upright, apparently perfectly composed save for a tell-tale twitch at the corner of her mouth to betray an inner satisfaction. Ana was worse, her pretty face twisted into a cruel leer of undisguised enjoyment. Xiuying's expression was hard to read, perhaps approval, perhaps indifference. Francesca was crying softly and biting her lower lip.

The eighth stroke had produced no more reaction than the others, and Miss Evans stood back, her face redder than ever, beaded with sweat and set in an angry scowl. Taking careful aim once more, she brought it around, this time lower still, to catch the tops of Tatiana's thighs and slam the soft flesh in against the protruberant lips between.

Now Tatiana screamed, loud and long, as she went into a wild, kicking dance, jumping up and down on her toes and beating her hands on the desk top. Miss Evans laughed, but allowed no time for recovery, whipping the tenth stroke in at the same spot as hard as ever. The eleventh came down, and the twelfth, applied without mercy, to keep the now broken girl in her writhing, helpless frenzy of pain, buttocks jiggling, fists drumming on the desk top, head shaking from side to side and bottom hole pulsing lewdly behind her.

Miss Evans laughed as she beat her charge, her anger forgotten, her audience forgotten, simply indulging her cruel lust on the poor girl's bouncing bottom cheeks. Nor did she stop at twelve, but continued, laying in stroke after stroke, across buttocks and thighs and hips, until at last Tatiana collapsed in a tear-stained heap on the classroom floor, clutching at the purple mess of her bottom and whimpering, with spittle and mucus running from her mouth and nose.

'Let that be a lesson to you all,' Miss Evans puffed, finally putting the tawse down. 'I am not a woman to be trifled with.'

'No, Miss Evans,' the girls chorused immediately, even Ana, whose delight in the whipping had turned to shock when Tatiana had lost control.

'What do you say, Tatiana?' Miss Evans enquired gently of the broken girl on the floor.

'Sorry, Miss Evans,' Tatiana managed, the words coming out in a trio of choking sobs. 'I – I shall be more respectful in future, Miss Evans.'

'So you shall,' Miss Evans answered her. 'Now go back to your desk, but remain standing and with your lower clothes down. So, where was I? Ah yes, the reasons for the ascendancy of the British Empire.'

Miss Evans continued the lesson as Tatiana returned to her desk to stand, her hands on her head and here well-smacked bottom directly in front of Thrift's face. The combination of the close view of the beaten girl's bottom and the strong and intensely feminine scent made concentration difficult, but fortunately it was not really necessary, with Miss Evans going over facts she had known for years.

The history lesson complete, Miss Evans moved on to geography, each lesson an hour long. Lunch followed, served in a well-appointed dining room with the senior girls also present, along with their Companions, of various nations and hues and modes of dress. Courteous servants served lamb chops, potatoes and greens, then jam pudding, all eaten with silverware and on fine china, both bearing the Foreign Office crest. Thrift found her fears of the morning subsiding, also her sense of shock at the outlandish clothing of the other girls.

After lunch there was a brief pause before they trooped back to the classroom and Miss Evans. Literature was followed by mathematics, and mathematics by Latin. Last came divinity, taken by Lady Newgate herself, to Thrift's profound relief. The Headmistress carried a cane, but her manner was ladylike and reserved, whereas with Miss Evans the tawse had seemed a constant threat. No other girls had been beaten, but both she, Xiuying and Ana had come to the point where one more wrong answer would have resulted in the application of six hard strokes to her bottom. It was a terrifying prospect, but more from the unendurable humiliation of being forced to expose herself than the pain.

With the final bell came a sense of relief so strong it left her feeling faint. Tea was served, for which their Companions and also the Mistresses joined them, allowing Thrift to cast an eye over yet more fascinating and alarming people. The other two Mistresses seemed no less formidable than Miss Evans. These were a great gaunt woman with red hair and a lipless mouth, Miss Peel, and a squat matron with fat arms and an evil glint in her eye, Mrs Leary. Then there was Francesca's Companion, who wore a hunting dress in bottle green, had a monocle in her left eye and carried a riding crop. Less frightening but more bizarre, was Xiuying's Companion, a man, to Thrift's amazement, small, stark bald and as fat and soft as butter. Perhaps most astonishing of all, Tatiana proved to have no Companion at all, and when tea was done she left alone, walking a little stiffly as she made her way across the square towards the Soviet Embassy.

Alone with Miss Challis, Thrift found her head still whirling with unexpected impressions, and began to ask questions as soon as they had passed through the gates of the Diplomatic Enclave.

'Why is it, my dear Miss Challis, that they adopt such peculiar costumes?'

'They are foreign,' Miss Challis answered, 'and they have not had our advantages. I am sure that our missionaries, both of the church and secular, do their best to bring much-needed reform. Meanwhile, we must take that attitude of Christian forbearance suitable to those less fortunate than ourselves. Now, it is a beautiful afternoon, and really quite clement. Shall we take a turn in the park?'

'As you please, Miss Challis,' Thrift answered.

'I think so, yes, the crocuses are so pretty. Now, you must tell me all about your day. The Welsh Lady, she is Miss Evans?'

'Yes, and she is a dreadful, coarse woman. How she could have been appointed to so consequential a post I cannot imagine!'

'I have no doubt that wiser minds than yours or mine have made that decision, Thrift. She is strict then?'

'Dreadfully! She carries a tawse, a huge thing, of which I am quite terrified, and she thinks nothing of our modesty.'

'That is only right and proper. As you well know, a girl who errs forfeits her modesty until her chastisement is complete.'

'Yes, but in front of foreigners – heathens even! The daughter of the Chinese under-secretary, Xiuying Shi, is not Christian!'

'So, you were beaten?'

'No, not I. Miss Tatiana Zhukov, who is the daughter of the Soviet Ambassador himself, and dresses in the most peculiar manner, in uniform, as if she were a man! She who left the school immediately before –'

'She was made to disrobe?'

'She was made to show herself behind, and to bend across Miss Evans's desk, in – in the most indecent posture one could possibly imagine. Miss Evans is a beast and, when Tatiana would not cry, she – she – I cannot bring myself to speak of it!'

'She would seem a most formidable Lady, this Miss Evans.'

'She is indeed, quite without mercy!'

'Nonsense, my dear, she is showing the best mercy she can. As the good book says, spare the rod and spoil –'

'She takes pleasure in it,' Thrift interrupted and stopped abruptly. More than once it had seemed to her that Miss Challis also took pleasure in delivering punishment.

They had crossed Wellington Place as they spoke, and moved on into the park. It was now busy, if not crowded, with both riders and strollers displaying themselves on the broad, tree-lined walks. For a space neither of them spoke, Thrift thinking of how she had escaped the hideous ordeal of a beating from Miss Evans, and wondering if she would be able to escape it for the entire year of her tuition. When she spoke again it was to make a firm resolution.

'I shall be faultless this year. I shall study hard, and perfect my manners and address.'

Miss Challis laughed. 'You see, my dear Thrift, already Miss Evans has inspired you. Still, is it not rather proud to say you will be faultless?'

There was a hint of amusement in Miss Challis's question, and Thrift felt a sudden and all-too-familiar sinking feeling. Hastily she apologised.

'I am sorry, Miss Challis, for showing unwarranted pride, yet I do feel –'

'No doubt,' her Companion interrupted her, 'you will be, once properly chastised. Come, this bench will do admirably.'

'Here!' Thrift gasped. 'No, Miss Challis, you cannot!'

'To the contrary,' Miss Challis answered, seating herself, 'it is my duty.'

Thrift stayed where she was, in the middle of the path. She was burning with consternation, blushing furiously, and shaking. Miss Challis had trapped her, she knew it, but she also knew there was no escape. To disobey was to invite worse punishment, perhaps held up across the cook's broad back while a bundle of birch twigs was applied to her naked buttocks. Yet to voluntarily go down across her Companion's lap in the park was something she simply could not bring herself to do.

'Thrift, come now,' Miss Challis said gently, patting her lap.

'Miss – Miss Challis –' Thrift stammered. 'I beg you, no! There are Gentlemen in view!'

'All the better to lessen that unreasonable pride,' Miss Challis answered. 'Come, come, Thrift, you have seen girls spanked in the park before.'

Thrift could find no answer, her words jamming in her throat as she tried to speak. She wanted to say that it was impossible, that merely because the occasional well-deserving brat had to have her bottom beaten in public it did not mean it should, or could, happen to her. She was good, obedient and mild, with the feminine virtues always uppermost in her mind. Yet she knew that any such protest would only lead to a further accusation of being prideful. She was trapped. Once more Miss Challis patted her lap, but now there was a touch of asperity to the gesture.

'Thrift, do not tell me that you need to be held down.'

'No, Miss Challis,' Thrift answered quickly, with a glance around at the various women nearby, all of whom she was sure would be more than happy to perform the task.

Already people had begun to notice her predicament. Two elderly gentlemen were pretending to examine a stand of crocuses just a few yards further down the path. Behind, a group of six, three Governesses and their charges, had stopped to talk, the young ladies glancing at her sidelong and hiding giggles behind gloved hands. One group or the other was going to see her bare bottom. She chose the women, and with hot tears of helpless frustration already threatening to spill from her eyes, she stepped forward to the bench.

'That is better, my dear,' Miss Challis stated and moved a little forward to make more space across her lap.

Thrift bent, the whalebone of her bustle and corset creaking as she moved, down and over Miss Challis's lap, to lift her bottom into a convenient position to be spanked. With it thrust high, her bustle lifted her skirts to make them bulge up to the level of her Companion's chest, a huge ball of material covering a ball of flesh that felt no less enormous. Her humiliation was already a physical pain, and suddenly too strong to bear. She burst into tears, her whole body shaking with great, wracking sobs, her eyes tight shut. A girlish titter sounded from behind her.

'There is no need to make quite such a fuss,' Miss Challis remarked, the mock disapproval in her voice completely failing to hide the underlying amusement. 'Why, you are not even bare yet.'

Thrift didn't answer, but clung on to the bench, praying that Miss Challis would change her mind, that the audience would realise how utterly unsuitable it was to watch her punished, that something, whatever it was, would happen to stop her being given the public spanking.

None of her prayers was answered. Instead, she felt her gown taken in Miss Challis's fingers, to be lifted, deliberately slowly to let her feelings sink in, and also, she was sure, to give other people a chance to come and see the fun. They were doing so too. As Thrift opened her eyes to peep out through a haze of tears, she saw that the two old men were walking past her, undoubtedly to get into a position where they would be able to inspect her bare bottom. A park keeper had stopped too, his blue uniform unmistakable even with her vision a wet blur. Added humiliation hit her as she realised she was to be watched by one of the lower orders, and fresh tears squirted from her eyes.

'My, what a fuss you make!' Miss Challis chided gently as Thrift's gown was laid on her back. 'Now, were you less proud, you would make less fuss, so do you see the reason you must be chastised?'

Thrift gave a single, miserable nod of her head, scattering tears over the bench beneath her. She could not see the reason, but only that she was all too obviously being punished for Miss Challis's private amusement, yet she knew better than to voice her feelings. Such things would never, ever be admitted too, any more than she would admit to her feelings of excitement and delight on watching other girls given the same treatment, or what she knew the spanking would do to her between her legs.

Her underdress had been lifted, exposing her taffeta petticoat. That followed, exposing the flannel one, and that too, lifted over the lowest, of cotton. With each exposure her crying grew more bitter and the choking sensation in her throat stronger, until she could barely breathe. As her last petticoat was lifted, she let out a wail of pure misery. Her bustle was showing, and her corset, brand new, the very first day she had worn them, and shown off in a public park, her intimate, female secrets revealed.

There was worse to come, no mere assembly of whalebone and satin, steel and lace, but her own, naked flesh. All Miss Challis had to do was open two layers and her bare flesh would be showing, to strangers, to men, providing the same unspeakably indecent view Tatiana had been forced to show in class . . .

She cried out again as the gudgeons on her corset seat were twisted loose. Suddenly the constriction of her waist had lessened, but it only seemed to make it more difficult still to draw her breath. Then the panel was being lifted, her drawers coming on show, the bulging flesh of her bottom cheeks all too obvious within, round and fat, so lewd, so improper, and about to be revealed in the flesh.

A disconsolate whimpering had set up in her throat, a noise over which she had no control whatsoever. As Miss Challis casually inverted the bustle and fastened the raised corset panel in place, it grew louder and more wretched still, ending in a fresh cry as she felt the Companion's finger on the first button of her drawers.

The button came loose. Her flesh was showing, a tiny triangle of soft bottom skin cool in the spring air. A second went and the triangle had become a slice, a third and the slice lengthened, a fourth and one whole side of her precious drawers was unfastened, with a full crescent of flesh revealed. It was a sight all too easy to imagine; plump, female flesh, her flesh, poking out from among the silk and lace, bare.

She burst into fresh sobs, but Miss Challis merely gave an admonitory click of her tongue. The fifth button came loose, on the far side of her panel, the sixth, seventh and eighth, each one taking her one step closer to the complete loss of her modesty. The crowd had grown, she knew, a ring of people, both male and female, now visible through her streaming tears, and her stomach and chest tightened in pain as Miss Challis took hold of the ninth button.

It came open, tweaked casually loose as if Thrift's exposure was nothing.

The tenth followed and the top of her bottom crease was showing. She began to wail brokenly, unable to stop herself for the agony of her shame.

The eleventh went and a good half of her crease was on show, and nearly all of one fleshy cheek. She began to beat her fists on the hard wooden slats of the bench in sheer frustration, and to shake her head from side to side.

The twelfth and last went and the panel fell away to expose the full expanse of her bottom. She screamed out in unbearable suffering, her hair shaking loose at the frantic tossing of her head, her boots drumming on the bench, her vision blind with tears.

Her unmentionable place showed from the rear, she knew it did, and as Miss Challis cocked up a knee to force Thrift's bottom into great prominence it grew abruptly worse, with cool air on the damp skin of her dirty place and the wet mouth and tangled flesh of her pee-pee wrinkles . . .

She screamed, loud and long, a wordless cry of agonised frustration at what had been done to her.

'Oh what nonsense,' Miss Challis said casually and began to spank.

Thrift hung her head low, her humiliation complete. She was bare, her bottom showing, her cheeks jumping and quivering to Miss Challis's slaps, the two rude holes between her thighs actually showing, in public. Yet after the agony of her exposure, the spanks came almost as a relief, almost. They hurt, a lot, and every one made her yet more self-conscious of the lewd display she was making of her rear end. Her feet continued to kick, her hands to drum on the bench, her head to shake, yet it was as if her feelings could grow no stronger.

Or so she thought, until the force of the slaps started to grow and the pain got worse, making her wriggle on Miss Challis's lap. At an abrupt change in the pressure in her tummy she realised with horrible certainty that something was about to happen that made her complete exposure seem trivial.

'No! Stop, I beg!' she screamed, but Miss Challis took no notice whatever, continuing to slap at Thrift's now wobbling buttocks.

In wild desperation Thrift clenched her cheeks, as tight as she could, the desire not to emit the air in her bowels stronger than all her other emotions, but compounded of them, and most of all, humiliation.

'Do not clench, Thrift,' Miss Challis admonished, still spanking. 'I am sure you would not wish me to have to fig you.'

'No!' Thrift wailed. 'I – I – I –'

She stopped, unable to voice her feelings. Instead her will broke under the overwhelming force of her emotions; her bottom cheeks went loose even as a hard slap caught them to make them bounce and spread; her anus opened in a long, rude fart, as unendurable humiliation hit her, and she collapsed into a faint.

When the tang of Miss Challis's smelling salts brought her round it was to find herself still across the Companion's lap, still bare bottomed, still being watched. Her vision was hazy, her body too weak to let her rise, her will broken. As the salts were removed from beneath her nose, she waited, in patient, miserable resignation, for her bottom to be covered or the spanking to continue, according to Miss Challis's wishes. Before either could happen, a voice penetrated the fog of her brain, high and nasal.

'Really, quite a little tantrum. How preposterous that a girl of her station should make such a commotion over a little public discipline. Quite unsuitable.'

Thrift looked up through a veil of tears. There, among the watchers was Decency Branksome-Brading, with her own Companion, Miss Buckleigh, their expressions cool, superior, and mildly amused.

2

London, June 2004

Spring passed to summer, the leaves on the imposing planes of the parks and squares growing a richer green and the London air becoming slowly hot with the smell of tarmac and ozone. Thrift continued with her studies, and maintained her resolve to achieve perfection, or at the very least to come sufficiently close so as to avoid Miss Evans's tawse. She was successful, as were most of the other girls: Decency through sycophancy and perfect manners; Xiuying through intelligence and extreme diffidence; Francesca through brilliance and stark fear. Tatiana failed, her inability to keep her opinions to herself leading to the exposure and thrashing of her neatly muscular bottom on average once a fortnight. Ana also failed, and had been obliged to put her full, black buttocks on display for tawsing three times.

If Thrift had managed to avoid chastisement from Miss Evans, she had failed miserably with Miss Challis. Her best efforts at politeness and proper conduct had come to nothing, and time and again she had found herself upended and her bottom stripped for spanking, and almost invariably in the most embarrassing possible circumstances. She had been spanked in the park, five times, until it had become such a regular occurrence that she was certain that some of the strollers were timing their afternoon walks in the hope of catching what they evidently regarded as a highly entertaining show. She had also been spanked on the front steps of the Albert and Victoria Museum, in the perfumery department of Messrs Humbert and Gorce's great emporium in Regent's Street, and in the stalls of the Theatre Royal in Shaftesbury Avenue. Each time the gap between the spankings had been just long enough to ensure that Thrift's shock and humiliation retained its full force, and she was now convinced that the punishments had far more to do with Miss Challis's enjoyment of them than her own need for discipline. The only relief was that the spankings in her own home had become rarer and gentler, seldom delivered hard enough to make her cry, and never to scream. With the outdoor spankings and the perpetual threat of Miss Evans's tawse, that was only so much consolation.

Her class had quickly divided itself into two cliques, led by the two dominant personalities, Decency Branksome-Brading and Tatiana Zhukov. With Decency so clearly Miss Evans's pet, Francesca had been quick to work herself into the British girl's favour. Xiuying, always meek and deferential, had quickly followed. Ana had not, preferring Tatiana's company and unwilling to grovel to quite the extent Decency expected. Thrift, frightened of being left out and knowing that Decency was sure to take every opportunity to belittle her, had had little choice but to look to Tatiana and Ana. The consequence had been Decency nicknaming Thrift 'the Brat'. The name had stuck, to her lasting resentment, but, with either Companions or Mistresses present or at least close by at all times, it had gone no further, until a Tuesday in early June.

Arriving back from lunch for the afternoon art class, she found that Miss Evans was not in the room, nor were Tatiana and Ana. Decency was, also Francesca and Xiuying. Thrift went to her desk as quickly as she was able, steering around the easels and drawings boards set up for their studies. As she seated herself, Decency spoke.

'Well, well, if it isn't the Brat, and without either her little Communist friend or the cannibal princess to look after her. Do you know something, Brat, something that offends me, that offends me deeply?'

'I am sure I do not,' Thrift answered coldly as she lowered herself into her chair with the inevitable creak of whalebone.

'It is this,' Decency went on. 'It is that you should have been admitted to this school. Really, your father can have no sense of place –'

'I am fully entitled to be here!' Thrift answered indignantly. 'As indeed the daughter of my father's assistant will be, when she has reached a proper age.'

'Entitled, perhaps.' Decency laughed. 'But with you for a daughter I would have thought your father would have been sufficiently mortified to apply for a place at a grammar, or one of those institutions where they carry out Universal Education, whatever it is they are called.'

'That would be most unsuitable!' Thrift snapped.

'Highly appropriate, I would have said,' Decency went on. 'I mean, your mother actually *works*! How extraordinarily common is that!'

'My mother,' Thrift replied, 'is the President of the Ladies' Society for the Dissemination of Gospel Truth.'

Decency merely sniffed and continued. 'Look at you. How many pairs of gloves do you possess? Three, four? You eat like a pig; your boots are a disgrace and you smell like a rubbish collector. Furthermore, you have no dress sense, none at all. Imagine wearing white with your sickly complexion, and it soils so easily – hardly the appropriate colour for a little ragamuffin to play in. What if you were to start to make mud pies, or your nose began to run in the disgusting manner it does after you have received a spanking?'

'I am very well able to look after my attire, thank you, Miss Branksome-Brading.'

Decency merely raised an eyebrow, reached out to take a tube of Burnt Sienna from the nearest easel and squeezed hard. Brown paint squirted from the tube, catching Thrift across the smooth curve of her corseted bosom before she could react, also spattering the lace of her collar and her face. Decency gave a peal of rich, musical laughter as Thrift sat back in shock, with Francesca tittering and even Xiuying's mouth curving briefly into a smile.

'I shall tell Miss Evans!' Thrift declared when she found her voice.

'Do,' Decency answered. 'Then you will be tawsed, something I should very much like to see, despite being already familiar with the contours of your grossly overweight sit-upon from your little exhibitions in the park.'

'Not at all! It is you who shall be tawsed, and properly bare!'

'No, Brat, it is you. You are a liar, you see, something Miss Evans cannot abide.'

'I am not a liar!'

'Ah, but I think you will find that you are. For, when you tell Miss Evans that I am responsible for the disgusting mess you have made of your front, both Miss Scaan and Miss Shi will assure her that it is not so.'

Decency turned to the others. Francesca didn't look happy but gave a quick nod. Xiuying merely looked down at her lap.

'You see?' Decency continued. 'You must tell everything, please do. It should be quite a spectacular beating, I would imagine, for lying and accusing me of playing such a wantonly childish and unladylike prank. I would be surprised if she gives you less than thirty-six strokes. Oh, how you will howl!'

Thrift made to answer, only to go quiet as the door swung open. It was Tatiana, and for a moment her hope rose, only to sink again as Miss Evans appeared a moment later. The Mistress noticed the state of Thrift's gown even before reaching the desk, and stopped.

'What is that disgusting mess down your front, Miss Moncrieff?' she demanded.

'Burnt Sienna, Miss Evans,' Thrift answered miserably.

'I can see that,' Miss Evans snapped. 'What I wish to know is, how did it come to be there?'

Thrift hesitated, torn between telling the truth, and being tawsed, and lying, something she had been brought up to abhor. At that moment Ana appeared, in company with a man, the artist Sullivan-Jones, who occasionally gave demonstrations or even lessons, although invariably under the close supervision of Miss Evans. Distracted, the Mistress merely snapped at Ana to sit down and ordered Thrift to clean up. Thrift left gratefully, only to discover that there was no way of removing the paint effectively and so was forced to return with the entire bosom of her gown stained brown. Decency gave no reaction, but her amusement showed in her eyes. Mr Sullivan-Jones spoke as she sat down.

'Ah, Miss Moncrieff, somewhat soiled, but present, which is what matters. So, if you have all finished playing with the paint, we shall proceed.'

He looked around the room, his bushy eyebrows raised, his moustache twitching with humour at his own joke. None of the girls responded as he had obviously hoped they would, and he went on.

'Today,' he stated, 'we shall endeavour to complete a study in perspective, a principle central to the depictive art.'

He paused for effect, his long moustaches quivering slightly at the tips, then went on.

'By good fortune, it is here in London, the greatest city of our world, that we have the ideal prospect for such a study. Indeed, one could well argue that it is in

Belgrave Square itself from which the perfect viewpoint exists. Come.'

He beckoned them and strode through the door, leaving Thrift and Decency struggling to rise in their restrictive clothing and so forcing Miss Evans and the others to wait. By the time they reached the pavement, Sullivan-Jones was already in the square, directing a group of school servants to set up the easels, paint stands and chairs. Thrift crossed to him with the others, wondering why he considered a view of the school to represent an ideal study in perspective. Only when she reached her chair and turned around did she discover the answer.

Looking north and west over the roof of the school, the vast bulk of the Empire Tower rose above everything, in perfect symmetry but in a proportion that was hard to take in until she managed to focus on the tiny human figures on the observation decks. Higher still, the cupola and the mooring mast above it appeared to challenge the few lazy wisps of cirrus drifting across the summer sky.

'There, Ladies,' Sullivan-Jones called out, gesturing dramatically with his arms, 'is your study in perspective!'

Thrift's gaze remained firmly towards the sky and a sight that, although familiar since she had moved to London in late childhood, never ceased to inspire her with awe. Even beside the great buildings of London the tower seemed entirely out of scale, and it was always visible, a firm and reassuring symbol of the greatness of Empire. She had also watched the great airships come and go, usually from the window of the nursery in the Dover Street house, although it was not considered a suitable activity for a young girl. Even now, the long shape of a ship was approaching from the east, glinting silver in the bright sunlight.

'Magnificent!' Sullivan-Jones called out. 'How timely! An airship approaches, the *Duchess Elizabeth* unless I am greatly mistaken. Do I not see the Union Flag on her mighty bows? Superb, is she not? Can any other nation boast such an imposing leviathan, such a colossus of the skies?'

'That is not your flag on the bow, Mr Sullivan-Jones,' Tatiana said quietly, 'but a red star. She is the *Stalin*, named after a dead hero of the October Revolution. Her length is four hundred and fifty metres, or approximately five hundred of your yards. The length of the *Duchess Elizabeth* is only four hundred and ten metres, or some four-hundred and fifty yards.'

'Preposterous!' Sullivan-Jones snorted. 'Can this be so? Are you lying, girl? I am an artist, I know nothing of engineering. You wouldn't want your, er ... ah ... pants to come down now, would you?'

His moustache had begun to twitch with excitement as he spoke, and with the final word he cast a questioning glance towards Miss Evans. She rose, holding the tawse.

'Do you wish her beaten for impudence, Mr Sullivan-Jones?' she asked. 'Although I fear it would not be strictly just. The *Stalin* is indeed larger than the *Duchess Elizabeth*, but the world's greatest airship is the *Sir Redvers Buller*, at something over six hundred yards. Nevertheless –'

She trailed off, holding the tawse out in obvious anticipation of being asked to use it. Sullivan-Jones glanced to Tatiana, and to Ana.

'Hrumph,' Sullivan-Jones grunted. 'No, I think not. Honour is satisfied.'

Tatiana had been about to speak, but hastily closed her mouth. Miss Evans sat back down, her face set in disappointment.

'Regardless of her nation of origin,' Sullivan-Jones went on, 'she will provide an admirable addition to our composition. Thus we have elements in the vertical and horizontal, the foreground and background, and yet in most unusual scale ...'

He went on, illustrating his points with a long paintbrush he had picked up. Thrift listened, careful to show polite attention, but more interested in watching the huge airship as it drifted slowly towards the Empire Tower. Tatiana, she suspected, knew it was due, as it was far too distant to make out the name, and Soviet airships were always made to more or less the same design. She also wondered why Tatiana had not been beaten, and why Sullivan-Jones had seemed to meet Ana's eye a moment before making his decision. It was certainly curious, but, more importantly, the incident had left Miss Evans itching to use her tawse.

She turned her attention to her drawing board, only to find that part of her grid was obscured by Decency's bonnet, a wide affair in the latest style and hung with pale blue ribbons to match her gown. She stood up and moved to adjust her view, and as she glanced down she saw that the ribbons decorating the hem of Decency's gown were lying against the leg of the chair. All it needed was the merest motion to loop one around another, and . . .

And it was impossible. Her corset was too restrictive to allow her to stoop quickly. Too many people were likely to see. Miss Evans was likely to guess what had happened, and she herself would end up being the one with her bottom stripped and whipped in front of the entire class and the open windows of half the embassies in London. Besides, if Decency upset her things, she was more likely to be admonished than beaten. She was Miss Evans's favourite, and it would take something more – an open lie, impudence, extreme stupidity.

She began to sketch, paying careful attention to Sullivan-Jones's instructions, yet with her anger and resentment of Decency always at the back of her mind. There were people about, many pausing to watch the girls draw, and she knew that every single one would see the ruined state of the front of her gown. Something had to be done.

It struck her as she began to mix paint to apply colour to her sketch. A wash was needed, a blue only a shade paler than Decency's gown. Stronger colours would lie over it. Abandoning her wash, she quickly took up some Primrose Yellow, applied a little to the trunk of one of the plain trees in her sketch and stirred it into her water jar. A touch of umber followed and she had what she wanted, only to find that Sullivan-Jones had begun to walk around the rear of the group. She smiled as he reached her side. He shook his head.

'No, Miss Moncrieff, no! Wash first, my dear girl, wash. I am surprised at you, to make so elementary a mistake. Normally you are among the most conscientious of students.'

'A foolish mistake, Sir, I see,' Thrift admitted quickly, but he had already passed on and was standing behind Ana, his hands on her shoulders as he studied her sketch.

To Thrift's surprise and shock, Ana responded to the liberty with a pleased smile.

'Now here,' Sullivan-Jones stated, 'we have potential. A bold style, my dear, and reminiscent of the French school, unlikely perhaps to win you much praise among the examiners, save for the fact that I am one of them and have an appreciation of art somewhat broader and deeper than is the norm.'

Thrift stole a glance at Ana's work, which showed the tower, buildings and trees in bright colour, the perspective correct but line almost entirely ignored. With a shrug she turned back to her own work, as Sullivan-Jones moved forward to inspect Francesca's efforts. Above them, the airship had docked, her insignia and name now plainly visible.

'She is the *Stalin* indeed,' Sullivan-Jones remarked, and Miss Evans turned to look up.

Quickly, Thrift took up her water jar, leaned forwards, and slowly tipped half of the rich yellow contents on to the rear of Decency's dress, immediately below where the bustle pushed out a great puff of pale blue silk. Sitting back, she composed herself, risking only a brief glance at Ana before returning to her work. The black girl had seen, and responded with a look of both amazement and delight, leaving Thrift struggling to prevent the corners of her mouth twitching up into a mischievous smile.

They painted for the remainder of the afternoon, Decency remaining completely unaware of the state of her gown. Sullivan-Jones noticed, but merely raised his eyebrows, comment on a young Lady's accident being unthinkable for a man. Thrift continued to work, pleased to see that her study was notably better than any but that of Xiuying Shi, who seemed to have a natural talent for art and a light and precise touch with her brush. Finally, as the school bell rang to announce tea, Miss Evans called a halt.

All rose, leaving the equipment to the school servants. Decency took Francesca's arm, began to walk towards the school and bobbed politely as she passed Miss Evans, who had stayed to supervise the servants.

Judging her moment to perfection, Thrift called out. 'Oh! Decency, my dear, are you all right? Here, let me help, and quickly! Oh you poor thing!'

She moved forwards. Miss Evans turned, her hard red face registering puzzlement, then shock and anger.

'Whatever –' Decency began, but was interrupted.

'Miss Branksome-Brading!' Miss Evans snapped. 'Really! If you were in need of the convenient facilities, you could have alerted me to the fact. I mean to say!'

'Whatever is the matter?' Decency demanded, turning.

'I think we can see that plainly enough!' Miss Evans answered. 'Indeed, it is visible for all to see on your gown. Are you not ashamed of yourself? Francesca, take her in immediately. You, girl, fetch Miss Branksome-Brading's Companion.'

As the servant Miss Evans had addressed hurried away, Decency finally realised what was wrong. Peering back, she had taken up the skirts of her gown, clutching a fold of the wet, yellow-stained material. Her mouth came open, the first words of an angry denial spilling out, only to change.

'I have n – never been so ashamed!'

Led by Francesca, Decency made for the school, walking as fast as her hobbled legs would permit and pink faced with anger and embarrassment. Thrift, inwardly laughing, forced herself to retain her composure and an expression of mild distaste suitable for the incident. She felt revenged, and Decency's humiliation was wonderful to see, yet there was some disappointment. Had Decency completed her denial, it would have been a plain lie, and without question it would have meant a bare-bottom tawsing, then and there, on the lawn, with not only Sullivan-Jones but also the school servants and several dozen foreigners watching.

It was a prospect to relish, yet, as she took Ana's offered arm and followed the others, she realised that it would have meant disaster. With Decency's corset panel showing, never mind her drawers, it would have been quite clear that she had not wet herself at all. Inevitably Thrift would have been discovered, and subjected to a punishment far worse than anything Decency might have expected for lying. Rumour had it that somewhere in the school there was a room where girls were stripped naked and fastened to a frame for severe beatings, and she had no desire to discover whether it was true.

'Very funny,' Ana whispered as they reached the gate of the square. 'You must come to dine with us, yes?'

'I should be delighted,' Thrift answered, flushing with pleasure at the invitation. 'We must have our Companions make the arrangements, perhaps for one evening next week?'

'No,' Ana answered, 'tonight.'

'Tonight? But, Ana, what of your father? Will he have time to present a formal invitation? I do not even know his correct address, or any of your country's form and etiquette!'

'It is simple,' Ana told her. 'My father is Sub-Chief Nago Lakoussan, Trade Spokesman to the Ashanti Embassy. A simple curtsey will suffice in greeting, we do not expect you to mimic every one of our customs, as you expect us to. His first wife, my mother, is –'

'First wife?' Thrift interrupted. 'He has more than one wife?'

'Twelve,' Ana answered, and went quiet as they reached the hall of the Diplomatic School, where Lady Newgate was in conversation with Sullivan-Jones.

Miss Challis was at tea, as was the stately and beautiful black girl who acted as Ana's companion. Thrift and Ana approached them, and accepted tea and slices of bread and butter from a hovering servant.

'I am greatly honoured by an invitation to dine with Mr Lakoussan, my dear Miss Challis,' Thrift announced. 'It is this evening; rather sudden, I know, but I am sure you will be able to make arrangements?'

'No doubt,' Miss Challis answered, smiling but with her irritation at the unexpected extra work showing in her eyes. 'You must change, of course. Whatever has happened to your dress?'

'An accident during art,' Thrift explained, praying inwardly that Miss Challis was got going to make it an excuse for yet another bare-bottom spanking. The last had been only four days before, and they were invariably spaced to make sure she never got used to it, or they had been so far.

'We must hurry home then,' Miss Challis stated. 'Mrs Lakoussan, I shall call presently, if I might have your address?'

Thrift, wondering if Ana's Companion was also her stepmother, turned to speak to Tatiana, who had entered the room. Decency was nowhere to be seen. Thrift began to linger over her tea, hoping for the opportunity to make a few telling remarks, only to realise that Decency would undoubtedly have been taken straight home, hopefully for a spanking across her Companion's knee.

The initial arrangements complete, Miss Challis collected Thrift, maintaining a bland smile until they had left the school, only then allowing her annoyance to show.

'Really, it is most thoughtless to issue an invitation at such short notice! Perhaps they do not have our advantages, but surely it is only common sense to allow a period of a few days? Never mind, you could hardly have refused, at least not graciously, but I do think you might have found some excuse for postponement.'

'I am sorry, Miss Challis,' Thrift answered, her stomach fluttering and her bladder suddenly weak with fear of what she was sure the conversation was leading to.

'So you should be,' Miss Challis answered. 'Had I the time, I would take you into the park for a thoroughly good spanking, to teach you a bit of courtesy. As it is, that will have to wait. Do come along!'

Thrift struggled to go faster, her boots already pattering on the pavement in the tiny steps her corset allowed. Miss Challis, her own corset covering her only from her bosom to her hips, had no such difficulty. Already hot in her heavy clothes, Thrift was out of breath by the time they reached Dover Street. Miss Challis disappeared back towards Belgravia, and Thrift was left to the care of a maid as she undressed, bathed and dressed once more. An evening gown of rich red silk was selected, cut so low at the front that the whole of her throat showed, filling her with embarrassment but also pride at the pale softness of her neck. Make-up, jewels and flowers followed, carefully selected by her mother to reflect age and status without appearing vulgar or unduly ostentatious. A bonnet and cape completed her ensemble, and she was escorted back downstairs and out to the mews, where the chauffeur waited beside the great black Bentley.

Miss Challis joined her within a few minutes and they were conveyed noiselessly down Piccadilly, through the gates of the Diplomatic Enclave once more, and to an elegant four storey mansion in Chester Square. A footman operated the door, a man darker of skin even than Ana, but in a uniform no different from any other save for being vivid green and with perhaps three times as much gold braid and polished brass. They were admitted to a drawing room typical of the others she had seen in London houses, with high double doors opening on to a dining room, the table already set out with a glittering array of silver and crystal.

Thrift curtseyed as a man stepped forwards to greet her, evidently Ana's father. He was tall, very straight, with a touch of grey in his hair and a stately yet affable manner, and his clothing was conventional to the point of obsession – a black three-piece suit, black shoes, white gloves, shirt, collar and spats in pristine white and heavily starched. What misgivings Thrift had had faded quickly as he returned her curtsey with a formal bow.

Ana joined them, then her mother, and a number of other wives, younger sisters and brothers and, last of all, Mr Sullivan-Jones. Thrift quickly hid her surprise, greeting him with carefully measured formality. Introductions complete, Miss Challis made to leave, only for Ana's mother to insist she stay. Clearly embarrassed by the lapse in etiquette, Miss Challis could only accept, and joined the others at the table.

Dinner began, again following a plan little different to that which Thrift was used to at home. The soup was perhaps a little richer than the typical British recipes, and the fish was unfamiliar, but both were delicious.

Legs of something similar to chicken in a delightfully spicy sauce followed, and then a haunch of meat she sincerely hoped was venison. Wine was served with each course, and poured for her as liberally as for any of the other guests. Thrift held back at first, after catching a meaningful look from Miss Challis, but soon found that, as they were on the same side of the table but well separated, it was not easy for her Companion to keep an eye on her. By the time the main course was over, she felt pleasantly mellow, and in thoroughly good company. As the servants cleared the dishes, Sullivan-Jones excused himself and Ana immediately leaned forwards, addressing the entire table in a loud and delighted voice.

'Thrift was wonderful today. I wish you could all have been there to see her. The dreadful Decency had been tormenting her, and do you know what Thrift did? She poured water with yellow paint in it down the back of Decency's gown to make it look as if the stupid girl had piddled her clothes! Can you imagine anything so funny?'

A gale of laughter greeted Ana's announcement as Thrift went abruptly scarlet. Ana went on, oblivious.

'And do you know? When silly Decency noticed, she as near as nothing denied it and earned herself a tawsing! Now that would truly have put the cap on it all.'

There was fresh laughter, and several compliments directed at Thrift. Despite her feelings, she found a smile creeping on to her face, only for it to be wiped off abruptly as she caught a furious glare from Miss Challis. Nothing was said, the conversation quickly changing, but Thrift was left feeling as if the meal she had just consumed was made of lead.

Ana excused herself, disappearing for what Thrift felt was a long time even for the intricate business of a visit to the convenient facilities. Sullivan-Jones also took a remarkably long time, and pudding had been served before the two were back in their seats. For one moment Thrift wondered if they could possibly have made an assignation, but the idea was so improper that she quickly dismissed it as a product of the wilfulness she was having more and more trouble keeping down. Moreover, neither Ana's father nor her mother nor any of the eleven stepmothers took the least notice.

A spread of cheese and summer fruits followed pudding, and the Ladies retired to the drawing room to leave the Gentlemen to their port. Thrift made a point of sitting as far away as possible from Miss Challis, although she knew it would make no difference to what was sure to happen in the end. Still, she struggled to delay the inevitable, providing a long recital from MacCauley and performing a piano duet with Ana. Still, the end came, Miss Challis rising to make their excuses a moment before Thrift could volunteer to give a second recital.

With her heart in her mouth she completed the round of thanks and courteous goodbyes, all the while thinking of the spanking she knew was coming, and of whether it would be done back at the house, in the car with the chauffeur watching or simply in the street. As Miss Challis took her arm on the steps and the door swung silently closed behind them, she found herself babbling.

'Please, no, Miss Challis. It was only a foolish joke, and no harm was meant, and yes, I know I should be punished, but, if you must, then please let it be at home in my bedroom, please, my dear Miss Challis, oh please!'

Miss Challis merely raised her eyebrows and began to steer Thrift towards the waiting Bentley, speaking only when they were in the car and moving smoothly away down the road.

'What remarkably pleasant and civilised people the Lakoussans are – for heathens – but that is more than I can say for you, Miss Thrift.'

'I know,' Thrift answered miserably, hanging her head. 'I am truly sorry.'

'So you should be,' Miss Challis answered, although there was more amusement than admonition in her voice, as usual. 'Well, I suppose we had better get what is so plainly necessary over and done with, don't you?'

'No, Miss Challis, not here, please,' Thrift begged. 'Not in the car, not in front of –'

'Of Henry?' Miss Challis queried. 'Yes, I take your point. Opinion is divided as to whether girls should or should not be punished in front of the lower servants. My own position . . . is that they should. Henry, stop the car. Thrift, come across my knee.'

Thrift could manage only a broken sob as she laid herself obediently across her Companion's lap. By good luck they were in a quiet street, but it was little consolation as the chauffeur parked and leaned nonchalantly back across his seat even as Miss Challis began the slow and elaborate task of exposing Thrift's bottom.

Thrift's beautiful evening gown came up, the underskirt beneath it, the taffeta petticoat, the flannel, the cotton. Her bustle on show, it was inverted and the panel of her corset opened, lifted and tied off. Her drawers were undone, button after button, each one bringing new agonies of embarrassment, until the final ghastly moment when her bottom was exposed and she burst into tears. A moment later, Miss Challis had begun to spank, Thrift's bottom bouncing merrily in the bright glow of the interior lights.

It was long, and slow, Miss Challis making little effort to bring Thrift's pain up, but taking her time, and all too obviously enjoying her task. It still hurt, and had Thrift crying into her hands and kicking her feet up and down just as far as the tight lacing of her corset would permit, all the time with the thought of the chauffeur's eyes on her bare, jiggling bottom burning in her head. After a while, dimly, through the pain and humiliation of her spanking, she became aware of a strange meaty noise, then a low moan. There was no more, and she was left to the misery of her punishment, her bottom slapped and slapped, until finally it stopped and Miss Challis spoke.

'Are you ready, Henry?'

'Quite ready, thank you, Miss Challis, Ma'am,' the chauffeur answered.

'Then pray proceed,' Miss Challis went on.

The car started. Thrift lay still, snivelling as she waited for her modesty to be restored. Nothing happened, save for Miss Challis's hand coming to rest on her warm bottom. Thrift gave a choking sob as the hand began to stroke, the cotton of her Companion's glove tickling her tender bottom skin.

It was not the first time Miss Challis had explored her bottom after a spanking, but it was something she had always thought of as intimate, for all the embarrassment it brought. Now it was being done in the car, with the chauffeur able to see in the mirror, and every likelihood that people would look in through the windows. To her utter relief Miss Challis stopped and began to sort out the disarranged clothes as they approached the gate to the Diplomatic Enclave.

'Oh dear, what am I to with you, dear Thrift?' Miss Challis sighed as she pulled Thrift's skirts back down.

It seemed an odd thing to say, but Thrift took no notice, only glad to be covered and so avoid having the guards and gate staff added to the growing list of people who had seen her bare. The brief conversation with the chauffeur was also strange, but then servants often said things that she could not understand, and she knew that it was inappropriate for her to do so.

Thrift was in no doubt where the responsibility for her latest humiliation lay, with Decency Branksome-Brading. She was equally sure that Decency would not see what had happened as a fair tit-for-tat. The next day she was cautious, staying close to Tatiana and Ana, and being careful never to give Decency an opportunity for revenge, while all the time plotting her own. To her surprise, Decency simply ignored her, behaving with an aloof dignity that would only have been appropriate towards somebody in trade or manual work.

She remained cautious on Thursday, but still nothing happened. Friday passed to the weekend, and on the Monday Decency even ventured a neutral remark on the weather. By Tuesday Thrift had begun to relax, and also to wonder if it might not be better to attempt to make friends with Decency after all. At lunch Decency made a point of being polite, and Thrift responded in kind.

After lunch she visited the convenient facilities, to go through the elaborate and embarrassing process of relieving herself. Once finished, she emerged from the cubicle to find Decency, Francesca and Xiuying also there. There was a moment of fear, but Decency's smile was frank and friendly as she spoke.

'Ah, there you are, Thrift. Did you know we are to visit the Natural History Museum this afternoon, in order that we may sketch? We are to consider both the bones of the beasts and their stuffed or reconstituted forms, while next week it is to be the Zoological Gardens at the Regent's Park. Will that not be the most exciting expedition?'

'Wonderful, I am sure,' Thrift answered, more surprised at being addressed by her name rather than as the Brat than at Decency's announcement. 'Will our Companions be joining us?'

'They will not,' Decency answered, 'and nor –'

She stopped as the door swung open. For one moment Thrift was sure that her tone had changed on the last word, but dismissed the idea as Ana entered the room. Decency gave the black girl a formal nod and left the room, Francesca and Xiuying following in train.

Ana waited until the door had closed and then came quickly forwards, speaking in an urgent whisper.

'Thrift, you and I are firm friends now, are we not?'

'Why certainly,' Thrift answered. 'What –'

'You must help me in the most important matter,' Ana went on. 'Say you will.'

'If I am able,' Thrift answered cautiously, concerned by both her friend's excitement and the secretive undertone in which she was speaking.

'It is a little thing,' Ana went on, 'but very important to me. Merely stay here, arrange your hair in the mirror, or whatever you might wish to do, but seem busy. I will be within a cubicle and, should another enter the room, you are to speak to them quickly, is that clear?'

'Yes,' Thrift answered, 'but why –'

'Sh!' Ana urged. 'We must be in the hall in one quarter of an hour. Please just do as I say. When I have finished, I shall signal you, and you may leave. Say you will do it.'

'Why of course,' Thrift answered, puzzled by why Ana, the boldest of all save Tatiana, should wish such exaggerated privacy for her necessities.

'Thank you,' Ana answered, and kissed Thrift, full on the lips.

Thrift stood back in surprise, both for the warmth of the kiss and the sudden fluttering in her chest that followed it, but, before she could say anything, Ana had darted away, not for a cubicle, but for the door. It swung wide, and Thrift was left gaping in astonishment and outrage as Mr Sullivan-Jones slid quickly within, pulled by Ana.

'Mr Sullivan-Jones!' Thrift exclaimed, her hands flying instinctively to her chest and belly despite being fully dressed.

'Sh!' Ana urged.

The artist tipped his hat and vanished, pulled into the cubicle closest to the door.

Thrift stood stock still, staring vacantly at the door, her mouth wide and her hands frozen in place at her bosom and lap. Her mind was whirling, in a vain effort to find any excuse for what she had just seen other than the obvious one. Then Ana giggled and the sound was answered by a deep chuckle from Sullivan-Jones, quite the lewdest sound Thrift had ever heard.

Angry, severely uncomfortable and feeling that she had been tricked, Thrift turned to the mirror and began to redo her hair as she had been instructed. From the cubicle came a soft rustling, cloth on cloth, another girlish giggle, then a wet sound Thrift could not identify, but which set her heart hammering and her nipples embarrassingly stiff. The sound did not stop either, and Sullivan-Jones gave a long, contented sigh.

Thrift stared angrily at her reflection in the mirror, furious, yet fascinated to know what was happening within the cubicle. It had to be something physical, something men and women did, and should only do in wedlock, although beyond that she had no idea what happened. Whatever it was, it obviously involved a lot of wet goings-on, and it smelled, the same rich, disturbing scent that always came when a girl was beaten, growing stronger as the lashes fell and as her unmentionable place grew damp. Thrift wondered if Ana was letting Sullivan-Jones touch her between the legs, but decided it was impossibly vulgar.

Yet *something* was happening, all too clearly. The wet sounds continued, and grew more rapid. Sullivan-Jones began to moan, and to mutter, something about a beautiful black doll, which Thrift realised could only refer to Ana. There was fresh rustling, then more wet sounds, but different, a smacking noise, oddly reminiscent of underdone steak. Sullivan-Jones's voice sounded again, now clear.

'Dirty wench! My, but you are wonderful!'

Ana didn't answer, but the wet sounds grew more urgent still. Once more Sullivan-Jones began to moan, sounds even more satisfied than before. At last Thrift's curiosity overcame her shock and anger. After pushing quickly into the neighbouring cubicle, she put her back to the squat chest of drawers in which the hygienics were stored and hauled herself up on to it, and sat down. With a lot of effort and much creaking of whalebone, she managed to roll over on to her knees, into a thoroughly indecent kneeling position that somehow felt appropriate, and at last to her feet. Gingerly, she peered over the partition between the cubicles.

Once more she froze in shock. Sullivan-Jones, the highly respected artist, had his back to the cubicle wall, and Ana, the daughter of an equally highly respected foreign diplomat, was on her knees in front of him, with a great rod of flesh sticking out from his belly, and into her mouth. To watch Ana's mouth work on the hideous thing was bad enough, but *it* was worse, terrifying, a great column of flesh that seemed unnaturally pale against the dark skin of Ana's face. There was a fat, hairy sac below, like dogs had, which she had always suspected, deep down, that men must have too. The sticking-out thing also resembled what she had seen on dogs but, if anything, it was uglier, with its fish-belly white colour, writhing purple veins and thick collar of puffy flesh.

The idea of any woman, let alone a Lady, taking such a thing in her mouth was inconceivable. Yet Ana was doing it, and plainly enjoying it, her eyes closed in bliss and one hand wrapped around the hideous thing as she tugged on it, and took it right into her mouth. Her other hand was invisible beneath her dress, which she'd lifted, and, from the jerking of her elbow and the way her big breasts quivered in her gown, it was all too plain that she was rubbing herself between her thighs.

Thrift could only stare, frozen with emotion – both shock and what she recognised only too well as a wanton reaction, a severely wanton reaction. She was wet between her legs, and not with pee-pee, but with the same sticky, slippery fluid that came out when Miss Challis spanked her, to her utter mortification. There was more now, and the split bulge where her belly curved under between her thighs felt oddly big and swollen.

Finally, she managed to get control of herself and moved back. Ana and Sullivan-Jones were being noisier than ever as Thrift climbed down quickly, and as she hurried from the cubicle he gave a cry as if of pain, then called Ana something Thrift could not bring herself to repeat even in her head. He finished with a long sigh expressing a satisfaction beyond anything of Thrift's experience. Another grunt sounded, this time from Ana; there was a last flurry of meaty slapping noises, a soft, female cry, then silence.

Thrift stood where she was, shaking with emotion, not sure if she should be angry or happy, upset or elated. Only by the strongest of efforts did she manage to compose herself before there was a tap from within the cubicle and an urgent hiss from Ana.

'Is all safe?'

'Quite safe,' Thrift answered, finding her voice oddly high.

Ana emerged. She was smiling, her eyes glittering, and she gave Thrift a knowing wink. Briefly Ana inspected herself in the mirror, adjusting her hair and wiping a bead of some white substance from her lower lip before scampering to the door. Sullivan-Jones emerged the instant Ana had given the all clear, tipped his hat to Thrift as politely as ever and left.

A week passed without undue incident. All six girls managed to avoid Miss Evans's wrath, although Francesca came close to getting a thrashing, which gave Thrift a sense of satisfaction she knew to be highly unsuitable. Miss Challis also held back, and gave nothing worse than admonitions and the occasional pat to the rear of Thrift's skirts. Decency remained polite and friendly, until Thrift was sure that she had, after all, decided it was best to be friends. Ana was more friendly still, embarrassingly so, more than once kissing Thrift with a warmth that set her tingling.

When Tuesday came, Thrift found herself ill at ease. Sullivan-Jones would be with them, and she was not at all sure how she would cope if Ana asked her to stand guard once more. As it was, there was no opportunity, the entire class being formed into a line and marched smartly around the corner to Hyde Park Underground Railway Station directly after lunch.

Sullivan-Jones accompanied them, as did Miss Evans and Lady Newgate also, the two women fiercely protective as the girls made their way down the moving stairs and to a first-class compartment. Two changes brought them to the Zoological Gardens Station, and a brief walk to the gardens themselves.

It was not Thrift's first visit, but she found herself fascinated as always. The area lay within an Enclave, yet most of the Zoological Gardens was open to the commonality. Those who lived there were also very different to the gentry and governmental people she was used to. There were citymen in their bowlers and pinstripes, engineers in stovepipe hats and cutaway waistcoats, even Empire traders, the Indians in white or pale-tan suits, the Burmese in vivid green or scarlet. The women, she was amused to see, wore the latest fashions, yet somehow never quite got it right. Here was a bustle with the central cleft a touch too deep, there a sleeve triple gored rather than single, creating an impression she found droll, clownish even. Then there was the canal, in a deep cutting, with long, brightly painted boats moored by the banks and moving with noiseless efficiency on the still water. The crews were more eccentric still, largely those who had chosen to abandon mainstream society, which, she was greatly amused to note, seemed to involve wearing colourful yet largely shapeless dresses, with no hint of an S curve. The men tended to thick shirts, coloured braces and, in some cases, to her shock and astonishment, even had their sleeves rolled up over bare arms.

Within the gardens, the animals were scarcely more remarkable, often less so. There was the conventional fauna of India, Africa, Australia and North America; tigers, elephants, kangaroos, lynx, each in a compound railed with black iron and ringed with a moat. In among them were those beasts recreated from frozen carcasses and bits of ancient bone; mammoths, glyptodon, a solitary sabre-toothed tiger, a huge ape with shaggy red fur that stared at the passing girls with a disturbing intelligence. More unusual, and certainly less smelly, were the exotic birds, whose brilliant plumage and curious calls could be noted from lines of wired cages, with each one bearing a plaque to announce its name and distribution.

For an hour the girls moved from cage to cage, enclosure to enclosure, making sketches and taking notes under the ever-watchful eyes of Miss Evans and Lady Newgate. Sullivan-Jones was at his most charming, pointing out the peculiarities of each animal and remarking on the relationships of anatomy and art. Behind them, three school servants carried the easels and other necessities, but they were not ordered to set them up until the group had come out of the common area and around to the rear of the great ape cages. Thrift, having accepted an ice cream from Decency and a large carton of chilled apple juice from Francesca, was beginning to feel in need of the convenient facilities. She was wondering where those reserved for Ladies of Quality were as Sullivan-Jones began to speak, indicating the huge red ape with a flourish of his arm.

'Here,' he declared, 'is our study for the day, *Sinopithecus andropovii*, or the Ural Ape. As you will no doubt have noted, this beast is among those retrieved from the nothingness of extinction by the wonders of modern science, and yes, Miss Zhukov, before you need make remark, the technique was developed by a Soviet team. He is not, however, as was originally thought, an ancestor of man, but more closely related to the Orang-utan of our Java and Borneo colonies. There is intelligence there, though, beneath the mighty dome of his skull, a glimmer, perhaps, compared with our own, but nonetheless intelligence. Note his eyes.'

The annoying pressure in Thrift's bladder was forgotten as she peered in at the creature. He was large, taller and heavier than any man, with a massive head, an enormous, heavy jaw, long arms set in solid muscle and stumpy, banded legs. Thick, red hair covered his entire body, save only his face, in which two bright, dark eyes shone with what she had no doubt at all was a clear understanding. Immediately she found herself trying to read an expression in his gaze, and wondering what he thought as he stared out at her, only for all such thoughts to be pushed instantly from her mind as he got to his feet.

His face was not, after all, the only part of his anatomy without hair. From among the thick red tangle between his thighs sprouted the same grotesque arrangement of wrinkled and obscene flesh she had noted on Sullivan-Jones, only on a much larger scale. A leathery sac the size of a large apple hung below a column of pale, taut flesh perhaps twice as long as that of the artist, but otherwise horribly, disgustingly similar. Thrift turned sharply about, her face flushing pink with embarrassment. The others were no different, save Tatiana, who was still looking, and Ana, who was giggling.

'Miss Zhukov, Miss Lakoussan!' Miss Evans snapped. 'Mr Sullivan-Jones, I think perhaps a more suitable subject might be found. Come, girls!'

Tatiana and Ana had come away from the cage, leaving the ape meditatively tugging on the monstrous bar of flesh that protruded from below his belly. Unable to stop herself, Thrift stole a final glance at him, to find him stroking his rod with his face set in a grotesque parody of human lust. Shock and disgust welled up in her, making her bladder twinge, then again as the truly revolting thought of how it would feel to take the creature's cock in her mouth as Ana had done Sullivan-Jones's forced itself into her mind.

Not a word was spoken as they trooped across to an enclosure in which a pair of monstrous birds with beaks like sickles stood motionless on a sun-whitened log. Sullivan-Jones went into a description of them and how their genetic code had been recovered from a tar pit in the North American colonies, but Thrift was no longer paying attention. Instead she was thinking of him and Ana, what they had done, the huge ape and what she could only suppose it had wanted to do. Her reaction was strong, there was no denying it, but she was still trying hard to tell herself that it was of disgust and not wanton.

By the time the easels had been set up the pressure in Thrift's bladder was growing extremely uncomfortable. She had to relieve herself and, short of letting it soak into her abundant undergarments, there was no choice but to go through the embarrassment of asking where the convenient facilities where. Any one of a number of small buildings within the area might hold them, but she had no idea which one. Only when her discomfort had turned to pain did her need finally overcome her embarrassment. She raised her hand.

'Yes, Thrift,' Miss Evans asked immediately, and loud enough to ensure that every one of the others heard.

'May I be excused, please, Miss Evans,' Thrift asked, blushing hot once again.

Miss Evans sighed, then answered. 'Very well, Thrift. Come with me.'

Even as the Mistress spoke Thrift had remembered the place, a small building beyond the gibbon enclosure, shielded within a thicket of laurel. Hot with shame, she rose, only to pause as Decency raised a hand.

'You also, Decency, my dear,' Miss Evans stated. 'Then you may go together for the sake of convenience. Will there be any further disturbances before we commence our study?'

Francesca rose immediately, followed by Xiuying after a moment's pause. Decency offered her arm, which Thrift took, unable to suppress a sense of pleasure at being shown such a favour. All four walked together, in two pairs, watching the antics of the gibbons as they passed the tall enclosure and pausing demurely until they were sure they were unobserved before entering the discreetly concealed path among the laurels.

The bushes were high enough to ensure that even the tallest woman with the most elaborate hat would be fully concealed. The building within was invisible from the outside, and from the path, which was designed to make absolutely sure that there was no possibility of any man catching an accidental glimpse of the door to the convenient facilities. Thrift and Decency took one tight turn, then another, to reach a little space with a bench, from which the path turned back once again.

'Here will serve admirably,' Decency remarked, and the next instant Thrift found that Francesca had taken her other arm.

'Decency!' Thrift protested, almost losing her balance as she was pulled in among the laurel bushes.

'Be quiet, Brat,' Decency answered.

'But – but, what are –' Thrift stammered, only to shut up as Decency took hold of her face, squeezing her cheeks.

'Be quiet, I said,' Decency hissed. 'We've brought you in here to teach you a lesson.'

Fear gripped Thrift's stomach, but she could do nothing, neither speak nor struggle. The two girls had her in a tight grip, and they had pulled her deep in among the bushes, to a little patch of dry earth, surrounded by high, green walls on every side. Decency went on, her beautiful eyes alight with excited cruelty.

'Cry out, Brat, and it will be a lot worse, I promise that. You are going to do as you are told, are you not?'

Thrift managed a nod, praying that whatever horrid fate they had in store for her it was not going to hurt too much. Decency nodded in return, with cruel satisfaction, speaking again as she let go of Thrift's face.

'Yes, I did not think we should have a great deal of fight from you. Now, what shall we do with you? I think, perhaps, we should whip that fat bulb of a bottom of yours.'

'No, please, not that!' Thrift begged. 'Be merciful, Decency!'

Decency merely laughed and went on. 'Don't be scared, my little coward. It will not be that. I know how you bleat from watching you get it from your Companion and, even if we might have you take a stocking in your mouth to stifle your cries, there would be sure to be trouble when you are inspected.'

'What then?' Thrift quavered.

'Tell her what she must do!' Xiuying said quickly, her tiny, mild voice suddenly full of cruel delight.

'What you are to do,' Decency said sweetly, 'will be a fitting response to what you did to me. You need to make water, do you not?'

'Yes,' Thrift answered. 'I must, Decency, please let me, before you . . . you –'

She was unable to finish, not knowing what horrible fate they were going to inflict on her. Decency smiled.

'Certainly you may relieve yourself, my dear Thrift. That is what we intend for you to do – in your clothes.'

'No!' Thrift gasped. 'You would not . . . you would not!'

She had begun to struggle, but the three of them were holding her and kept their grips. A rustle of skirts sounded from the path, but Decency's gloved hand was immediately clamped tight over Thrift's mouth and she was held still and silent as the woman passed on into the convenient facilities.

'Do it, Brat!' Decency hissed.

Thrift managed only a muffled sob in denial. Her tummy hurt, and she was straining to stop it happening, but determined not to give in, anger and helpless frustration boiling inside her as she squirmed in their grip.

'Do it!' Decency repeated. 'Do it now, Brat, do your pee-pee, right in your clothes, like the dirty, common little she-cat you are!'

At the same instant Decency twisted hard on the arm she held trapped behind Thrift's back. Thrift cried out in pain, and for one instant her concentration was off her bladder. As pee-pee squirted out into her beautiful white silk drawers she let out a wail of misery, and it was coming, full force, so hard they could hear the hiss and tinkle of her stream as it gushed out. They let go of her, Decency to step back with a peel of delighted laughter, Francesca with a quiet and satisfied smile, Xiuying to jump up and down on her toes in sheer glee.

Unable to stop herself, all Thrift could do was hang her head in miserable defeat as she piddled her clothes. It was coming fast, gushing out into her drawers and trickling down her thighs to wet her stockings. She was sobbing bitterly as it came, and her mouth opened in disgust and disgrace as the hot fluid continued to spurt from her body, soaking her drawers, her stockings and her corset, also slowly filling her boots.

Her tears started, hot and copious, running down her cheeks to splash on the ground, into the pool of piddle that was expanding slowly from beneath her skirts. Decency greeted the sight with fresh laughter, and suddenly took a handful of Thrift's skirts, to haul them up and reveal the heavy lace frill of her corset hem, now with yellow piddle dripping from the fringe. Overwhelmed by misery and shame, Thrift didn't even try to prevent the added humiliation of having her boots and a slice of stocking-clad calf exposed. Suddenly it had got a lot further, with Thrift's skirts and petticoats hauled high and her corset exposed, with the yellow stain still spreading at front and rear.

'What a revolting little brat you are!' Decency laughed. 'Just look at you, pee-pee all over yourself, and still running! How very droll! Come, do you have a little more, or is that the end of our entertainment?'

Thrift gave a miserable, choking sob and squeezed out a final spurt of urine from her bladder into her drawers, unable to stop herself from obeying the awful command. With her legs soaked and her feet squelching in her piddle as she made little treading motions in her boots from sheer embarrassment, she stood for them to inspect her, front and back, all three girls giggling over the mess she had made.

'Oh look!' Decency called as she came behind Thrift. 'It has soaked up her corset panel to outline the shape of her bottom! How simply ludicrous she does look!'

'And how she smells!' Francesca added, pinching her tiny nose in a gesture of exaggerated revulsion. 'I wonder if Miss Evans will beat her for being so vulgar.'

'With luck, yes,' Decency answered, dropping Thrift's skirts, 'and naturally it is our duty to report so disgustingly unladylike an incident.'

'Without question,' Francesca answered.

'No!' Thrift managed, finding her voice at last through pure fear.

'Why ever not?' Decency queried. 'It will be fun to see you flogged. Who knows, with any luck you might get it in public.'

'No!' Thrift wailed. 'Please, Decency, I beg you, do

not tell! I will do anything you ask, just do not tell Miss Evans, please! I could not bear to be so humiliated!'

'It will do you good,' Decency answered coolly. 'Come, girl, we have a task to perform, disagreeable of course, but necessary.'

'No, please!' Thrift begged. 'I shall say you made me, I shall!'

'Pray do,' Decency answered her. 'You will get double for lying as well as soiling yourself. Come.'

'No, please, Decency,' Thrift went on, now babbling. 'Do not do it, I beg you! I will do anything, I mean it, anything!'

'Shall I test, to see?' Xiuying said suddenly. 'It might amuse, I think, if she were to drink up my own pee-pee.'

Thrift turned to stare in horror at the little Chinese girl, her mouth falling open in amazement at the outrageous suggestion. Francesca had given a shocked gasp, and had her hand over her mouth and a pink face. Even Decency looked taken aback, but quickly rallied.

'You would pee-pee, on her?'

'In her mouth,' Xiuying explained. 'We do this at home to punish a woman who has sought to rise above her status. She is taken out to a field, where the peasants can see as the pee-pee is made in her mouth. It is very comic.'

'What of your own exposure?' Francesca demanded.

'To us, this is no shame,' Xiuying answered.

Neither Decency nor Francesca answered, both staring at the Chinese girl in disbelief. Thrift could only stare, the impossible disgrace of having another woman urinate into her mouth slowly sinking in. Francesca thought it had gone too far, Thrift could see, but it was Decency who eventually spoke.

'Well, I suppose for the Brat it might really be quite appropriate. Certainly she gives herself airs far above her station.'

'No, Decency, have some thought!' Thrift declared in horror. 'You cannot . . . you simply cannot . . . I shall tell Miss Evans, I shall, and you can't pretend I wet myself, not after that!'

'Frankly,' Decency answered, 'I doubt you have the courage, but yes, I can see there might be difficulties –'

'No difficulty,' Xiuying stated. 'She must push out her head, to be sure none falls on her bosom, and do her best to drink.'

Thrift gave a muffled sob, once more beyond speech.

'I see,' Decency said thoughtfully. 'Yes, why not then? So be it, Brat, you may choose, either let our little heathen friend do her business in your mouth, or we shall inform Miss Evans that you have wet your clothes.'

'I – I – please no, Decency,' Thrift managed to say.

'Choose,' Decency answered.

Thrift looked at them. Francesca was blushing and shamefaced, standing pressed back into the laurels. Decency looked amused, shocked, but determined too. Cruel humour showed on Xiuying's normally impassive features, with no trace of modesty or mercy. Weak with fear, her stomach and throat twitching, Thrift tried to fight down the horrible compulsion rising up in her to accept Xiuying's revolting suggestion, and yet with a public beating if she refused it was hard, too hard . . .

'I – I'll do it – drink it,' she said, choking out the words.

'Oh how foul!' Decency exclaimed, and immediately turned away. 'Give the common little whelp what she wants then, Xiuying, you Godless creature. How truly disgusting!'

For all her words, Decency had not turned fully, and still had a clear view of Thrift and Xiuying. Francesca had covered her face with her hands, but was peeping out from between her fingers. Xiuying's expression had become crueller than ever as she gestured to the ground and spoke.

'Squat at my feet, Brat, and push out your face.'

Thrift went down, her stomach crawling, her mind screaming at her to stop, but her body following the order, and also her hideous, unthinkable compulsion. Then Xiuying had begun to hitch up the dress of tight, brilliant green silk she was wearing, exposing neat, slim thighs, and then the plump swell of her belly with the little split fig of flesh in the V beneath, hairless and unencumbered by drawers.

'Push it out more,' Xiuying commanded, now imperious. 'Open your mouth.'

Numb, blindly obedient, Thrift obeyed, all the while with her eyes fixed on the delicate, fleshy groove below her persecutor's belly. Xiuying pushed out her tummy even more, as she reached down to spread her puffy little lips wide and reveal folds of wet, pink flesh between and a tiny hole.

'Wider!' Xiuying snapped, and yellow, pungent fluid squirted out from her, full into Thrift's mouth.

Francesca squealed in shock and disgust. Decency gave a sharp exclamation. Xiuying laughed. Thrift let out a single, choking sob as her mouth began to fill with piddle, unable to bring herself to swallow.

'Is she not funny!' Xiuying laughed. 'Look, look, how it comes out at the sides to fall down her chin! Swallow, you daughter of a pig, swallow my pee-pee!'

Thrift struggled to obey, gulping down the piddle in her mouth. Immediately her stomach revolted, tightening hard, to bring her acrid mouthful back up. Once more she forced it down, terrified of letting it out all over the front of her dress. Xiuying's laughter grew louder, the stream of urine stronger, Thrift sobbing in her misery as she took it in, before gulping it down when her mouth was full, then breaking into deeper, harsher sobs as the thick, acrid taste caught her throat; again letting her mouth fill, then swallowing.

'Pig-girl, she-dog, wanton piece of cattle dung!' Xiuying crowed. 'See, she enjoys it! How funny, how very funny, yes!'

'Never could I have imagined it!' Decency said as Thrift leaned forward to catch the last trickle of Xiuying's piddle in her mouth. 'How disgraceful! How truly revolting!'

'What do you want, dirt-girl?' Xiuying cackled. 'You want to lick my cunt?'

'Xiuying!' Decency exclaimed as Francesca gave another gasp of shock. 'How could –'

She stopped, struck dumb. Xiuying had snatched Thrift by the hair, dragging her in. Thrift gave a last frantic squeal and then her face was between Xiuying's thighs, being rubbed against the wet, pee-soaked folds between. Struggling to get away, she began to flap her arms, and to beat them against Xiuying's legs.

'Lick it, pig dirt!' Xiuying screeched.

'Xiuying!' Decency snapped. 'What are you thinking of? We shall be overheard!'

For a moment Xiuying took no notice, still rubbing herself in Thrift's face, only to stop abruptly and step away.

'It is true,' she said. 'Then the mother of pigs Evans will beat me, and that I could not bear.'

'Well, quite,' Decency answered, sounding anything but in control. 'Now I think that is quite enough. Thrift, do clean your face up! You are a disgrace, to yourself, to your family, to the Empire! Imagine drinking pee-pee! You disgust me!'

'But –' Thrift began, and stopped, utterly overwhelmed by the sheer injustice of Decency's words as she began to cry again.

'Do stop snivelling!' Decency snapped. 'We were only having a little fun with you, and there is no reason to go making an exhibition of yourself. Now do hurry, or they will wonder what we have been doing.'

Thrift could not find an answer, but pulled a handkerchief from her sleeve and began to clean the sticky mess of Xiuying's urine and juice from her nose and round her lips. She felt beaten, utterly defeated, yet also utterly wanton, and to her inner horror she knew that had it not been for her audience she would have done as she had been ordered, and licked what Xiuying had called her 'cunt'.

Francesca was also shaken, red faced and silent as they pushed their way back out of the laurels. The woman who had gone into the convenient facilities had still not emerged, and they hurried back to the open ground. All was as before, the warm air heavy with the scents and cries of animals, the people walking among the cages and enclosures, their own group around the easels. Thrift realised that what had seemed like an age of being helpless as they bullied her had in reality been perhaps less than ten minutes. Decency spoke quietly as they reached the gibbon enclosure.

'Now, remember, what happened is this. Thrift here was unable to reach the convenient facilities in time, and made water in her clothes. We three, naturally –'

'No,' Thrift broke in. 'You said that if –'

'That if what, my dear?' Decency enquired calmly. 'That if you were to drink Xiuying's pee-pee we would keep your little secret? Nonsense! How could anybody believe such a vulgar absurdity for a moment? Besides, I think you will find that you are obliged to tell the truth. You are dripping.'

'The truth!' Thrift exclaimed, but she was already looking back.

Behind her, leading directly to where the path opened among the laurel bushes, was a trail of spots, dark against the dusty grey of the sun-dried tarmac. Her hand went to her mouth in horror.

'It is always best to be truthful, Thrift, my dear,' Decency said. 'Come, let us make a clean breast of your little accident. Perhaps if you make your own confession, the consequences may prove to be less severe?'

Decency took her arm, to lead her forwards. She went meekly, unable to decide on any other course of action. As they approached the group, Xiuying and Francesca went quickly to their seats, Decency staying with Thrift. Miss Evans looked around, puzzled, then outraged.

'Miss Moncrieff,' she demanded. 'What is this?'

'I – I am so dreadfully sorry, Miss Evans,' Thrift answered, her voice meek even as she burned with consternation inside. 'I had an . . . a little accident.'

'She could not help herself,' Decency added, still holding firmly to Thrift's arm.

'Really!' Miss Evans sighed as Lady Newgate turned from where she had been studying Tatiana's drawing. 'It is too much, Thrift, a disgrace. Decency, I realise that you are only trying to be helpful to your friend, but kindly stand aside. Thrift, you are to be beaten. Bend across your chair.'

For a moment Thrift thought to respond, only to abandon the thought. It was hopeless. She was to be beaten, in public, hard, and any protest would only make it worse. Meekly, her face set in abject misery, fresh tears rolling down her cheeks, she bent down to take hold of the seat of her stool. For a moment she caught a look of triumph on Decency's face, and then it had changed to concern, as Miss Evans moved around, the monstrous tawse she favoured already drawn from somewhere in the recesses of her clothing.

Thrift closed her eyes, already in agonies of emotion, filled with humiliation, feeling small and stupid in the knowledge that she had been tricked into drinking Xiuying's piddle for nothing. Yet that was not the worst of it. The experience had left her damp between the legs, and not just with pee. It would show, she was sure, the slimy white stuff that came out when she had wilful thoughts. As she knew only too well, it came out when she was spanked too, as it did with other girls, but that was simply one of those many things that were never,

ever mentioned. Now she was like that before her punishment, and Miss Evans was going to see.

So were other people. Her face was to the class, who had turned to watch the punishment as they were supposed to for the sake of their own humility. That left a good many people behind her, between the bird enclosure and that which held the great shaggy ape and, for that matter, the beast itself. A peep showed her that he had come forward to the bars of his cage to investigate, and then she had shut her eyes tightly in fresh humiliation.

'Six will suffice, I feel,' Miss Evans announced, 'as you did at least have the decency to confess to your disgusting crime. Now, up with your haunches.'

Thrift obeyed, lifting her bottom into position for beating even as her gown was taken. It came up and the stripping had begun. Thrift was already pink faced and tearful, and growing swiftly pinker and more tearful as her underdress came, her petticoats, one, two and three, and her corset was put on show, with the big, bottom-shaped stain wet and yellow behind her.

'Revolting,' Miss Evans remarked and Thrift's bustle had been inverted with a single, practised motion.

Miss Evans gave a fresh sniff of distaste as she bent to unfasten the gudgeons of Thrift's corset panel. It came loose, open and up, to leave her drawers showing, the wet silk plastered tight to her bottom. The scent of her own piddle caught her, sharp and clear even beside the all-pervasive smell of animals. Wincing in shame, she could only wait and endure the agony of being unbuttoned. Miss Evans opened them with evident disgust, one by one, until at last the panel of Thrift's drawers fell away and her bottom was laid bare, wet and sticky in the hot sunlight. With the tears streaming from her eyes, she hung her head in mute, broken submission, every moment expecting the horrible sting of the tawse.

Nothing happened.

Miss Evans spoke. 'A Cantlemere and Lucas, I see. Well, we shall just have to do our best.'

'The recommended technique,' Lady Newgate broke in, 'is to have the young Lady lie on her back and to turn up her legs. Thus the posteriors become more readily available.'

'Most estimable advice, Lady Newgate,' Miss Evans answered. 'Thrift, you are to lie on your back upon the chair. Sharp now!'

Thrift moved as quickly as the disarray of her clothing allowed, her fear of Miss Evans overcoming her reluctance to get into the unfamiliar and possibly even more humiliating position. Bending back, with her whalebone creaking in protest, she laid herself on the chair and took hold of the back to steady herself. As she pulled up her thighs her emotional hurt rose to pain, making it hard to breathe. Her skirts dropped, spreading out like a flower around her middle and she was exposed, her bottom thrust out, wet and glistening, through the hole in her corset. Everything showed, she knew – the full spread of her bottom, the lips of what she could not stop herself thinking of as her cunt protruding rudely, her dirty place, spread wide for all to see.

It hurt, too, the bones of her corset digging into her midriff and tight across the small of her back, forcing her to hold up her legs as if presenting herself for inspection. There were plenty to inspect her too. Sullivan-Jones had moved to Xiuying's chair, as if casually, but providing himself with a prime view of Thrift's exposure. Others had stopped too, some furtive, some casual, the latter mainly ladies, who whispered together in delight and disgust from behind gloved hands.

'I see, yes,' Miss Evans remarked, 'now she is quite unobstructed.'

'It is a position I quite frequently employ,' Lady Newgate responded.

'I also shall do so, in the future,' Miss Evans agreed. 'Now, six strokes, I think we said.'

She had brought the tawse up as she spoke. Thrift winced, closing her eyes in stark terror as it whistled down, then opened them sharply as it hit, cracking down across her spread buttocks with a meaty smack. She screamed as the pain hit her, let go of her legs and almost fell from the chair, only to be caught by Lady Newgate and quickly hauled back into position.

'Do try and keep still!' the Headmistress snapped. 'I shall hold her, Miss Evans, if you would care to proceed.'

'Much obliged, Lady Newgate,' Miss Evans answered and laid the second stroke in.

Thrift screamed as the crack of leather on flesh rang out, louder, enough to startle birds and send the gibbons hooting away among their swings and ropes. It left her whimpering, teeth clenched, eyes tight shut to squeeze hot tears out from beneath the lips, briefly kicking in Lady Newgate's grip as her muscles jerked against the pain.

'Hold still, girl!' Lady Newgate snapped. 'We shall make it a round dozen should you not behave!'

'No – please, no –' Thrift whined, bubbles breaking from her lips as she spoke, and ending in a long, snotty sniff.

'Miss Evans,' Lady Newgate said quietly.

The third stroke came down on the instant, catching Thrift plum across the thighs and the plump lips sticking out from between them. Again she screamed, writhing in her pain and completely unable to control her body. Lady Newgate gave only a sniff of disapproval, and the instant the spasmodic jerking of Thrift's muscles had stilled to a hard, steady trembling, the fourth stroke came in.

As leather smacked to flesh, mucus exploded from Thrift's nose as the breath was knocked from her body, her scream cut off in a burbling, choking noise; a spurt of urine erupted from her tight-stretched cunt. Behind her a girl giggled, a sound that might as well have come from watching the ludicrous antics of a clown, and Thrift was left shaking her head in her pain and misery as Lady Newgate's grip tightened once more.

'Revolting girl,' Miss Evans commented. 'Control yourself! As it seems that she is incontinent, Lady Newgate, it would be best, I believe, if I were to deliver the last few in rapid sequence. If you would be so good as to hold her well.'

'Absolutely,' the Headmistress agreed. 'Eight more, I think, in the hope of teaching her the virtues of self-control.'

'I could not agree more, my dear Lady Newgate,' Miss Evans answered, and laid in.

Thrift was screaming from the first blow, completely unable to control herself, her legs kicking in the Headmistress's grip, her head shaking to dislodge her bonnet and hair net, her arms snatching at air, spittle and mucus bubbling from her mouth and nose, drops of piddle from her wet clothes spraying in every direction. Fresh urine spurted from her cunt with each stroke, and with the third she began to fart, the little dirty hole between her bottom cheeks opening and closing in helpless spasm. Nor was that all that was in spasm. Her cunt had begun to contract, of its own accord, independent of the rhythm of the beating.

A touch of horrified self-disgust hit her through the pain as she realised that more than anything else in the world she wanted to put her hands on to the swollen fig of flesh between her thighs and rub as her buttocks were whipped. For one second her eyes came open, just in time to catch sight of the huge Ural Ape, his shaggy body close to the bars, the monstrous rod of flesh in his hand, with some thick white substance trickling down over his hairy fingers.

Then it had happened, something extraordinary, something totally unexpected. Every muscle in her body locked tight, as fluid erupted from her pee-pee hole in a high arc and her anus opened in a long, rasped fart. The tawse cracked down, full across her cunt lips, and she was screaming louder than ever. Only it was not in pain, but in blinding pleasure far beyond anything she could have thought possible as her head filled with images; the cruelty of Decency's face, Sullivan-Jones's rod in Ana's mouth, the ape's cock in its hand and Xiuying's cunt spraying piddle into her open mouth.

3

London, July 2004

The incident at the Zoological Gardens left Thrift more confused than she had ever felt. Impropriety, and the exposure and punishment it brought, should cause pain and humiliation, as was only suitable if her behaviour was to be corrected. That such things should bring the rapture she had experienced under Miss Evans's tawse ran contrary to everything she had been taught. Almost as dreadful and incomprehensible was that the horrible way the three girls had bullied her had brought on similar feelings. While her reaction to the Ural Ape was something she did not even dare bring to the front of her mind.

Deep down, she knew what it meant. She was a wanton, and what's more, she now understood what being a wanton really meant. However, it was quite simply not something that happened to young Ladies. Wantonness was something she faintly understood to occur among the commonality, and even then it was a disgrace. For her it was unthinkable, and to admit to it equally so.

Both her parents, she was certain, would be quite unable to cope with such an admission. Her mother was calm, stately, proper, the very picture of British womanhood, and undoubtedly had never experienced any such feelings in her life. To think of speaking to her father was simply absurd. He was aloof, serious, his mind always on higher matters.

Miss Challis, Thrift suspected, might have at least an inkling of understanding, but not sympathy. If Thrift confessed, her Companion's response would be to beat the improper feelings out of her.

Miss Evans, she was sure, would understand it only as something that needed prompt correction. If Thrift confessed, the teacher's response would be to beat the improper feelings out of her.

Lady Newgate could be relied on to be both shocked and vengeful, more so even than Miss Evans. If Thrift confessed, the Headmistress's response would be to beat the improper feelings out of her.

Her Priest, the Very Reverend Judgement Huxtable, Deacon of St James's, could be relied on only in one sense. If Thrift confessed, his response would be to beat the improper feelings out of her.

Only one possibility remained, her friends. These did not include Francesca and Xiuying, let alone Decency Branksome-Brading. Tatiana, Thrift was certain, would merely laugh and make it an excuse for a lecture on the superiority of the Soviet moral system. That left Ana, a girl who took unabashed pleasure in taking a man's rod in her mouth, and played with her cunt. Ana was clearly wanton as well and, if that hardly boded well for a way to get rid of Thrift's uncomfortable feelings, at least it suggested sympathy.

Broaching the subject was a very different matter. Not only was it hideously embarrassing, but the chances to speak in private were few and far between. Tatiana invariably joined them at lunch, while even in the all-too-brief gaps between lunch and afternoon lessons there was little opportunity. Even when opportunities did present themselves she found it far easier to find an excuse to put off the conversation than to begin it. At last, with the summer holidays only two weeks away and the prospect of eight weeks in Scotland with no intimate company but her parents and Miss Challis, she found the time and courage to approach Ana in one of the school's less frequented passages after lunch.

'Might we speak, Ana?' she began as she caught up with her friend.

'We do often enough,' Ana answered, with what Thrift was aware was in some curious way a joke.

'I have a secret,' Thrift went on, her face growing steadily hotter as the words came out. 'I am – I believe I must be – a – a wanton.'

It came out with a gasp and a great surge of relief, but also intense embarrassment, and her skin was burning as she looked up for Ana's response. She found sympathy, but mainly puzzlement.

'What is a wanton, Thrift?' Ana asked.

'It ... is –' Thrift began, and stopped. 'You must know, Ana. You – you suffer the same ... maybe you do not suffer, but what you do with Mr Sullivan-Jones, that is wanton, terribly wanton!'

'And you want the same? To suck pego? Why, of course, my dear, you need only ask!'

'No! Absolutely not! I could never ... ever ... No, Ana, that is not what I meant! That is wanton, to – to take his – what you said in your mouth. I do not want to do it though, never, yet I have those same feelings.'

'You wish to suck a man but not Sullivan-Jones?'

'No! No, of course not, how could – yes ... maybe ... I do not know, Ana. I do not understand my own feelings any more! Since that day in the Zoological Gardens. Perhaps before, I have found myself wanting to do terrible, ungodly things, and these awful pictures come to trouble me at night, and –'

'You British!' Ana laughed. 'There is nothing unGodly in this, nothing even strange. You are a woman. It is natural you should want a man. Not Sullivan-Jones, perhaps, but the old ones do as they are told, and are polite and grateful. Young ones tend to be impetuous, and to want to stick their pegos where they do not belong.'

'Where they do not belong? They do not belong in a girl's mouth, surely?'

'They are best in a girl's mouth, but yes, perhaps my English failed me. The pego goes in the cunt, yes, but only when –'

'In the cunt!'

'Sh! Thrift! What do you think Miss Evans would do to us if she caught us using such words!'

Thrift shuddered. 'Thrash us, hard, with both classes as witness and the servants too.'

'At the least! Now speak quietly. Do you mean to say you do not even know how babies come about?'

'Certainly I do. Between man and wife, by the will of God.'

'Between man and wife, yes. God has little to do with it. The man's pego is pushed into the woman's cunt, to –'

'Ana! What a dreadful lie!'

'It is the plain truth!'

'That such a wanton act – and surely there can be no act more wanton – should lead to the product of Holy Union?'

'It is truth, Thrift. The man's pego makes seed, which resembles cream, only has a taste of salt. This seed conjoins with the woman's egg, and thus their child is begun.'

'Oh what nonsense, Ana! Somebody has been teasing you, and in what a horrid way! Be sensible, I have seen Mr Sullivan-Jones's rod . . . his pego. It is too large by far to be put in any woman's cunt.'

'No, for there is a piece of skin, the maidenhead, which you may see with the aid of a mirror, and –'

'I could not! What a thought!'

'As you like. It is there and, when first a pego is introduced, it tears.'

'Oh, what nonsense!'

'I speak plain truth, Thrift.'

'No . . . You – you would swear on the Holy Bible?'

'That would have no meaning for me. I would take an oath on my Ka.'

Ana's voice was absolutely serious, and Thrift realised that the impossible, blasphemous piece of wantonness the black girl had described was, in fact, the truth. For a moment she could say nothing, her head spinning with the effort of accepting the utter contradiction of such a filthy act being in any way related to the miracle of procreation. At last a new thought penetrated.

'You have done this?' she demanded.

'No, no!' Ana answered hastily. 'I must come to my wedding couch pure.'

'Then how do you know it is the truth?' Thrift questioned.

'In Ashanti,' Ana responded, 'these things are taught, from mother to daughter, from sister to sister. I am the eldest, and much I have learned has been from my father's lesser wives. I have seen Ejura's cunt, with what remains of the membrane, and my own, with the membrane intact. It hurts, so she says, and will bleed also. That blood is a crucial proof of maidenhood, and after my first fucking the stained sheet will be hung from my man's window for all to see.'

'Oh my! How could you bear the shame?'

'There is no shame, only pride. As to what I do with Sullivan-Jones, a girl has a right to some recreation, for the satisfaction of her needs, and so that she may achieve skills for her husband. What man would want a girl who is innocent of her body, and his, of pleasure?'

'Every man, to be sure! Is it not right that a girl should be pure in thought, word and deed as she stands before God to take her vows? The ways of your country are – are so peculiar – so improper! I do not mean to offend, dear Ana, for I have grown especially fond of you, but it is so!'

'Our ways are peculiar?' Ana laughed. 'What of yours?'

'Ours?' Thrift queried. 'Our ways represent the culmination of all that is civilised and Godly –'

'They do?' Ana broke in, still with a laugh in her voice. 'What of the way you hide your bodies in shame, yet at the same time you claim you are made in the image of your God? What of your bustles, which exaggerate what you consider the most indecent part of all, your fat white bottoms?'

'You also wear a bustle!'

'I do. It is expected of me, by my father, who is wise enough to know the benefits of imitating your ways.'

'What are these? Tatiana dresses in the style of her homeland, outrageous though it is, Xiuying also, and with nothing beneath!'

'That, Thrift, my dear, is because neither the Soviets nor the Chinese Empire fear you. With my people it is different. On every side are your colonies and, if the British Empire thinks of the Ashanti people as savages, you will swallow us at a gulp, as you did Togo, d'Ivoire, and others.'

'Oh . . . but would you not be honoured to be a part of the British Empire?'

'We prefer independence. There is more than your supposed decency to our choice of clothes as well. Here it is so cold! That is really why you wear six layers over your skin, Thrift, to keep out the cold.'

'Nonsense! In London the weather is most clement. In Inverness, where I was brought up as a little girl, and in Edinburgh, where my father was First Secretary to the Consul, the weather is a great deal colder.'

'I have been to Scotland, when my father was with a party shooting the Red Deer. It is a freezing waste of bog and dank woodland and mist.'

'It is quite the most beautiful place on the earth!'

Ana merely gave a dismissive laugh and Thrift decided not to labour the point.

'What then,' she asked, 'would you wear at home in Ashanti?'

'Much what I do here, within the Diplomatic Enclave,' Ana answered, 'but of lighter material and with fewer layers and no stupid bustle. In the high country I would wear a simple wrap.'

'A wrap?'

'A piece of cloth, light, but of great richness. It is the simplest and most comfortable of garments, while to dress takes a moment and not a full half-hour!'

'How is it worn?'

'It is wrapped around the hips. Hence the name in your language, a wrap.'

'You mean your – that you are bare, here?' Thrift asked incredulously as she indicated her chest.

'As a maiden, yes,' Ana answered. 'I am proud to show what is mine. When I marry, I will fold it differently so that the men may know my status, over my shoulder, so that a piece runs down, like so.'

She indicated a line of her chest, making it clear that even as a married woman she would have one breast showing. For a moment Thrift found herself too shocked to reply, only to burst out laughing.

'Oh, my dear Ana, how funny you are, and how perfectly straight you kept your face! I was truly taken in, but what an immodest joke, have a care, for Miss Evans –'

'It was no joke,' Ana broke in. 'I dress that way. Visit me, if you do not believe what I say, and I shall show you.'

Thrift went instantly pink as an image of Ana in nothing but a single piece of folded cloth rose up in her mind. The black girl went on, not noticing Thrift's blushes, but with new warmth in her voice.

'I might also show you a little more, if you wish?'

There was no mistaking the implication of Ana's words, nor the honeyed warmth of their tone. Her skin burning from the crown of her head to the slope of her bosom, Thrift turned quickly away, unable to accept the offer, but also unable to refuse.

With the end of term approaching, it proved simpler than Thrift had hoped or feared to arrange a private visit to Ana. Miss Challis, entirely ignorant of the relationship between Ana and her stepmother-cum-Companion, Ejura, gladly accepted the latter's suggestion that she might enjoy an afternoon to herself. Thus, on the afternoon of the Saturday before the Diplomatic School broke up for the summer, Thrift found herself at the Chester Square mansion. The day was balmy, and only a handful of servants, Ejura and a couple of other wives were in, and each busy about her own affairs. Thrift's heart was pounding at the prospect of what Ana had suggested they do, but the black girl, while clearly pleased, betrayed not the slightest unease.

Ana's room was her own, but small, on the second storey of the house beside the long dormitory which housed her younger sisters. Unlike the rooms of the ground floor, it was not furnished to the British taste, but in that of Ashanti, with rich furs spread over a French divan, and chairs and tables of dark wood supported by elongated human carvings. Decorations of exotic feathers and brilliantly coloured silks adorned the walls, also statuettes of ivory, ebony and cinnabar, all of it in striking contrast to the typically British pattern of the pale blue wallpaper. Thrift stared around herself in wonder, unsure whether the impression was of richness, or vulgarity, or both, only to have her attention brought sharply back to her friend as Ana began to undress.

There was no hesitation, no shame, not even a sense that what she was doing was inappropriate. She simply began to unfasten the long row of buttons that held her gown closed at the front while Thrift watched in fascination, unable to tear her eyes away as the opening grew slowly wider to reveal the taut curves of the corset beneath.

Ana's corset was old fashioned, the bust tight to the lower slopes of her big breasts, accentuating them rather than creating the smooth, undivided bosom currently in fashion. Lower, as Thrift saw as the gown dropped to the floor, it flared at the hip, making a broad half-bell to the black girl's rear. Nor was it decently long, but ended no more than halfway down Ana's thighs at the front, and, rather than a panel, the rear was cut away to leave the seat of her drawers bare, while the trim was a single layer of puffed lace. When Ana had been beaten she had been in a far more conventional garment, and Thrift exclaimed in surprise as it was revealed.

'Wherever did you buy that?'

'Accra,' Ana replied proudly, 'in the English Boutique.'

'There is very little English about it!' Thrift answered. 'Why, it is open at the back!'

'And ever so much more convenient for being so,' Ana answered, turned, casually flipped up her bustle and spread the flaps of her split-seam drawers to show off the full width of her bottom, pushed out far enough to make her heavy black buttocks part.

Thrift's hand went to her mouth in shock as she caught the scent of Ana's cunt, and a glimpse of twin lips, plump and dark and deeply cleft around a moist pink centre. Then Ana had let her drawers close and the deliciously rude vision was hidden. Thrift found herself trembling, her own cunt warm and tingling as she sat down on the divan. Ana continued to undress, tugging her corset laces loose and sighing as they came. Immediately both her breasts popped free of the inadequate cups. She took them in her hands, to rub at the marks where the whalebone had pressed into her flesh. They were full and dark, perhaps twice the size of Thrift's, each of which made an ample handful as it was, also very round and heavy. They were topped by big, deeply wrinkled nipples of a brown so dark as to seem true black, which came erect as Ana stroked herself.

'The relief of taking it off almost makes it worth wearing,' she sighed, then giggled as she noticed the quality of Thrift's attention.

Thrift's blushes grew abruptly stronger and she looked quickly away. Ana laughed and pushed her chest out.

'You like them, yes? Would you like to kiss them?'

Thrift wanted to, desperately, but could not find the words. Ana simply chuckled and stepped forward, cupping one big breast even as she cradled Thrift's head to her chest. Overcome by her own feelings, Thrift began to suckle. Her sense of impropriety was burning in her head, but faded against the sheer pleasure of having the full, plump breast pressed to her face, the long, firm, nipple in her mouth, and her head full of the taste and smell of Ana's skin. Her own arms came up by instinct, to take Ana into her embrace. Now feeding greedily at the big, dark breast, she began to stroke the black girl's body, her back, her waist, the swell of a hip. Ana pulled gently back, chuckling.

'Later, my darling. It is nice, I know, but we have all afternoon!'

'Please, Ana,' Thrift answered, barely able to believe it was her own voice. 'I need to hold you, now. Please?'

'You British girls!' Ana laughed. 'So demure, and inside you it is like a coiled spring. Can't you even wait until we are undressed? And you also, don't you think I might like to hold your titties, and to see how you look bare? Now, if you are going to get rude with me, I had better lock the door.'

'I –' Thrift answered, her confusion and shame warring with her desire. She wanted Ana to lead, to make her do the dirty things her mind was telling her she needed, but it was not something she could bring herself to express.

'Come,' Ana went on, pushing her corset and bustle down over her hips as she walked back from the door, 'off with your clothes. I want to see your body.'

It was an order, something Thrift found far, far easier to follow than a request. Her fingers were trembling hard as they went to the buttons of her dress, but she began to open them for all her rising shame and fear of discovery.

'What – what if Ejura should come?' she asked suddenly. 'You must open the door to her, surely? There will be no time to dress.'

'I have locked the door to keep my nosy little brothers and sisters out, should they come back,' Ana answered as she stepped from the mess of clothing around her feet. 'Besides, Ejura knows.'

'She knows that we desired a little privacy, yes.'

'She knows,' Ana said, quickly rolling down a stocking, 'what we plan to do with that privacy. She is my Companion, remember, and my teacher.'

'It was she who taught you to – to know your body?' Thrift queried.

'Largely,' Ana answered, and kicked her second stocking free with her boot.

The black girl stood forward, naked but for the voluminous drawers that covered her from waist to below the knees. With no chemise, her upper body was lined with the impression of her corset bones, but her waist had changed very little, while her breasts seemed bigger than ever. She put her hands on her hips, shameless in her nudity, watching Thrift, whose dress was undone to the navel.

'You now, everything.'

Thrift nodded and went back to undressing. It felt impossibly rude, with no screen, and with Ana looking on, yet also impossibly exciting. Her gown came loose, and she stood to shrug it off. Ana gave a pleased nod and stepped back a little, folding her arms. Thrift removed her gloves, her ladyspats, her boots, the underdress, the sense of exposure growing with each garment although she had bared almost none of her flesh. Her petticoats followed, first, second and third, each opened and carefully folded on the growing pile behind her. The shaking in her fingers was growing worse, and she had to ask Ana to undo the knots of her laces, and to help remove her corset. With it gone, the sense of exposure became too strong to bear, and she stopped, looking at Ana.

'Here I am.'

'No you are not,' Ana chided. 'You are in your chemise and drawers and stockings. I can see nothing!'

'Well –' Thrift began, only to break off with a squeak as Ana's fingers went to her chemise buttons. 'What are you doing?'

'Undressing you. Now stop being silly.'

Thrift swallowed hard, but gave no resistance as her chemise was quickly unbuttoned and hauled wide, spilling out her breasts, bare and round, nothing hidden, her nipples as eagerly erect as Ana's. Crimson faced in her embarrassment, she closed her eyes, unable even to look. Ana chuckled and ducked down, her agile fingers working on the panel of Thrift's drawers, popping the buttons one by one until it fell loose. Immediately Thrift's buttocks were taken in Ana's hands, the soft flesh kneaded, stroked, patted. Thrift sighed, lost in pleasure as her bottom was explored, dizzy with her need, and quite unable to stop what was happening to her.

'Now you can hold me,' Ana sighed, and pushed Thrift back on to the divan.

They came down together, in a tangle of soft, round limbs and disarranged cotton, brown and cream and white, black and auburn as their hair came loose. Thrift abandoned herself as she was mounted, her thighs spreading wide to let Ana's body between them. Her shoulders were taken, Ana's lips pressed to her belly, her breasts, her nipples, kissing, suckling, nibbling, and something deep within Thrift's soul seemed to break.

The next instant she was grappling with Ana, her hands stuffed into the split of the black girl's drawers. Ana squeaked in surprise as her bottom was laid suddenly bare and her cheeks hauled apart, then in ecstasy as Thrift's fingers penetrated the sticky holes of cunt and anus. Their mouths met and opened, in a hard, urgent kiss as Ana rolled to her side, dragging Thrift with her. Thrift cocked one thigh up, spreading her cunt for Ana's hand as it wriggled down the front of her drawers.

Ana began to rub, her fingers right on the little bump between Thrift's spread cunt lips. Thrift was pushed down gently, on to her back, her fingers slipping from the juicy holes into which she had pushed them as the black girl took over. Still kissing, Ana manipulated Thrift's cunt, teasing and flicking, exploring the hole. One finger slipped lower to tickle Thrift's anus, then to probe, pushing up into the sensitive little hole. Another finger slid up into her eager cunt. A thumb found her bump again, rubbing. Thrift felt her muscles start to tighten, and the same wonderful feeling she had experienced as her cunt was whipped came over her. She moaned into Ana's mouth, clutching tight. Her thighs came up and open. Her cunt and bottom hole began to tighten on Ana's fingers, once, again and in a sudden flurry of hard contractions as her whole body shook and quivered in ecstasy and hot fluid spurted from her pee hole, over Ana's hand and into her drawers.

Shudder after shudder went through Thrift's body, Ana holding her tight all the while, only breaking away when it was finally done. Still Thrift held on, never wanting to let go, but Ana gently detached herself, kissing Thrift's mouth before propping herself up on one elbow.

'Wonderful . . . beautiful . . .' Thrift sighed. 'Truly the Devil commands all temptation.'

'That was no devil,' Ana answered. 'That was me. You have come to climax, and now it is my turn.'

'Whatever you wish,' Thrift sighed. 'I can refuse nothing, if I suffer eternal damnation in conseq –'

'Oh, sh!' Ana interrupted, bounced up, swung one leg across Thrift's head and hauled the curtains of her drawers wide, exposing the full, dark spread of her bottom, her cunt and anus showing between the ripe cheeks, her scent strong in Thrift's nose.

'Wha –' Thrift began, only for her words to end in a muffled grunt as Ana's bottom was settled in her face.

Barely able to breathe, with the tip of her nose actually poked a little way up the black girl's bottom hole, she began to flap her hands in protest. Ana moaned.

'Shut up and lick!'

Thrift obeyed, her shock and revulsion at having her face smothered in plump black bottom overcome by her arousal and the curt tone of Ana's order. Telling herself that she was now undoubtedly damned, she began to lick at the juicy cunt over her mouth, wiggling her tongue in among the fleshy folds and poking it in and out of the hole. Ana wiggled, squirming her bottom in Thrift's face.

'And my bottom,' Ana demanded hoarsely.

Again Ana wiggled, and Thrift's nose pushed deeper up the wet, open bottom hole. A last, faint twinge of revulsion hit her and she was doing it, licking at the soft, wrinkling little ring of Ana's dirty place, lapping, then probing, to feel the little round muscle open to her tongue tip. Ana cried out in ecstasy, said something unintelligible in her own language, and suddenly moved back, cunt to face, squirming herself about and babbling what Thrift was certain were obscenities.

Thrift licked anyway, completely abandoned as her nose and lips and tongue were used for Ana to rub on. Her arms came up, to take Ana by the thighs as the black girl's wriggling motion became frantic. Her own thighs came open, spreading her cunt for the sheer joy of putting herself in an available position, and Ana's climax had begun.

It was noisy, long and dirty, the black girl squirming her spread buttocks and soaking cunt in Thrift's face, using nose, mouth and chin to pleasure herself. Thrift struggled to lick, and to breathe, gasping in air thick with the scent of Ana's sex and swallowing down the pungent juices running from the open hole above her. Ana stopped only when she was thoroughly spent, and then collapsed on to the divan with a long, satisfied sigh. For a moment neither girl spoke, both recovering their breath and Thrift trying to reconcile the ecstasy she had just experienced with everything she had been taught. At length, Ana gave a mischievous giggle and rolled on to her side, then spoke as she reached out to tweak one of Thrift's nipples.

'So, you are willing to lick a bottom? You are quite a find, Thrift.'

'You gave me little choice!' Thrift protested.

Ana merely chuckled, then stretched, catlike on the bed, with a purr of deep satisfaction before speaking again.

'Do not be ashamed. If you did it for kindness, I thank you. If for your own joy, it was mine too.'

'I do not know – I did not want to, but then I did. It was the same with everything we did. I am a wanton, Ana, a fallen woman.'

Thrift sniffed, struggling to hold back sudden tears. Ana rolled close to her once more, hugging Thrift's body to hers.

'Sh! Don't cry, Thrift. That was beautiful, a lovely thing.'

'It was wrong, Ana, the Devil's work. I am wanton, I surrendered to my base needs, like an animal, like –'

'Oh stop it!' Ana chided. 'Or I will spank your bottom, here and now!'

'Yes,' Thrift sniffed, her eyes now cloudy with tears. 'Do it. Make me strip, beat me hard. It is no less than I deserve.'

'What nonsense!' Ana laughed. 'How your people have come to master half the world and more is beyond my understanding, when you cannot even master your own feelings. Was it not pleasant what we did?'

'Yes,' Thrift answered miserably. 'Such pleasure is sin, terrible sin. I will burn now, for eternity, in the Pit of Fornicators of which Reverend Huxtable speaks.'

She began to cry openly, feeling more intensely sorry for herself even than after taking bare-bottom spankings in public. Ana sat up.

'I shall spank you, Thrift!' she warned.

Thrift looked away, snivelling.

'I shall sit on your face again,' Ana went on, her voice laughing yet full of concern.

Thrift managed a weak smile but shook her head. She rolled on to her side, away from Ana, who gave a deep sigh.

'Then I shall tickle you, until I see that pretty smile once more,' Ana stated, and on the instant slid a hand under the tuck of Thrift's bottom to tickle at the plump underside of her cheeks.

Thrift squealed in shock, tried to roll, only for Ana to push her forwards, face down on the divan. An instant later one powerful leg had been thrown over Thrift's back and she was pinned in place, with Ana's hand still down her drawers, tickling the swell of her bottom. It was maddening, and she began to kick immediately, and to babble protests.

Ana took no notice, still tickling, and laughing as Thrift's struggles grew more frantic still. Kicking, shaking her head, thumping her hands on the divan, Thrift struggled to break free, to breathe, and not to laugh. Then it was too late, and she was giggling stupidly as the long, agonising fingernails danced on her skin, and writhing too, completely helpless to speak, or to stop the torture. Ana just laughed, then suddenly, completely unexpectedly, pushed one finger firmly into the slimy cavity of Thrift's bottom hole, where she began to wiggle it about. Thrift gasped in response, unable to stop herself, but then found her voice.

'You won't, Ana, please?' she begged.

'Won't what?' Ana demanded. 'Say it, Thrift!'

'Won't – won't make me climax!' Thrift wailed. 'Please!'

'Oh but I will,' Ana answered. 'I will wiggle my finger about in you, and I will rub on your cunt. When you start to climax, I will pull my finger out and make you suck it. You will do it, I know. Unless you tell me you are being silly.'

'No!' Thrift wailed.

'I will,' Ana answered.

The finger probed deeper into Thrift's bottom. A second slid into her cunt, and a third, in the same wet hole. They twisted. Thrift gasped and she was being rubbed, her pleasure rising on the instant, and on the same instant she knew full well that when Ana's hand was offered to her mouth she would suck.

'I was being silly!' she gasped. 'I'm sorry, Ana . . . I'm sorry!'

'That is the wrong answer, Miss Moncrieff,' Ana answered, her accent a parody of Miss Evans's Welsh lilt.

'What then?' Thrift wailed.

'The answer,' Ana went on, 'is that there is no reason to feel shame for taking pleasure in your body, and that it would be kind and generous of me to help you to a second climax.'

'That . . . anything!' Thrift gasped.

'Then I shall do it,' Ana answered and Thrift's answering whimper of defeat turned into a gasp.

Ana had begun to rub, as expertly as before, and to probe at Thrift's holes, both at once, pushing deep into cunt and anus and laughing as she masturbated her helpless victim. Thrift could do nothing, only lie, shaking her head in despair as her ecstasy rose up once more, higher and higher, until her cunt and bottom had begun to twitch on the intruding fingers.

'It – it's going to happen!' she wailed, and it had, her muscles tightening in climax even as the fingers were snatched from her body. 'You big cow!' she yelled. 'Don't stop! Do me! Do m –'

Her mouth was filled. Her eyes went wide at the taste of her own fluids.

Ana broke into a peel of laughter as Thrift began to suck, and to buck her bottom up and down in urgent need to be helped to climax. The help came, Ana twisting to rub at Thrift's cunt even as her fingers were sucked. Thrift came, her whole body jerking under her tormentor as the climax went through her, on and on, to finally leave her exhausted and panting as the fingers were pulled from her mouth.

'That was good, was it not?' Ana asked.

Thrift nodded weakly.

'Good is good,' Ana went on. 'Bad is bad. Now smile, and stop worrying about your stupid Pit of Fornicators. It sounds rather fun to me.'

Thrift managed a weak smile as Ana climbed off her back. Being masturbated a second time had not changed her mind, but she no longer wanted to air her feelings. Ana sat back on the divan, legs flung carelessly wide to show off the split of her drawers and the moist crevice of her cunt.

'Do you – should I lick?' Thrift asked, sitting up.

'Later,' Ana answered her. 'For now, let us talk. Be truthful. Have you come to climax before?'

'Once,' Thrift answered, hesitated, then went on. 'At the Zoological Gardens, when Miss Evans tawsed my cunt.'

Ana winced. 'When she tawsed your cunt? You are truly wanton!'

'I know,' Thrift admitted.

'So then, why not play with others? What of Miss Challis? Does she not like to make you lick her?'

'No! She would never dream of – Well, not lick no, but I am sure she likes to humble me. Always she spanks me outdoors, and in front of an audience if she can. Before it was private, usually, but since I have been corsetted it has changed. She likes to stroke my bottom too.'

'She would like to do more, be sure of it. I doubt she dares. Offer your tongue and perhaps she would be kinder to you.'

'I could not . . . never!'

'Please yourself. What of men? None have ever made you take their pegos in your hand, nor your mouth? Speak honestly.'

'No! I had never even seen a man's pego until I peeped on you and Mr Sullivan-Jones.'

'Amazing! Are British boys such cowards then, that they will not urge a girl to tug them?'

'That is not cowardice; that is simple decency!'

'It would not surprise me. Still, some day, you will have a husband, and no doubt he will be pleased if you prove skilled in the use of your mouth to pleasure him.'

'No Gentleman would ever want such a thing!'

'Would you care to risk, say, five guineas on that?'

'I do not wager! I – no, I would not.'

'That is just as well, as you would lose. So, listen. There is an art to sucking a man's pego. First, you must know which parts provide the most lascivious feelings. These are the bulb and the collar of flesh below the neck, notably on the underside. Whether tugging or sucking, these are the areas to attend to if you wish him to climax. If you wish to tease –'

'Ana! I should not know these things!'

'Be quiet! If you wish to tease, touch only the base of his shaft and his balls. It is wise, because then you may reach your own climax before his. Few men will lick cunt, so seek one who will.'

'How would I do that!?'

'Ask him ... no, I do not suppose you could. I am getting ahead of myself anyway ... back to sucking a pego. Now, if a man should take control of you, be prepared for nasty and often painful tricks. Some like to make us choke, to feel our throats tighten and gulp on their bulbs. Others go further, to make us sick for the pleasure of the heat on their pegos. Be sure of one thing. If you can no longer bear it, you can always bite.'

As she finished she curled her thick, dark lips back to expose the perfect white of her teeth and gnashed them suddenly together. Thrift managed an uneasy giggle.

'It is better,' Ana went on, 'and ever so much more pleasurable not to relinquish control to the man. Thus you may enjoy the taste and feel of his pego, until you yourself are ready for your climax, although it is considerate to allow him his after you are done. Indeed, that is an important general point. Even if you are lucky enough to have a man who will lick cunt, ensure that your climax is first, as few men will trouble to aid you once they have spent their seed.'

Thrift nodded, amazed at how casually Ana was going into so improper a subject, but fascinated despite herself.

'Another trick they play,' Ana said, 'is to make sure you are stained with their seed. All men like to boast, and many to show that they have had you suck on them or whatever it might be. These will do their seed not in your mouth, where it may be swallowed without ill-effect – save occasionally for a little sickness – but in your face or hair, perhaps across your breasts. Even if you clean up, your make-up will be quite spoiled or your clothes stained, and people will guess what you have done. Still, here in Britain the men are more discreet, and tend to fear others knowing rather than court it.'

'So I should think!'

'Then there are those who must have your bosom bare, or even see you strip for their satisfaction. Others prefer clothes, perhaps as you are now, in chemise and drawers but with nothing hidden, or dressed strangely. Mr Sullivan-Jones wishes to paint a portrait of me wearing a leopard skin and nothing besides. Why, I do not know. Then there are those men who like to place their pegos between your breasts, or along the crease of your bottom, which is dangerous as some might be tempted to slip it into your cunt, and in an instant your maidenhead would be gone. Some, Ejura tells me, like to poke it up a girl's bottom, but this too risks being deflowered.'

Ana sighed and stretched, spreading her legs yet further apart.

'Enough for now, telling you this has made me feel rude. Lick my cunt.'

The Monday found Thrift if anything more ill at ease with what she had done than when she had left the house in Chester Square. Ana had made it seem so natural, really nothing more than a game, albeit one only suitable for adults. Each had climaxed three times before they had dressed, and for a while they had lain stark naked together, exploring each other's bodies and responses. Being nude was something Thrift was completely unaccustomed to. Even when washing she wore her rubber bathing gown, and it had felt very strange indeed. Yet Ana had made it acceptable, and Thrift had even managed to push her fears of damnation back for a while.

On Sunday they had come back with a vengeance. The Very Reverend Judgement Huxtable had preached a sermon on Hell. Before, Thrift had listened to the descriptions of the agonising tortures dished out to sinners with a blend of fear and virtue. His remarks were never clear and, while she had occasionally wondered if she might not have committed one or two of the sins covered in such vague terms, she had always trusted to the mercy of God for her salvation, as she was told to do.

Now it was different. She not only knew exactly what fornication was, but had picked up more detail on the specific acts involved in it than she would previously have imagined existed. She had sinned in thought, word and deed, without question, and, just as surely without question, she was damned.

She had left the church shaking so badly that Miss Challis had been on the point of calling for a physician, but Thrift had managed to explain it away as fear of God. For the rest of the day she had felt weak, and Huxtable's words had gone round and round in her head, her near-perfect memory for once a curse rather than a blessing. By dinner time she had been a nervous wreck, and had consumed her food in a reflective silence that had earned a murmur of praise from her father.

Night had been worse, with her fears vying with a near-intolerable urge to test what Ana had taught her and masturbate over some of her dirty memories. She had held back, finally drifting to sleep only to dream of being caught by the great Ural Ape she had seen at the Zoological Gardens and masturbated to climax in front of the entire class. She had woken to find her nightie and modesty gown up and her hands down her pyjamas. Giving in, she had brought herself to climax over the dream, and as she had come she had imagined the creature's huge pego being thrust into her cunt.

In the morning she had been guiltier than ever, so much so that she had been unable to eat her breakfast. Only after dressing had a new thought occurred to her – if she was already damned to eternal torture in the Pit of Fornicators, being tossed on red hot pitchforks and so forth, surely it would make no difference how she lived the remainder of her life.

The Very Reverend Judgement Huxtable had been very clear on the point. Confession and absolution of sins were heresies practised by certain decadent peoples in Europe and Southern America. A sin, any sin, and even a sin of thought, would be punished comprehensively. She was therefore damned without hope of absolution, and eternity was eternity, so what she did for the remainder of her life made no difference, just so long as she did not commit one of those few sins that would ensure she was hurled into a yet deeper pit. It seemed unlikely, unGodly murder, evil counsel and treachery all being things she was sure would never arise as an option in her life, while she was uncertain exactly what simony involved.

All morning she thought the argument through, nearly catching a dose of the tawse from Miss Evans for inattention. The logic was perfect, classic in fact. Had she dared, she felt she could have placed the argument before Lady Newgate without fear of a flaw being exposed. It worked, and that was that. There was still the prospect of eternal damnation to face, but at least it could get no worse.

She did full justice to a lunch of lamb chops, boiled greens and spotted dick, and even managed to swap a joke or two with Tatiana and Ana. Both were in good humour, Tatiana in particular, and afterwards she made a point of accompanying Thrift to the convenient facilities.

'I learn,' Tatiana said the moment the door had closed behind them, 'that you spent Saturday afternoon at Ana's, alone.'

'I did, yes,' Thrift answered. 'It was most agreeable.'

'So I hear,' Tatiana answered. 'Ana tells me you are very good . . . very obedient, passionate too.'

Tatiana laughed at the instant reddening of Thrift's face, then went on. 'There is no cause to blush, Thrift, well, not much. Ana tells me you were willing to kiss her anus?'

Thrift found herself nodding, the lump in her throat far too large to allow her to speak. Tatiana paused to light a cigarette, then spoke again.

'I too like to be licked, on my genitals . . . my cunt, I think, is the word you use. My first lover had great skill, but –'

'Your lover?' Thrift queried, finding her voice. 'A girl?'

'A man,' Tatiana answered. 'We Soviets do not share your foolish embarrassment for your bodies, nor the people of Ashanti's obsession with virginity. I fuck, Thrift.'

'Fuck?'

Tatiana paused in surprise, shook her head, took a deep drag on her cigarette and went on.

'You do not even know the word in your own language! Truly it is extraordinary how a capitalist Imperialist government exploits its own people. To fuck, little Thrift, when a woman takes a man's penis in her vagina. I do it with two men at the embassy, but both would think it degrading for a Soviet citizen to put his tongue to a girl's anus, just as I would to put mine to theirs. You, on the other hand, feel no such qualms, do you?'

'It – is was not like that!' Thrift stammered. 'Ana made me! She sat down on my face, as if it were a stool, and told me –'

'You obeyed?'

Thrift made a face, knowing she was trapped. Tatiana laughed, blew a smoke ring, watched it rise slowly into the still, hot air of the room and went on. 'I am hoping, little Thrift, that you will do me the same favour.'

'I – I could not – not possibly,' Thrift stammered.

'No?' Tatiana queried. 'Must I make you? Is that how you like to be treated? You enjoyed it, and you need not pretend otherwise.'

Thrift shrugged, her lips pursed, unable to deny what Tatiana was saying. The Soviet girl went on. 'Or do you have some difficulty with me?'

Thrift hastily shook her head.

'You are in love with Ana?'

Again Thrift shook her head.

'Then, what?'

Thrift shrugged.

'Good,' Tatiana stated, 'come then, we are wasting precious time, which would be far better employed with your tongue busy between my buttocks.'

She beckoned as she stepped to one of the cubicles. Thrift followed, resigned to her fate and wondering how it was going to feel spending time over the next two years licking other girls' bottoms. One last possible means of escape, or at least postponement, occurred to her as Tatiana shut the door behind them.

'What if somebody were to come?'

'Lick quietly,' Tatiana answered her, 'and we will be safe. It is a shame, though. If it were not so noisy, I would beat you first to make you more eager. Yes, Thrift, Ana told me that too, how you came to climax under Miss Evans's tawse.'

Tatiana chuckled as Thrift's blush grew a shade deeper. Her cigarette holder clamped firmly between her teeth, she put her hands to her belt, tugging the buckle wide. The button came loose, the fastener down, and both trousers and the peculiar abbreviated drawers beneath were pushed down, and off, along with boots and socks. As Thrift caught a glimpse of the hammer and sickle tattoo on the mound of Tatiana's cunt, a thought flashed through her mind, that it might be unpatriotic to lick a Soviet girl's bottom. She promised herself that she would not kiss the communist symbol as she sank down into a squat, balancing herself on her heels.

With an approving nod to Thrift, Tatiana turned and bent at the waist, bracing her legs to either side of the broad china facility. The tails of her uniform jacket and shirt rose with the movement, leaving her firm, muscular bottom quite bare, her cunt on plain show between well-parted thighs and her anus revealed as a deeply dimpled star in the groove between her cheeks. Thrift licked her suddenly dry lips, but shuffled forwards obediently, catching the scent of Tatiana's sex as she went. Tatiana's bottom was directly in front of her face, her cunt and anus on offer, the urge to lick both strong, yet not as strong as the barrier of propriety that prevented her from making the final move. Then the words she wanted to say had come from her lips, unbidden.

'You – you must make me, Tatiana.'

The Soviet girl gave a grunt of indifference and reached back to take Thrift by the hair. Thrift squeaked as her head was pulled firmly in between Tatiana's buttocks, and it was done, her lips to the hot cunt lips, her nose stuck in the soft, damp bottom hole. Her tongue came out and she was licking, taking up the juice from between Tatiana's lips and probing the already moist hole. Tatiana sighed in pleasure, then spoke softly.

'Yes, just like that. I could wish it was a man, but you will do. Deeper then, get your tongue right in, and see to my clitoris, then my anus.'

Immediately Thrift obeyed, pushing her tongue deep into Tatiana's cunt. Abandoned, she took hold of the firm, rounded buttocks in front of her, kneading and stroking as she licked cunt and wiggled her nose in Tatiana's bottom hole. The hand was removed from her head, but she did not stop, moving instead to the firm bead of flesh between Tatiana's pee-pee wrinkles and lapping at it, now with real need. Again Tatiana sighed and spoke, now both soft and breathless.

'Maybe I do not need a man after all. Like that, yes ... now to my anus.'

Thrift did not need to be asked. Her own cunt was in need of attention, but lay deep within her clothing and unreachable. Urgent for what friction she could get, she began to squirm her thighs together, producing a delicious sensation as she moved her mouth to the little moist hole her nose had already been up and began to lick, taking in the taste, acrid, musky and deeply feminine.

Tatiana let out a long, ecstatic sigh. Thrusting her bottom out into Thrift's face, she reached down to snatch at her cunt. In an instant her fingers were busy, rubbing among the wet fleshy folds. Thrift responded by pushing her tongue deeper up the rubbery little bottom hole, as far as she could, while using her lips to kiss at the puckered anal ring. Again Tatiana moaned, rubbing harder, until Thrift could hear the meaty slapping of urgent fingers on cunt flesh. Tatiana's bottom tightened in Thrift's face and she was there, cunt and anus in spasm, panting and shivering as she went into climax. Thrift licked and kissed and groped, doing her best, as Ana had taught her, and with an urgency driven by the hot need in her own cunt.

When Tatiana stopped, Thrift pulled back, reluctantly extracting her tongue from her friend's now gaping anus. Thrift's face was a slimy mess, and the muscles of her tongue and cheeks ached, but she was smiling as the Soviet girl turned, eager for praise and wondering if she dare ask for the rear panel of her corset to be unfastened for her own cunt to be masturbated. It had to be done.

'Would – would you?' she said, her voice barely audible.

'Lick a British girl's bottom?' Tatiana queried. 'No.'

'Rub me?' Thrift asked hopefully.

Tatiana shrugged and took a draw on her cigarette holder.

Thrift climbed to her feet, burning with embarrassment, yet more with need. Bending quickly over the facility as Tatiana watched in amusement, Thrift threw up her skirts, petticoats and all, exposing the globous bulge at the rear of her corset. Four quick motions and her bustle was inverted, the gudgeons twisted open and the panel pulled up. With trembling hands she tied the panel strings into place, but as she began to fumble with the buttons of her drawers Tatiana gave an understanding nod.

'I will help you,' she offered. 'How it must feel to be in such absurd clothes.'

Grateful, and not wanting to argue, Thrift simply hung her head and braced herself against the facility as Tatiana began to pop the buttons. Her shame grew strong as slices of bottom flesh were exposed, and near to unbearable as the panel fell away to expose her naked cheeks, but she clung tight to the seat of the facility and, with her bottom bare, pushed it well out. A moment later Tatiana had cupped her cunt from the rear, slid a thumb up the hole and she was being masturbated.

The climax came almost immediately. Tatiana's fingers had found her bump, and were rubbing, kicking Thrift's reaction in on the instant. She began to gasp, to wiggle her bottom against Tatiana's hand, and as it hit her she thought of how she had put her tongue up other girls' bottom holes, and how it felt so right. The image held as she climaxed: Tatiana and Ana's bottoms, together, black and white, the cheeks spread, the puckered bottom holes ready for her tongue.

Guilt hit her, breaking the climax at the very peak, but Tatiana did not stop, ignoring Thrift's sudden explosion of sobs and continuing to manipulate the sticky, open cunt until at last it had ceased to twitch. Thrift stayed down, crying softly and unable to speak as her clothes were rearranged. Tatiana said nothing, but shook her head in bewilderment at Thrift's reaction, then nodded at the door and put her finger to her lips.

Both girls stood stock still, listening. There was no sound. Again Tatiana nodded, quickly opened the door and both girls nipped smartly out. Thrift blew her breath out, only for her heart to jump at a sudden rush of water. She and Tatiana exchanged a glance, then the Soviet girl was gone, leaving the room at a speed impossible for Thrift in her elaborate clothes and tight corset. A moment later a cubicle door swung open. Xiuying Shi emerged, making a polite bob of her head as she moved to the basins beside Thrift.

Quickly the Chinese girl washed her hands. Thrift did the same, but was still adjusting her gloves by the time Xiuying had left. Thrift followed, her mind whirling with questions and the possible implications of their answers – How long had Xiuying been in the cubicle? Had she heard? If so, what had she heard? Had there been the trace of a smirk on her face as she came out, or a touch of mockery in her formal bow?

It seemed unlikely that Xiuying had been there all the time, but, if she had, then she had heard everything: Thrift's admission of licking Ana's bottom, Tatiana's demand for the same lewd treatment, Thrift's acquiescence. It would be disastrous.

Even if Xiuying had come in while Thrift had her tongue up Tatiana's bottom hole, then the Chinese girl would have overheard something, maybe whispers, maybe words. They had spoken quietly, at least for most of the time, and there was no reason to think that Xiuying would be able to interpret the faint slurping sounds as so lewd an act. Possibly Xiuying didn't know Tatiana had been there at all, and would assume Thrift had been masturbating. That was bad enough, but nothing beside the full truth.

She left the room with her stomach fluttering in fear. If Xiuying told Miss Evans, she could deny it, but more likely than not the teacher would assume she was lying and simply double the punishment. Miss Evans hated to feel anybody might have got away with something, and felt it far preferable to risk giving an unjust beating than allowing a crime to go unpunished. As she had often explained, there was always some good to be derived from a beating.

All five other girls were already in the classroom. So was Miss Evans, and Thrift's heart jumped once more as the teacher turned to her. Under the steely gaze she came within an instant of blurting out a full confession, but held back, and nothing was said as she went to her chair. The class started, a triple dose of Classical Language, with all six girls stumbling over their translations and declensions as Miss Evans fingered her tawse.

Nothing was said, nor afterwards at tea, and Thrift found herself filled with relief as she left the building. Evidently Xiuying had not heard or, if she had, she was not going to use the information to have Thrift beaten. Nevertheless, as she walked home with Miss Challis she held a nasty suspicion that before long she was likely to have her tongue up Xiuying's bottom hole. As they reached the park, her Companion spoke. 'You are very thoughtful today, my dear.'

'I do beg your pardon, Miss Challis,' Thrift answered. 'I was thinking of the Very Reverend Huxtable's sermon.'

'He is a most forceful speaker,' Miss Challis stated.

Thrift was going to make some bland comment in return, but paused, thinking of what Ana had said, about how the offer of a licked cunt might make her Companion less cruel. The idea appealed, there was no denying it for all the shame it brought, and yet what appealed more was more shameful still: the thought of being spanked and then made to lick cunt. Possibly a carefully phrased remark might make her feelings clear.

'There was much I did not understand,' she said, picking her words carefully. 'Why, for instance, is it sinful to take pleasure in that place from which God's greatest gift derives. Is that pleasure not also a gift?'

'I am not certain I follow you, Thrift, my dear,' Miss Challis answered. 'To what place do you refer? Church?'

'No, my dear Miss Challis.' Thrift laughed, the sheer absurdity of the contradiction breaking through her caution for one instance. 'I mean my cunt.'

'How – how dare you!' Miss Challis spat, her face going from pale cream to purple in an instant. 'Where did you hear that disgusting word? How dare you use it, how dare you, how dare you!'

Miss Challis went wild, slapping Thrift's face and chest, her arms a whirlwind of random blows. Thrift staggered back, her hands up to protect her face, stumbled on the verge and went over, to fall on her back on the grass. Miss Challis came forwards, to stand over Thrift, her face set in fury.

'Never, ever say such a –' the Companion shouted, and stopped, controlling herself with an effort, before going on in a low, angry hiss. 'Never are you to use such foul language, Thrift, never! It would break your poor mother's heart even to think you *knew* such a word. Now get up!'

Thrift pulled herself up, her stomach fluttering at the prospect of the inevitable public spanking she was about to get. The park was crowded, and to her horror she saw Decency approaching, arm in arm with her Miss Buckleigh. Immediately she was babbling.

'Not now, please, Miss Challis ... please ... I beg you! Beat me, beat me well, but at home, not here!'

'Quiet!' Miss Challis snapped in fury. 'Brush yourself down! You are a slattern, Thrift Moncrieff, a disgrace! You do not deserve a spanking, not here, nor later!'

Miss Challis walked on, faster than Thrift could keep up. Decency was coming towards them, her face set in a smirk of amusement. Brushing frantically at her skirt, Thrift followed her companion with quick, tiny steps, her shoes clattering on the path. Having expected at that instant to have been laying herself across Miss Challis's lap in full view of Decency, it was impossible not to feel relief, and, if there was a touch of disappointment blended with it, she was beginning to understand why. Yet neither was her principal emotion: that was astonishment for her escape.

It was raining when Thrift awoke the next day, a warm drizzle still falling some two hours after it should have finished. As she ate breakfast she watched the runnels of water on the window panes, strange in daylight and without the distorted glimmers and reflections of the streetlights. Miss Challis seemed absorbed, and barely spoke, failing even to react when Thrift deliberately used the last corner of her toast to mop up the egg from her plate, leaving nothing whatever for Mr Manners and little enough for an ant. Surprised and disappointed, she washed and dressed, greeted her mother and paused a moment in the drawing room until the rain had finally stopped.

Outside, the day was fresh and bright, with the clouds clearing quickly to the east and a stiff breeze blowing into her face. Miss Challis remained taciturn as they walked down Piccadilly, commenting only on the sudden lapse in reliability of the weathermen. They had arrived at the school a little early and, with Miss Challis gone, Thrift found herself in the classroom alone. The next to arrive was Decency, who gave a wicked smile at the sight of Thrift on her own and bent to whisper.

'I hear the most disgraceful story, Brat, so disgraceful indeed, that I find it hard to credit, even of a wanton like you.'

Decency stood quickly, and before Thrift could answer Miss Evans had appeared in the doorway. Thrift's stomach began to churn in fear as the huge tawse was laid on the Mistress's desk, but Miss Evans merely went to the board and began to write down the names of the principal battles of the Napoleonic Wars. Thrift relaxed a little, still sure that what Decency had said could only relate to the incident in the convenient facilities the day before.

Determined to stick close by Tatiana and Ana for the rest of the day, she was horrified when neither girl turned up. As the lesson began, Miss Evans explained the absences, stating that both had been invited to a reception held by the Soviet Embassy for an Ashanti trade delegation.

The morning passed with depressing speed and, when Thrift made a point of selecting a table of her own at lunch, Decency, Xiuying and Francesca immediately vacated their own to join her. She managed a polite bob as the three girls sat down.

'I trust we may join you,' Decency stated. 'It is such a shame to be seated all alone, when between us we might make such interesting conversation.'

'I would be most pleased, I assure you,' Thrift answered formally.

'That I doubt,' Decency answered. 'As I mentioned earlier, I hear a truly revolting story about you, to the effect that you licked Tatiana's sit-upon, and also Black Ana's. Xiuying assured me it is the truth.'

'Very true,' Xiuying put in, and Thrift caught the cruelty and excitement in her voice.

'And quite revolting,' Francesca added.

Thrift lowered her eyes, unable to find an answer, her bottom cheeks already twitching at the prospect of the tawse.

Decency went on. 'What, I wonder, would happen to you should your repulsive behaviour become known to

Miss Evans? For a wanton act with another girl, and a foreigner at that, never mind such a dirty one? I could not even begin to imagine. Ten dozen strokes of the tawse, stripped naked? That at least, I should have thought. I myself would recommend more, but Miss Evans has no real idea of how to keep discipline, and certainly your Miss Challis does not, or you would never have become the wanton little trull that you are. Well, answer me!'

'I do not know,' Thrift admitted sulkily.

'Well,' Decency went on, 'it is just possible you may never find out, that is, if you are a very, very good girl.'

'How do you mean?' Thrift queried.

'I mean, that I might consider forgetting my duty, but only on one condition. From now one you are to do exactly as I say, and I mean exactly. Don't worry, I shall do nothing that might puncture your precious reputation, but I can assure you that it will be both painful and thoroughly debased. Do you remember how we made you wet your clothes, how Xiuying made pee-pee in your mouth? That was a start, no more.'

'No!' Thrift answered. 'You will merely amuse yourself at my expense, and then, when I have done whatever horrid and inappropriate task you devise, you will report me and I shall be beaten just the same.'

'Perhaps,' Decency admitted coolly, 'and, yet, what choice do you have? If you do not obey me, you may be very sure I will tell everything I know, and promptly. If you do obey me, maybe, just maybe, I will not.'

'You will, I know,' Thrift answered her.

'Now you are just being difficult,' Decency went on. 'You see, I would far rather have you as my little slave than see you beaten, although naturally it would be ideal to see both. So, this is what I propose. If you do not agree to my terms immediately, then I shall have Miss Challis informed of your behaviour with the cannibal Princess. You will be beaten, probably in public, as I will be sure that the information reaches her in a suitable place. Then, I will allow you a second chance to make yourself my slave. Refuse it, and I will tell Miss Evans everything. There, is that not rather clever?'

'Ever so clever, Decency!' Francesca answered immediately, Xiuying adding a little cruel smile.

'Well?' Decency enquired.

Thrift stood irresolute, tears of frustration already welling in her eyes. To refuse meant two beatings at the least, both harsh and both public. It was more than she could bear, even with her new feelings, yet to accept meant the humiliation of acting as something lower than a servant to Decency while still risking the beatings. Meekly she nodded her head.

'I knew you would see sense,' Decency answered in triumph. 'However, it is clear I must test your obedience. Let me see . . . yes, a fitting task for a guttersnipe. You will lick my boots clean. Finish your lunch, as quick as you may, and we should have plenty of time before art this afternoon. We are going to make a study of symmetry, the King Albert II bridge, I believe. It should be most instructive.'

Thrift turned her attention back to her meal, eating slowly at first, but more rapidly once Decency began to tap her fingers meaningfully on the table top. With the last mouthful of apple pie and custard swallowed, she rose, the three girls keeping close to her as they left the room, and her anxiety and misery rising step by step as they made for the convenient facilities.

It was empty, to Thrift's disappointment, the row of big, square cubicles each showing a little green symbol beside the lock. Decency selected the middle cubicle and pulled Thrift quickly inside, leaving the door open.

'You two must watch,' she instructed her friends, 'the Brat will hate it so much more that way, but be quick with the door should anyone come.'

'Yes, Decency,' Francesca answered, quickly taking hold of the door.

'On the floor, Brat,' Decency ordered, pointing to the tiles in front of the facility. 'Kneel to me.'

Thrift dropped slowly to her knees, leaving her corset taut across her legs. With an almost regal calm, Decency sat back on the seat of the facility. Crossing one knee over the over, she allowed the richly layered lace trim of her gown and petticoats to rise just far enough to expose the lower part of her boot, yet to leave the upper surface of her ladyspat covered and not so much as hint at her ankle. Her boot was far from clean, with mud spattered on to the highly polished black leather and caked around the edges of the sole. Thrift hesitated, knowing that it was pointless to plead for mercy, and that the more reluctance she showed the more Decency would enjoy it, yet unable to put her mouth to the dirty boot in front of her face.

'Come, come,' Decency chided. 'You would not be being disobedient now, would you, Brat?'

Thrift shook her head, but was still unable to make herself go forwards.

'Lick it up, Brat!' Decency snapped. 'I will count to three, and –'

She stopped, laughing as Thrift immediately bent forwards to poke her tongue out on to the dirty boot sole. The taste of mud caught Thrift as she began to lick, quickly filling her mouth as bits of wet soil and leaf mould came loose on her tongue. Decency watched, bright eyed in sadistic glee, her mouth twitching in laughter. Shame and misery welled up in Thrift's breast as she licked, growing stronger with the taste of dirt and the mounting humiliation of cleaning Decency's boots with her tongue. Soon she had begun to cry, heavy tears running slowly down her cheeks to splash on the tiled floor. Decency merely grinned more widely still.

With the first boot shiny and clean, the second, dirtier still, was presented to Thrift's mouth. Decency showed no mercy, ordering it licked completely clean. Soon Thrift's mouth was full of gritty earth, bits of leaf and a thick, acrid slime, so foul tasting that she was sure that if she tried to swallow she would be sick. When her cheeks had begun to bulge with it and a trickle of dirty saliva was running down her chin she stopped, sitting back, unable to speak for her foul mouthful but imploring her tormentor with her eyes.

'Well?' Decency demanded. 'Why have you stopped? You still have the heel to do.'

Thrift pointed at her mouth and at the facility, indicating that she wanted to spit.

'No,' Decency answered her. 'How dare you suggest that you spit out the dirt from my boots? You should be privileged to swallow it, Brat, and don't think of doing it on the floor as, if you do, you will simply have to lick it up. Now come on, with me you must learn to behave as befits your new station.'

Thrift leaned forwards, determined not to swallow, and once more began to lick at Decency's boots, now picking off bits of muck with her lips in an effort to keep her dirty mouthful from spilling out. Decency watched for a while, then shook her head in disappointment.

'I believe I told you to swallow, Brat,' she said. 'Now swallow!'

So sudden and so sharp was the command that Thrift found herself gulping by instinct. Her throat filled with acrid slime, contracted in rebellion and she was forced to clap her hand to her mouth to prevent herself from being sick on the floor. All three watching girls burst into laughter as Thrift forced herself to swallow once more, this time taking it down, to leave her with her eyes watering profusely, more so even than with her tears.

'How very droll!' Decency called when she had recovered her breath. 'You are not entirely stupid, are you, Brat? You know that I would have made you very sorry indeed if you had soiled my gown, don't you?'

Thrift managed a weak nod.

'There,' Decency went on, 'you see, you can do it, and it is not so very bad, is it? At least not for you. Now finish and you may do the same for Francesca.'

Completely broken, Thrift pushed out her tongue once more to lick the sole of Decency's boot, firmly, to take up a patch of compressed mud. She still felt sick, and her eyes were blind with tears, but to complete her shame she could feel that her cunt had begun to swell and juice.

With the last trace of mud removed from her boots, Decency handed Thrift some paper from the dispenser. Thrift took it and began to polish without having to be told, quickly leaving both boots shiny. Satisfied, Decency stood up, to allow Francesca to sit and offer one booted foot in the same commanding pose. Her boots were, if anything, worse than Decency's, not merely spattered and fringed with mud, but with clots of it caked into deep grooves that ran across the thick sole. This time there was no hesitation as Thrift began to lick and kiss at the mud, using her lips to pull the bigger bits off and even her teeth. Soon her mouth was full of dirt and brown saliva had once more begun to trickle down her chin. She sat back. For a moment her cheeks bulged in disgust, and then she had done it, swallowing down her filthy mouthful.

She went back to her boot licking to the sound of their laughter. Decency kicked her bottom and called her a pig, but the words barely sank in and the vicious little prod only seemed to make her cunt more urgent. Barely aware of what she was doing, she took hold of Francesca's boot, to kiss and nibble at the filthy sole, sucking mud from the cracks and rubbing her face into the mess until her lips and chin, her nose and cheeks were streaked and foul.

The girls watched, in silence now, Francesca even a little scared, until, with the mud sucked and licked from both boots, Thrift stopped and sat back to swallow one last mouthful of filth. She felt dizzy, her head spinning, her stomach bloated with the mud she had swallowed on top of her lunch. Her mouth stayed open, hanging slack with brown dribble running down over her lower lip. Some mud had gone on the floor, and she bent to lick it up, pressing her face to the tiles and lapping at the dirty brown stains. Francesca rose to step over Thrift's prone body. Again Decency kicked Thrift's bottom, harder this time, a display of her control.

'Get up from the floor, you wanton trull! Xiuying, it is your turn. Lick her boots, Brat, and swallow it all. Up!'

'Not boots,' Xiuying demanded, stepping forward. 'She must lick my cunt.'

'Must you really be so foul?' Decency sighed. 'Oh very well, do it, Thrift, although after what you did with Ana Lakoussan I very much doubt it will be much in the way of a torment.'

'My arse too,' Xiuying added. 'Yes, Brat, you will lick arse and cunt. Make me climax!'

Thrift hung her head, defeated, not even able to put up a token resistance or to beg to be let off, needing it and unable to hide that need. Xiuying wasted no time, but closed the lid of the facility and scrambled up, turning to present the neatly rounded shape of her rump to the room. Her hands went back to grip the hem of her tight dress of embroidered purple silk and tugged it high, showing off her bare bottom, the lips of her hairless cunt peeping out from between her thighs, her anus a star of yellowish flesh with a brown centre. Thrift stuck her tongue in, deep, licking up the acrid taste of Xiuying's bottom, letting it fill her mouth, before swallowing and swallowing again.

'Suck on my hole, dirt-pig!' Xiuying demanded.

Francesca squeaked in disgust as Thrift responded immediately, puckering her lips up to kiss Xiuying's anus, and then sucking as she wiggled her tongue in the slimy little hole. Xiuying farted, full in Thrift's mouth, and broke into a peel of high-pitched laughter as both Decency and Francesca exclaimed in disgust.

'Now cunt!' Xiuying demanded. 'Nose in arsehole, tongue up cunt!'

Thrift obeyed, her mouth slipping lower to lap up the thick juice running from the tight hole in Xiuying's hymen as she poked her nose into the slippery little bottom hole. Xiuying cried out in delight and began to wiggle in Thrift's face. Thrift licked deeper, harder, indifferent to the sticky juice plastered over her face, compounded of tears and mud and cunt juice and spit.

'Now, dirt-pig!' Xiuying squealed. 'Make climax, now!'

Again Xiuying farted in Thrift's face, and again she laughed. Thrift moved down, pressing her face well into Xiuying's bottom, to lap at the little bud of flesh. Xiuying gasped in ecstasy and her wiggling became more urgent, her trim buttocks wobbling and the flesh of her cunt bumping against Thrift's lips and nose. Still Thrift licked, struggling to get it right, her own need so high she thought she might climax anyway, and higher still as Xiuying did it in her face, squealing and calling out insults in Mandarin as her cunt went into spasm.

'You are pigs, both of you,' Decency remarked from above and behind, yet much of the haughty calm was gone from her voice.

'No,' Xiuying gasped as she came down. 'Brat is pig, dirt-pig.'

'You are both pigs,' Decency stated firmly. 'Wanton little pigs, her for doing it, you for wanting it.'

'The Brat is pig,' Xiuying replied. 'She is peasant girl, fit only to lick arsehole. I am not a pig. I am a Lady.'

'Foreigners!' Decency sighed. 'Come, Francesca, I feel a trifle uncomfortable.'

Thrift had sat up, dizzy with reaction, so wet between her thighs that she could feel her cunt juice where it had soaked into her drawers. Her need to climax was desperate, and she knew full well why Decency felt uncomfortable. She, like Thrift, and doubtless Francesca too, needed her cunt manipulated. Wanting to offer, and to beg help for herself, Thrift turned, only to find both Decency and Francesca already at the sinks, making a deliberate show of adjusting their coiffures and make-up. Xiuying got up, casually rolled her dress down to cover herself and left the cubicle, looking thoroughly pleased with herself.

'She will be a good slave for us, the Brat,' Xiuying said to Decency, her English perfect once more and the high-pitched excitement gone from her voice. 'You should make her attend to your cunts, my dears. It is a most pleasurable experience.'

'It is hardly decent for an Englishwoman,' Decency replied, but with a strong catch in her voice.

'Not decent at all,' Francesca agreed. 'For any woman of sensibility.'

Thrift had risen as they spoke. Her whole body ached, especially where the bones of her corset had dug into her flesh, and she felt sweaty and sticky, also sick. She composed herself, forcing her raging emotions down, and went to the sink. Decency threw her a look and, if there was disgust, there was complicity also.

'Clean yourself up, Brat,' Decency ordered. 'We must be ready for class in a just a few minutes. You have dirt in your hair, and a little on your left ear.'

'Thank you,' Thrift answered, turning to inspect the side of her face.

'That,' Decency went on, 'was the most vulgar, revolting display I have ever witnessed, that I could ever have imagined. Still, it was certainly amusing, at least to see you licking up the dirt from my boots. It does, I think, amuse me more to have you as my slave than to watch your fat sit-upon whipped. After all, that is becoming rather a common sight, in more ways than one.'

Francesca broke into giggles at the joke.

Decency went on. 'So, I shall not inform Miss Evans, at least, not for now. Perhaps I will write to Lady Newgate over the summer, telling her all about it. There, that should give you something to think about over the holidays.'

4

Edinburgh, July 2004

Thrift approached the summer holidays with both trepidation and guilt, trepidation for the inevitable spankings from Miss Challis, guilt for her equally inevitable response to them. She had begun to masturbate regularly, almost every night and sometimes more than once. When she did it, with her nightie and modesty gown pulled up and her hands thrust down the front of her pyjamas, she would think rude thoughts. Sometimes it would be taking a man's pego into her body, mouth, bottom or even cunt. At other times it would be what she had done with Ana and the others, licking boots and bottom holes as she kneeled at their feet. Most frequently it was over the way she felt as she was exposed and beaten in public, and especially by Miss Challis.

With term over and London hot, sticky and filled with tourists from all across the Empire, some of high status, even within the Quality Enclave, her father had taken a house in Edinburgh for the summer. They had relatives and friends there, which Thrift knew would mean at-homes and dinners and luncheon parties in addition to family picnics and excursions into the countryside. All that was welcome and, if at some point Miss Challis was sure to find an excuse to turn Thrift over her knee in front of an audience, then she knew what the consequences of the pain and humiliation would be. So, she was certain, would Miss Challis, but from the Companion's reaction to the use of the word 'cunt', it was all too plain that their real feelings were never, ever to be admitted to.

The journey north was made by airship, as was suitable for persons of her station, hurry being appropriate only for the commonality. The ship was the *Commodore*, a middle-sized yet luxuriously appointed vessel designed for short-haul routes within the British Isles themselves. For the moment of their smooth and noiseless ascent to the top of the Empire Tower to their corresponding descent down the only marginally less impressive King James Mast, Thrift spent her time admiring the view. From three thousand feet, all England spread below her in a twisted checkerboard of summer fields cut by the lines of roads, rivers and railways, while the sky above was pure blue crisscrossed by the vapour trails of jets carrying merchandise and common travellers.

Edinburgh was mercifully cooler than London, and her mother's mood almost light-hearted. They took tea on the veranda of the house as the servants scurried about their tasks, then a walk along a stroll reserved for the Quality beside the edge of the Firth of Forth. By dinner time Thrift already felt relaxed, and the ill treatment and threats she had received from Decency Branksome-Brading little more than a dream.

The next two weeks were spent in a round of visits and receptions, each made in strict order of priority. They moved from one finely appointed brownstone house to another, among crescents and squares and short streets, always within the city's Quality Enclave. Each hostess attempted to outdo her rivals, with every event in the exact traditional style. Sunday luncheon followed an exact formula depending on whether beef, mutton, pork or chicken was served, each one coming with appropriate vegetables and sauces. Weekday luncheon involved a choice of potted meats, ham or salmon, cucumber, tomato, dressing and bread, varying once only when Thrift's eccentric Aunt Piety served salad potatoes. Tea was simpler: the tea itself, thinly sliced brown bread, which had to be taken first, and a cake of one sort or another. Dinner was more varied, but always the five courses – soup, fish, meat, pudding and cheese.

To her surprise, Thrift was not spanked, despite several accidental errors and a growing failure of respectfulness of which she was fully aware. Gradually the ambiguity of her feelings shifted, her trepidation fading to be replaced by expectancy and even disappointment. Many times she had done things that she was sure were deserving of the full public, bare-bottom punishment, but in each case either her mother or Miss Challis simple corrected her with a quiet word. It grew more puzzling still after their first picnic, when she not only disappeared on her own for a while, but spoke to a commoner who made a remark on the view, and thereby caused them to be late and to have to hurry for their dinner appointment. Had the same happened the previous year, she knew full well it would have been skirts up and drawers open for a thorough spanking, and no thought to who was watching or how she howled. Now, she was merely reprimanded by her mother and instructed to change only her gown and underdress for the evening.

The dinner was with a set of second cousins, and no different from any other save that with the evening being particularly clement, it was suggested that they take their coffee on the terrace. The garden was very fine and, having drunk her cup of Jamaican Blue Mountain with one lump of Demerara sugar and a teaspoonful of cream, Thrift suggested a walk to the eldest daughter, Chastity.

It was brief, a stroll to the end of the garden, arm in arm, and a moment talking as they took turns on an old wooden swing beneath a fine oak in the shade of holly bushes. No notice was taken of their return, until Chastity walked on past the main group and it became evident that the rear of her gown was marred by a broad, green stain from algae on the swing seat. Thrift immediately put her hand back, to discover her own gown damp and undoubtedly soiled, even as Chastity's mother gave a single, sharp nod to the family Governess.

Chastity was spanked. It was a sharp, no-nonsense punishment – hauled squeaking across the Governess's knee, her skirts lifted, her drawers unbuttoned and her fleshy little bottom exposed for fifty vigorous swats as she was lectured on decorum. She took it badly, squealing and begging during preparation, whimpering as she was exposed, bursting into tears even before the first smack had fallen and wailing continuously as the slaps fell.

Thrift watched in expectant shock, knowing she was next, with her stomach fluttering and the juice from her cunt running down the insides of her thighs. By the time Chastity had run blubbering into the house, Thrift was standing with her hands folded in her lap and her head hung, waiting for the inevitable command and wondering if it would be her mother or Miss Challis who carried out the punishment. Her mother spoke.

'Do sit down, Thrift, dear, and do be careful where you sit. This is the most excellent coffee, my dear Hope, certainly as good as anything available in London.'

Completely bemused, Thrift sat down. It made no sense. She had committed the same sin as Chastity, and there was no question that she had been noticed. Yet Chastity had been spanked and she had barely been reprimanded. The disappointment was impossible to deny, as was the effect it had had on her, both watching and in anticipation of her own fate. There was guilt too, but, after wine at dinner and with an aching need between her thighs, it was not so very strong.

For the rest of the evening she thought about the spanking. Chastity had hated it, performing if anything worse than Thrift would have done. It seemed quite wrong that she should enjoy her younger cousin's pain and humiliation when she herself had escaped, yet there was no denying the pleasure in it, pleasure that had always been there. By bedtime she could barely contain the trembling of her hands for the state she was in, and her mind had turned to other spankings she had seen, particularly in Inverness, where occasionally the old-fashioned habit of making the girls strip naked was still observed.

By the time she was alone in her darkened room, the urge to play with her cunt had become unbearable. She was thinking of what had happened to Chastity, and embroidering the event in her mind. Best, she had decided, would have been for both of them to have been made to strip stark naked in front of everyone, even the servants. They could then have been spanked side by side and face to face, watching each other's reactions as the Governess and Miss Challis walloped their bottoms. Then, tear stained and red bottomed, they would have been made to stay shamefully nude for the rest of the evening.

Thrift knew it would never have happened, yet it made a wonderful fantasy, and she simply had to climax, and it had to be done naked, without a stitch on. Slowly, deliberately teasing herself and very fearful of Miss Challis, she began to peel off her clothes beneath the covers. Her sense of daring rose with her sense of excitement as she wiggled out of her nightie, her modesty gown and at last her pyjamas, to leave her as she wanted to be, and so excited that her breath was already coming in long, deep gulps.

She lay listening, but the only sounds were the ticking of a clock and the occasional low purr of an engine. Finally she decided that Miss Challis was definitely asleep and that she could masturbate in safety. It felt so nice to be nude that she spent a moment just wriggling gently in her bed to get the feel of the sheets on bare flesh, then she began. Her thighs came up, and wide, her fingers burrowing into the warm, fleshy folds of her cunt, to find the all-important little bead at the top, and she let her mind turn to her fantasy.

First it was what had happened to Chastity. She was so pretty, with a pert, delicate face and a cloud of soft black hair still worn loose. Just her beauty made the spanking that much more exciting, but best of all was the way she had responded. There was the shock, the urgent entreaties as her clothes were disarranged, the pitiful whimpering as her bottom was exposed, the miserable snivelling tears as her little fat cheeks bounced and wobbled under the spanking.

Thrift stopped rubbing. She had been close to climax, close enough to need only a few more touches to get there. Her cunt was soaking, and it had run down between her bottom cheeks to wet her anus and the sheet beneath. Stains would mean trouble, she was sure, and hopefully that trouble would involve a trip across Miss Challis's knee, something she now felt she needed more than anything else.

Again she began to rub, now thinking of how she herself should have been treated, her bottom exposed and smacked for all to see, left in tears just like Chastity, perhaps to comfort each other, stroking hot bottoms and wet, eager cunts. It would have felt so good, stripped and dancing in her pain, her face dirty with tears, her bottom bouncing, the rear view of her cunt on plain show. Then Chastity's warm embrace and a good lick of each other's hot little bottoms, tongues up the holes, only to be caught by the footman and both roundly fucked.

Once more she stopped, now panting with lust. The thought of having her maidenhead taken was simply too much. She had to climax. Pushing the bedclothes down, she spread herself, her cunt gaping to the air, open and wanton, ready for a big, fat pego to be pushed up the hole, splitting her maidenhead and pushing deep in to pump her full of hot seed. The footman would have been perfect, a man young and handsome, yet a commoner. The thought of a fucking from him provided her with exactly the mixture of virility and shame she wanted, and the muscles of her cunt had already begun to jump as she started to masturbate once more.

The footman would have come in, to catch Thrift with her tongue well up Chastity's bottom hole. He would have ordered them over the bed, bare bottoms up, with a choice of their families being told. They would have obeyed, sobbing with humiliation as they presented their naked bottoms for fucking, and for the loss of their most precious gift to a mere commoner and a servant at that. Chastity would have been first, made to suck his big, dirty pego and then rudely deflowered, only for him to pull out and stick it in Thrift's mouth, hot and wet with her cousin's virgin blood. At last he'd have fucked her, pushing his fat wet pego to the precious membrane that held her inviolate, pressing in, to make her gasp, to burst her cunt, to make her scream.

She did, out loud, the terrible, wonderful fantasy too much to contain, bucking up and down on the bed with her fingers snatching over and over at her sopping cunt and her spare hand gripped tight on to one breast. In complete ecstasy, she was lost to everything save that overwhelming pleasure. She saw nothing, and heard nothing, until the light clicked on and Miss Challis appeared above her, mouth wide in wordless horror for one long instant before finding her voice.

'Abuser! Oh for shame! Lady Moncrieff, Lady Moncrieff, come quickly!

Thrift's ecstasy broke and she was snatching for her sheets even as Miss Challis collapsed sobbing to the floor. Then her mother was in the room, face white with horror before she too slid senseless to the carpet, and her father, stern and angry as he struggled to cope with both fainted women. Servants arrived, bustling around with salts and cold flannels and brandy, not one able to so much as glance at Thrift.

She did nothing, merely sat in her bed, still naked, numb with shock and confusion. Only when the cook ordered her sharply to make herself decent did she pull on her nightie. The cook also stayed when all the others had gone, the normally friendly old woman sat red faced and silent in a chair, looking fixedly at a print of Ben Nevis on the opposite wall.

Not one word was spoken to Thrift for the remainder of the night. Many people came in, her parents, Miss Challis, servants. Her bed was changed and the sheets taken away to be burned, new night clothes were provided to replace those in which she had disgraced herself, conversations were held in urgent whispers with many sidelong glances, her tears and entreaties were ignored. Finally left alone but for the cook, she drifted into an uneasy sleep, only to wake with the first brilliant rays of the rising sun just striking in through the window and Miss Challis standing over her bed, looking drawn and dressed in black bombazine. Her gaze was directed a little to the side of Thrift's head, and when she spoke her voice was flat and emotionless.

'An appointment has been made with Dr Culverton, an expert in this field. There is no breakfast as he has recommended that you do without, and nor will you wear a corset.'

Thrift got up, washed and dressed in the gown of plain grey wool Miss Challis had laid out for her. A thousand questions were running through her head, and a hundred emotions, none of which she voiced. Once ready, she was led downstairs by Miss Challis. Her mother joined them, to escort her through the streets of Edinburgh to a row of houses in the professional quarter, on one of which was a discreet brass plaque announcing the doctor's name and nothing else.

Within there was an air of silence and guilt, with white painted walls and a smell of antiseptic. Nobody spoke, and those few others they saw passed with the same downcast looks and cold formality they themselves bore. Only in the waiting room did Thrift encounter the slightest hint of emotion, a single glance of pain and sympathy from a pretty red-haired girl sat opposite her, also between two older, silent women. At precisely ten o'clock they were admitted.

Dr Culverton proved to be an elderly man with a long face and a grave manner. His outer office was comfortably furnished, with several chairs upholstered in dark green leather and a single straight-backed, wooden chair to which Thrift was motioned. Beyond the doctor's desk a door stood slightly ajar, revealing a second room, brightly lit and tiled in white, with an assortment of bright steel implements visible on an enamelled tray. Without so much as a glance at Thrift, Dr Culverton addressed her mother.

'Good morning, Lady Moncrieff. Miss Challis, I presume?'

Both greeted him, their voices stern, their chins held rigid.

Dr Culverton went on. 'Pray do not be overly concerned, Lady Moncrieff. Such cases, while regrettable, are by no means uncommon. They are also curable, by one or another regime.'

'A regime, Dr Culverton?'

'Indeed, Lady Moncrieff, a regime. Pray do not be concerned, this is not the Albertian era! Neither electrical probes nor spikes are widely employed these days. Generally, a measure of nocturnal restraint proves sufficient.'

'I trust that it will be so, Dr Culverton. Did you have a particular regime in mind?'

'It is a little early for that, my dear Lady Moncrieff. First, I must ask a few questions and make an examination.'

'Very well.'

'Firstly then, how long has this been going on?'

The question was not aimed at Thrift, who remained silent.

Miss Challis answered. 'I discovered her last night, Doctor.'

'Indeed, yet are you certain that this is the first occasion? Think back, Miss Challis, have you noticed that she has become sullen or morose? Does she exhibit shyness or a reluctance for the company of her peers?'

'Perhaps,' Miss Challis admitted. 'She has been sulky, certainly, and I have noticed that she shows a disinclination for the company of Miss Decency Branksome-Brading, who also attends the Diplomatic School in London and is a most suitable young Lady.'

'Typical symptoms,' Dr Culverton remarked, making a note. 'For how long would you say they have been manifest?'

'A while, certainly,' Miss Challis replied. 'Since the spring, perhaps.'

'Several months in any case,' the doctor said thoughtfully. 'Hmm, it is a shame this could not have been brought to my attention earlier, yet doubtless it is not too late. Now, the examination, if Miss Challis would perhaps care to accompany me?'

Miss Challis rose immediately, Thrift also, despite the fact that she had not been addressed nor so much as mentioned. They entered the second room, at the centre of which stood a peculiar device halfway between a chair and a table. It was as ominous as it was strange, with thick leather straps fitted at the upper corners to a pair of steel semicircles projecting on adjustable struts.

'If you would be so kind as to disrobe the patient and place her in the chair,' Dr Culverton remarked, busying himself with the assorted implements on the bench.

Miss Challis took Thrift's arm without a word and led her behind a high white screen. Fresh tears of sheer misery sprang up in Thrift's eyes as she began to undress, with Miss Challis standing pink faced and nervous beside her. Once in her chemise, drawers and stockings, she stopped, unable to countenance going further or imagine it could be expected of her.

'Quite naked,' Dr Culverton said casually, never turning, as if he had anticipated her inability to make the final exposure.

'Must I?' Thrift quavered.

'You must,' Miss Challis said sharply.

'But, Miss Challis –'

'You forfeited your right to modesty when – last night,' Miss Challis answered, blushing scarlet. 'Now hold your tongue. You need only do as the doctor says, no more, no less.'

Shivering with shame and unhappiness, Thrift began to remove her final garments. Her stockings went first, leaving her feeling exposed as the air touched the skin of her bare calves, but it was as nothing with the agony of revealing her breasts, and that in turn paled beside the final exposure, her bottom and cunt as she let her drawers fall.

'On the chair, if you please,' Dr Culverton stated, again seeming to anticipate Thrift's emotions.

She found herself unable to emerge from behind the screen, but Miss Challis took her firmly by the arm and dragged her from cover to the huge and menacing chair. Climbing into it, she discovered to her horror that the projecting shafts were all too clearly designed to take her feet, leaving her with her cunt spread to the room. Completely unable to adopt so lewd a position, she crossed her legs and put her hands over her breasts and

cunt, to sit, utterly miserable, shamefaced and crying while
the doctor pulled on a pair of thin, white rubber gloves.

He turned, his face set in disapproval, and he spoke.
'Young Lady, as your good and patient Companion has
so rightly pointed out, you have forfeited all claim to
modesty. Now, pray place your feet in the stirrups and
your hands above your head, or I shall be obliged to call
the attendants.'

Physically incapable of uncovering herself, Thrift
simply sat as she was, numb with the humiliation of her
position. The doctor sighed and reached out to press a
button. A moment later two massively built women in
blue uniform gowns appeared. Without a word, their
faces emotionless, they took hold of Thrift's arms,
forcing them high above her head and fixing them into
the straps even as she kicked and squealed in protest. It
did no good. Her arms were secured and her legs hauled
wide, forced down into the metal stirrups and strapped
securely in place, leaving her panting and forlorn, tears
of unspeakable anguish streaming down her burning
cheeks, her cunt flaunted to the room. The attendants
left, each with a brief nod to the doctor.

'Obedience is much the easiest course of action,' Dr
Culverton stated and depressed a lever on the side of the
chair.

Thrift squealed as her legs were hauled higher and
wider, the stirrup shafts moving under power. She was
powerless to resist, and was left with her thighs at right
angles to one another and hauled so high that her
bottom cheeks had spread to add the exposure of her
anus to her woes. Snivelling, she watched through a
curtain of tears as the doctor picked a large thermometer up from a tray, pushed it into a pot of some greasy
substance and quite casually poked it up her bottom.
Again she squealed as her anus gave, louder and more
miserably than before. Dr Culverton gave the bell a
brief, irritable push and turned back to the bench.

Once more the two huge attendants came into the room. Worried, Thrift made to speak, only for one woman to pinch her nose while the other forced a fat ball of foul-tasting white rubber between her jaws, forcing them wide. She struggled briefly before the strap was fastened behind her head and her gagging was complete. Miss Challis had watched her bound and gagged without so much as a twitch of a single muscle.

Completely helpless, her bumhole twitching on the intruding thermometer, Thrift could only wriggle feebly in her bonds as the doctor turned back to her. His face was a mask of detachment as he bent close to inspect her cunt, for all that she could feel the muscles around her hole pulsing in the agony of her shame. A finger was poked into the tiny hole at the centre of her hymen and her shame grew worse still, tears spurting from her eyes as she shook her head in a futile effort to dispel her feelings.

'*Virgo intacta*,' Dr Culverton remarked, as he picked up a steel clipboard and placed a tick on the form attached to it. 'Peculiar ... I would have expected otherwise from the density and copiosity of discharge. Some other factor, then is at work ...'

He was talking to himself, and pulling at his chin as he spoke, all the while with his eyes fixed on Thrift's spread cunt. Her bottom hole was still clutching rebelliously on the shaft of the thermometer, but as he trailed off with a thoughtful nod he reached down. Thrift let out a soft, weak fart as the thermometer was extracted from her rectum. Fresh shame filled her head, and grew abruptly worse as the doctor's finger found her anus, first to touch gently on her ring, and then to push roughly inside and up into her rectum. After a moment he attempted to push a second finger in, but stopped as Thrift winced in pain.

'No,' he stated, with a shake of his head, 'no instinctive dilation, no evidence of enlargement, not anal. Hmm, a most singular case.'

Thrift's reaction to the slow, methodical inspection of all her most intimate places was so strong that she was running sweat as well as tears, while she knew full well that her cunt was juicing copiously. Still she was ignored, as the doctor pulled on new gloves, then turned to her once more, clipboard in hand.

Her nipples were erect and he made a note of the fact. He peered close to her cunt once more and made another note. Shaking his head in apparent perplexity he tapped the end of his pencil to her anus, then made yet another note. Shaking badly, wet with sweat and tears, the need in her bladder now urgent, Thrift lay shivering in the chair. For all his calm and professional manner, there was a notable bulge beneath the doctor's white coat, at crotch level, and she was wondering why he didn't simply find some excuse to send Miss Challis out. Then he could relieve his pego in her mouth or up the tight hole between her bottom cheeks he evidently found so fascinating.

He didn't, but contented himself with a squeeze of her breasts and bottom cheeks. Then, with a sudden, thoughtful nod, he twitched open the strap securing her right leg in the stirrup. Thrift winced, sure he was about to use her bottom, Miss Challis or no Miss Challis, but he merely bent her leg, until the ball of her foot was pressed to her open cunt. She winced in fresh pain but he took no notice, merely nodding once more and returning her foot to the stirrup.

She was given a final lingering touch to her anus before he once more pressed the bell. He made notes as the two attendants unstrapped her and took out her gag, all without a word. Hugging herself, she walked miserably back behind the screen, only to find a trolley there with a squat glass beaker on it.

'Fill the beaker and replace the lid,' the doctor ordered from behind the screen.

Thrift found her face setting in still deeper misery and resentment as she picked up the beaker. To fill it she was forced to squat while she held the wide rim to her open cunt, and when she let go the stream of her piddle produced a loud hiss and a peculiarly disgusting gurgling noise, wringing fresh tears of humiliation from her eyes. The instant she had finished the doctor's voice sounded again.

'Very good, you may dress.'

She put the beaker down, wondering what on earth they expected to discover about her self-abuse from a sample of her pee-pee. Doubtless there would be something, when doctors could create living animals from those long dead, but she was sure that, whatever it was, it would be to her disadvantage. She shook her head, struggling to dispel her overwhelming feelings of shame, but even as she did so a tiny thought pushed itself up in her mind. She was soaking between her legs and violated in both holes. She touched herself, the sheer sensitivity of her cunt flesh sending a shiver the length of her spine. A few quick rubs and she would be at climax . . .

'Stop that!' the doctor's voice snapped out from beyond the screen.

Thrift jumped, nearly upsetting the beaker of urine on the trolley. For an instant she was amazed, only to catch a sudden spark of sunlight from above her. There, in the corner of the ceiling and walls, a tiny lens was visible, set among the curlicues of the plaster frieze, and quite invisible save for the chance angle of the morning sun. Horrified, she realised that her every motion behind the screen had been watched and possibly even recorded, undressing, urinating in the beaker, the guilty touch of her cunt.

Weeping forlornly at what seemed the final intrusion into her privacy, she dressed as fast as she could. Outside the screen, Miss Challis sat as motionless and imperturbable as before, hands folded in her lap and face set in icy detachment. As Thrift emerged Miss

Challis rose, thanked the doctor with a polite inclination of her head and left the room. The doctor followed and sat back down in his chair. Frowning at the notes he had made, he spent a moment in reflection, then addressed Thrift's mother.

'It is a difficult case, Lady Moncrieff. Indeed, it might even be said to be singular. Fortunately, neither of the two principal symptoms associated with severe delinquency are present, and yet by the strength of her reaction I would have expected both. Yes, definitely singular.'

'No doubt, Dr Culverton,' Thrift's mother answered, 'but what is to be done?'

'What indeed, Lady Moncrieff?' he responded. 'Well, I am pleased to say that nocturnal restriction should prove sufficient. However, to make certain of our cure, I am going to prescribe Dr Molloy's Primary Regime. Essentially, this combines restraint with a measure of minor physical discomfort, thus both preventing physical agitation and turning the mind away from all such topics. Thus, one set of standard Lady's restraints, wrist and ankles in combination, and a bottle of Dr Molloy's Efficacious Pessaries, in the large or economy bottle.'

He had scribbled out a note as he spoke, and passed it to Miss Challis, who secreted it quickly in the recesses of her dress. Thrift rose, eager to be out of the horrible place, waited as her mother thanked the doctor and trooped out, sharing a pitiful glance with the red-haired girl in the waiting room as she went. The apothecary's counter was in a side room on the lower floor, and they collected their prescription on the way out, before walking back to the house without a word exchanged.

They themselves were entertaining at luncheon, and despite the stresses of the night and morning it proceeded as normal, the only difference being that Thrift was now forbidden to help pass the sandwiches. Afterwards, they went down to stroll, took tea with an old friend of her father's and dinner with the new Secretary to the Consul. Only afterwards did the routine break.

As always, Miss Challis accompanied Thrift up the stairs once the evening had come to a close. As always, she waited as Thrift completed her ablutions and changed from her day clothes into those suitable for the night. As always she brushed Thrift's hair out and tied it back. As always she led the recital of evening prayer. Then, rather than folding back Thrift's bedcovers, she went briefly to her own room and returned with the two brown paper packages they had collected at the doctor's that morning. With a face like stone she addressed Thrift.

'First, for the application of one of Dr Molloy's Efficacious Pessaries, it will be necessary for you to kneel on the bed.'

Thrift obeyed, somewhat puzzled as she climbed on to the bed and kneeled down, as if in prayer once more.

'The other way, girl,' Miss Challis sighed.

Quickly Thrift turned her bottom to her Companion, more puzzled than ever and also a touch worried.

'On all fours might prove most efficient,' Miss Challis said wearily.

Thrift went down, acutely conscious of the display she was making of her bottom as she adopted the position and wondering why such a lewd pose was required in order that she take a pill. There had been no mention of spankings before bed by the doctor, to her surprise, yet it seemed likely that she was going to get one anyway.

'Lift your gowns and pop down your pyjamas then,' Miss Challis went on, now sounding somewhat impatient.

Thrift reached back quickly, muddled emotions swirling inside her as she realised that she was to be spanked, and what it was certain to do to her. Despite the indignities of the morning, baring her bottom was no less shameful, and her cheeks were burning by the time she had gathered up her nightie and modesty gown on to her back and pushed down her pyjamas to show off her bare bottom. Immediately Miss Challis gave a sharp push at the centre of Thrift's back, forcing her to spread her cheeks and show off both cunt and bottom hole. Thrift shut her eyes, waiting for the pain and wondering if the beating would be delivered by hand, with a hairbrush or even if she would be made to hold her humiliating pose while a cane was fetched.

Nothing happened, but she kept her eyes tightly shut, sure Miss Challis was simply giving her a little time to let the indignity of her position sink in. Then came a noise, a soft pop followed by a grating sound, a chink as if of stone on glass and another pop. Puzzled, Thrift opened her eyes to look back. Behind her Miss Challis was holding the jar of pills, with one in her fingers, a dull green lozenge easily as thick as a thumb.

'Hold still,' Miss Challis instructed, and the horrible thing was pressed to Thrift's anus.

She winced as it was pushed in, her hole resisting the unwelcome invasion. 'Do stop it, Thrift!' Miss Challis snapped. 'You are holding yourself.'

'I can't help it!' Thrift wailed. 'It's – it's big, and I'm – I'm dry.'

'Honest to goodness!' Miss Challis snapped and stood, leaving the big pill wedged halfway into Thrift's anus.

Her Companion walked briskly from the room, leaving Thrift to endure the agonies of having to hold such a lewd position when at any moment a servant might come in on some errand, to find her bare bottomed with the pill projecting from her anus. Miss Challis was mercifully quick, though, returning a minute or so later with a jar of cream. Knowing full well what it was for, Thrift hung her head, and had to endure the further indignity of having her anus smeared with cream before the big pill was at last forced up into her rectum. Again Thrift was left, as Miss Challis washed her hands.

'Why haven't you covered yourself?' the Companion demanded, emerging from behind the wash screen. 'In all honesty, Thrift, I do wonder if you are truly wanton or simply too dull witted to overcome your base instincts. Not that I am at all certain any real difference exists between the two concepts. Now, place your hands behind your back.'

Thrift had already covered her bottom, and quickly crossed her wrists behind her back as ordered. Miss Challis came to her again and wrapped a thick, padded cuff around each wrist, tightened the buckle and locked it off. The process was repeated with Thrift's ankles and the two sets of cuffs fastened together by means of a short chain. Helpless, her arms and feet bound behind her back, Thrift had to be rolled over and the bedclothes pulled up to cover her body. Only then did Miss Challis give a quiet nod of satisfaction, the first positive emotion she had registered all day.

'There,' she stated, 'now you shall keep your hands to yourself, Miss Thrift Moncrieff, although if I had my way I'd give you two dozen of the cane every night and put you in a spiked belt as well. So, is there anything you have to say for yourself?'

'I am truly sorry, Miss Challis,' Thrift answered meekly. 'Please believe that I had no wish to bring you distress, nor inconvenience, much less to Mama.'

Miss Challis merely sniffed and turned away, before walking quickly to the door. After a curt 'good night' she extinguished the light and Thrift was left alone in the dark, feeling confused and thoroughly sorry for herself.

Not only were her straps uncomfortable, but the pellet in her anus had started to itch, and there was no possible way of reliving the sensation. Half-an-hour later, despite the long and exhausting day, she was still awake and the itching was rapidly becoming unbearable. With no doubt in her mind that to call for Miss Challis would only bring worse suffering, she held her silence, merely wriggling her bottom against the chain that connected her wrist and ankle cuffs in an ineffectual effort to relieve herself.

An hour later and it had become very plain to her that Dr Culverton was completely wrong in his assertion that the combination of restriction and Dr Molloy's infernal pessary would reduce her need to masturbate. The cuffs prevented her from getting at her cunt, yes, but being tied up only made her feelings of helpless submission stronger, while the pessary simply made her desperate to have something, anything, thrust up her bottom and jammed firmly in and out.

In no time she was thinking not of having her cunt fucked, but her bottom hole, and by the doctor himself. It was only appropriate after all, when he was the one responsible for her suffering. He had seen her strip too, and examined her in minute and hideously embarrassing detail. He had even probed her anus, and she was absolutely certain that it had only been the presence of Miss Challis that had prevented him from using his pego as a probe instead of his finger.

Just thinking about it had her cunt sodden with juice, producing a stickiness that rapidly started to make her itching worse. Soon she was wriggling against her chain and crying tears of pure frustration, while scheme after useless scheme to bring her torment to an end flashed through her brain. She tried to get the chain to her cunt, then her heels, but both positions proved so painful it was impossible to masturbate. Exhausted, and more frustrated than ever by the brief touches she had managed, she gave up, and at some point in the dark of the middle night she finally fell asleep.

Thrift woke cramped and sore, her thighs stuck together with dried cunt juice and her bladder straining for relief.

It was plainly impossible for her to reach the facility and, for all that the dim grey light of dawn had only just begun to filter through the gaps in the curtains, she was soon calling urgently for Miss Challis, who eventually appeared, still clad in her long nightie.

An irritable cluck greeted Thrift's pleas, but Miss Challis condescended to unfasten the links between the cuffs. Painfully stiff, Thrift hobbled to the facility, to squat low and let everything inside her out in one great, ecstatic rush. So strong was her reaction that it left her dizzy and as she wiped herself she found that the urge to bring herself to climax had scarcely faded. It was impossible, and she was obliged to allow Miss Challis to fasten her links once more and roll her back into bed. An uncomfortable hour followed before her Companion came back and she was at last released to wash and dress.

The rest of the day passed in trepidation of the night and, despite her best efforts not to seem sullen or listless and so exhibit further evidence of her complaint, it proved impossible to hide. More than once she caught whispered comments on how pale and tired she seemed, both of which she was sure would be put down as symptoms of her self-abuse rather than of the cure for it. By evening she was exhausted, and was sent to bed early and with yet more whispering, this time from the servants.

Her second night in restraints was marginally less terrible than the first, the third less again. Within a week she had learned to accept the agonising tickling sensation in her bottom hole and the pained restriction of her arms and legs in stoic resignation. Within a month it felt normal, and being free at night as distant as taking a doll to bed. For all that, her vivid dreams and imaginings of lewd conduct did not fade.

Not once was she spanked, and she had come to suspect that there had to be a reason for this strange conduct. No matter what she did, she was always corrected with a word, sometimes gentle, sometimes sharp. Even her self-abuse had not earned the expected beating, yet the result was for her wanton fixations to move slowly from a desire for spanking towards having her body used while she lay helpless in bondage.

By late August her lewd thoughts came with every moment alone, and could be triggered by the smallest thing. Usually it would be the sight of some particularly well-formed young man in the Edinburgh streets, sometimes the rosy bottom and pained squeals of a girl undergoing punishment, occasionally nothing more than the sight of a riding whip or a piece of rope.

Tied at night and accompanied at all other times, there was no chance to relieve her yearnings until one morning on the last day of the month. It had been a bad night and she had woken at some dark hour from a dream of having her bottom and mouth used by burglars. Her bladder was tense and she knew that a visit to the facility was needed, but with not so much as a hint of dawn light outside she felt reluctant to call for Miss Challis. For a long while she had lain still in bed, struggling to control both her body and mind. It had been no good, the pain in her bladder growing and the lewd fantasy also. Finally she decided that if she could only get out of bed it might just be possible to crawl into the shower basin and bare her cunt, enabling her to spray her piddle down the drain hole without soiling her pyjamas.

It was not easy. By dint of frantic wriggling she managed to squirm free of the covers and crawl, caterpillar-like, on to the floor. Then, moving in the same undignified fashion, she shuffled slowly across the room, behind the wash screen and into the shower, but not before bruising her hips and shoulder on the hard china. Kneeling up was harder still, and left her in a ludicrous position, her feet and back to the wall, her knees spread, her cunt thrust out forwards.

Baring herself was harder still, with the pain of her need growing stronger by the moment as she struggled to inch her nightie up at the back. It came, bit by bit, with Thrift forced to make little treading motions with her knees to let the cotton out from beneath them. By the time it was up around her belly and bunched over her bound wrists at the back she was in agony, but there was still the modesty gown to go. It was no easier than the nightie, and she had barely got it past her calves when she slipped, fell sideways and at the impact her bladder burst, spraying pee-pee into the gusset of her pyjamas.

With a little cry of despair she gave up, surrendering herself to the inevitable as hot piddle gushed out of her cunt and into her night clothes. For all her awful shame, the sense of relief was overwhelming, and brought the fantasy back to her head, this time with the burglars making her wet herself and laughing as her piddle sprayed and spurted from between her legs before they used her.

She let it all come, until she was lying in a warm pool of her own making, her garments soaked and her cunt sticky and ready. Discovery was inevitable, cleaning herself up an impossibility, hiding the evidence little easier. Now, she was certain, Miss Challis must finally spank her, and with that knowledge the need in her cunt grew greater still.

It was sure to happen, there was simply no option, and when she at last called out for help it was in the knowledge of what that help would bring, exposure, probably complete, and a sore bottom. Miss Challis arrived, still in her nightie, sleepy and irritable, but merely lectured Thrift on her lack of consideration for others as she cleaned up.

The shower was turned on over Thrift's prostrate body, cold, and left running until the piddle had been thoroughly rinsed away. She was left shivering with cold as Miss Challis disappeared on some errand, to return perhaps twenty minutes later, now dressed. Thrift was untied and ordered to strip and get into her bathing gown, then to wash properly.

She obeyed, her fear growing with the certainty that the spanking would come once she was dry, and her need from the necessity of cleansing and powdering her cunt. She was just pulling up her drawers beneath her modesty gown when the bell rang to summon Miss Challis. It was highly irregular, never mind so early, and more likely to be a mistake than anything. Miss Challis went in any case, leaving Thrift alone and unrestrained with an already tingling cunt.

It was impossible not to do it. Her frustration and need were simply too great, with her dream, wetting herself and the threat of punishment. The opportunity was too good to miss, and in an instant her fingers were in the sticky slot of her cunt and her eyes shut as she lowered herself to the seat of the facility.

It was simple. The burglars had broken in, the near impossibility of this with enclave security conveniently forgotten for the sake of her pleasure. They had found her sleeping and in restraint. They had gagged her, forcing her bundled stockings into her mouth and tying them off around her head. They had pawed her body, muttering in their common, guttural speech as they explored her breasts and bottom, her belly and at last, her cunt. They had broken the link between ankle and wrist cuffs in strong, rough hands. They had ordered her to wet herself, promising to spare her maidenhead if she made a good show. She had done it, spreading her cunt to them to show off as the piddle spurted high in the air and back over her body, soiling her belly and breasts and face as they laughed at her. They had fucked her anyway, rolled up on her side to leave both her holes available, cunt and bottom hole too, forcing her ring, bursting her precious maidenhead . . .

She came with a little cry of joy, a climax so quick, yet so powerful that it left her panting, as she still was when the screen was pulled roughly back to reveal Miss Challis and her mother.

It was as before. She was locked in her room with the cook, then marched in stony silence to the house where Dr Culverton made his practice. There was the same embarrassing wait, admission to the doctor's room, the questions, differing only when her incontinence was revealed. Then it was into the white tiled room, where there was the strip, the probing of her anus and the awful inspection of her cunt. Afterwards, more miserable than ever, she found herself listening to the doctor's remarks in his outer room, immediately discovering that she had been left deliberately to see if she would masturbate.

'... and at the very first opportunity presented,' he was saying. 'She is a hopeless recidivist, I fear. In some eighty-four per cent of such cases a girl will resist the first occasion, and in seventy-one per cent the second. A full sixty-four per cent never again descend to such wilfulness in the case of this regime.'

'Clearly then Dr Molloy's Regime is inadequate,' Lady Moncrieff replied frostily.

'Clearly,' Dr Culverton replied. 'I admit as much. I fear that my natural inclination is towards lenience, but, now, I see that we must not hesitate to employ the most severe methods of correction, my dear Lady Moncrieff. At the time it may seem cruel, but we must harden our hearts. Rest assured, in the fullness of time she will come to thank us.'

'I expect nothing less, Dr Culverton,' Lady Moncrieff answered.

'You shall have it, rest assured, my dear Lady Moncrieff,' he answered. 'I intend a prescription of Dr Lloyd's Improved Regime, which is certain to be effective.'

'Dr Lloyd's Regime? I believe I am acquainted with the procedure. Is it not somewhat old fashioned?'

'Yes, yet this must not necessarily be seen as a failing. Many authorities consider the modern techniques too lenient, and it must be said that figures for both offence and recidivism have gone up in recent years.'

Lady Moncrieff gave a delicate shudder.

Dr Culverton went on. 'My most profuse apologies, my dear Lady Moncrieff, for venturing upon such a distasteful and inappropriate subject, yet sadly we are brought to such straits.'

He cast Thrift a look of disgust, utterly indifferent to her tear-streaked face and trembling fingers. After digging into a filing cabinet, he pulled out a booklet, black covered with no title, and passed it to Miss Challis.

'Dr Lloyd's Improved Regime,' he stated. 'The necessary equipment may be collected from the apothecary. Instructions are given in detail, so I may spare you the distress of a recital. Clearly incontinence pants of compatible design will be required in addition. For these I recommend Madame Frobisher in Bruce Street. The mews entrance naturally.'

He gave Lady Moncrieff an unctuous smile, scribbled a prescription note and tore it free of the pad. Miss Challis took it and they left the room. Downstairs the note was handed in, drawing a glance of distaste for Thrift from the apothecary, who handed over a bag both large and heavy to Miss Challis.

Another silent walk through the streets followed, down the hill to one of the spotless thoroughfares designated as shopping areas for the Quality. Madame Frobisher's was easy to find, a Lady's outfitters with the windows closed off by heavy drapes of richly embroidered plush. A narrow, covered alley led down to one side, into the mews behind. Lady Moncrieff simply walked on, not so much as glancing at the dark archway that led into alley. A moment later Miss Challis had steered Thrift into it, herself blushing and angry as they once more emerged into the light.

'The shame you have put your poor mother through!' Miss Challis snapped. 'Really, is there no end to your mischief?'

Thrift simply hung her head. A large Alvis delivery van stood to one side, half-blocking a plain doorway that evidently led into the rear of Madame Frobisher's premises. Red faced but haughty, Miss Challis rang the bell. A moment later the door swung open and they were admitted by a silent maid who led them to a windowless box of a room lined with numbered drawers and compartments. A leather-topped table stood to one side, with two plain wooden chairs beside it. Without a word Miss Challis handed Dr Culverton's prescription note to the maid.

There was a wait, ten minutes, then twenty, marked by the ticking of a cheap, dusty clock fixed above the doorway. Miss Challis passed the time by studying the instructions for Dr Lloyd's Improved Regime, the expression on her face growing increasingly puzzled and increasingly irritable with time. At last the door swung open once more, to admit a huge, raw-boned woman with a sharp face and grey hair confined in a plain net. Ignoring Thrift completely, she addressed Miss Challis.

'Mrs Brodie, at your service, Miss . . .?'

'Miss Challis,' the Companion answered.

'A disagreeable task, ours, Miss Challis,' Mrs Brodie went on, 'but a necessary one. Would I be correct in assuming that Dr Lloyd's Improved Regime has been prescribed?'

'Quite so,' Miss Challis replied and both women cast Thrift a dirty look. Mrs Brodie shook her head.

'Recidivism, a terrible problem these days, yet I think you may be assured of efficacy in this case. Now, as to the fitting, it must be snug, naturally, and I find full removal of the garments important.'

Miss Challis threw Thrift another glance. Thrift understood immediately and began to undress, folding her garments one by one on a chair as the two women continued to discuss her.

'Possibly you wish the full fitting, Miss Challis?' Mrs Brodie enquired. 'Many Ladies find the process both personally distasteful and of exaggerated complexity.'

'I freely confess to both,' Miss Challis answered, 'and would be most grateful to you.'

'To claim that it is my pleasure would be to pronounce a falsehood,' Mrs Brodie replied, 'yet it is an element of my profession and as such must be borne with all good grace.'

She had turned to the compartments on the wall, opening one to reveal a number of bags, each of which bulged unpleasantly with some pink substance that moved as it was touched.

'The latest in this product line,' Mrs Brodie explained as she drew one of the bags down. 'An organic substance akin to rubber but capable of moulding precisely to the form. You may be assured that there will be no spillage, nor abrasion, the contact point being self-lubricating.'

Thrift watched sidelong, but in horror, as she began to unfasten her corset. Whatever was in the bag appeared to be alive, and squirmed disturbingly at the big woman's touch. It looked like flesh, but transparent, some smooth, some wrinkled, while a tube with a tiny spigot of the same pink substance was visible to one side of the package. Just the thought of being put in the thing was making her stomach twitch, but she knew better than to speak and continued to strip as Mrs Brodie went on.

'The self-sterilising catheter is an integral part of the mechanism and need only be changed once a week, a distasteful process but one with which you will quickly become familiar. I presume you have already collected your containment pants?'

'Certainly,' Miss Challis answered and bent to the bag she had brought from the doctor's to extract a bizarre object, made of what appeared to be thick black rubber and designed like the upper part of a man's trousers.

Thrift was shaking hard as she continued her strip, peeling off her corset, chemise, stockings and drawers with no less embarrassment than at any other time, but with the absolutely certainty that if she did not do as she was told it would be done for her. Nude, she stood red faced and shivering, one hand over her cunt, the other concealing her breasts.

'On the table, girl, legs apart,' Mrs Brodie ordered, and Thrift scrambled up hastily, before assuming the lewd position, her cunt spread to the room.

'Obedient, at the least,' Mrs Brodie remarked as she split the seal on the bag. 'So many have to be held down, especially for catheterisation.'

'She has learned her lesson,' Miss Challis explained. 'At Dr Culverton's, the first time, it was necessary for the attendants to hold her. Not since.'

'You have chastised her?' Mrs Brodie queried, drawing the flabby pink object from the bag.

Miss Challis made to answer, but hesitated.

Mrs Brodie went on. 'It is nothing but a foolish modern fad. Chastisement is chastisement.'

'I entirely agree,' Miss Challis answered with sympathy.

Some understanding had passed between the two women, Thrift was sure, and also sure that it had something to do with her recent lack of spankings. Then, as Mrs Brodie held up the incontinence pants for inspection, all thoughts of the puzzle were pushed from her mind. The things squirmed in the woman's hands, as if alive, filling her with the same crawling feeling as when she saw a worm or slug. Suddenly her self-control had broken.

'No . . . please,' she stammered. 'Miss Challis, stop her . . . I beg of you . . . wait, at least –'

'Be silent!' Miss Challis snapped. 'Are matters not bad enough without you making a scene? Remember that it is your own disgusting behaviour that has brought you to this sorry strait.'

'But –' Thrift answered, and broke down, tears bursting from her eyes, the shame, contrition and the total lack of sympathy from all others simply too much for her.

Her tears were ignored. Mrs Brodie took the black garment and threaded a long pink tube through a central plaque around which Thrift could see metal studs in the shape of low cones and in a pattern suspiciously similar to the outline of her cunt. Her ankles were taken, one, then the other, pushed into the leg holes of the black garment, then the pink. Both writhed against her skin, making her think of worms once more.

They were pulled up to the level of her knees, both stretched wide as Mrs Brodie took the long pink tube and, with a look compounded of intense concentration and deep disgust, spread Thrift's cunt with her fingers. Fresh tears came at the intrusion, blinding Thrift, so that it came as a complete surprise when the tip of the tube was introduced to her pee-hole. She gasped, her mouth coming open in wordless shame and disgust as the tube slid up into her body, waves of motion running down it as it burrowed inside her.

Mrs Brodie took no notice of the sudden twitching motion of Thrift's cunt, nor of the increasingly bitter tears as she carefully pulled up the black pants. Thrift lifted her bottom without having to be asked, now surrendered to the indignity of what was happening to her. The pants were fitted snugly around her hips, and tightened as Mrs Brodie released them, taking her in a rubbery grip and making her stomach jump in fresh revulsion.

'Naturally,' Mrs Brodie stated, as she took hold of the pink pants, 'even in so advanced a case of delinquency we would not wish to spoil the line of the girl's waist. Both garments therefore fit low about the upper hips, immediately below the bustle line.'

'I see,' Miss Challis remarked, peering close as the pink pants were pulled up over the snivelling Thrift's hips. 'It seems straightforward enough, I must say.'

'Practice is essential,' Mrs Brodie assured her, 'especially in the fitting of the catheter. It must also be admitted that the manual is couched in language perhaps unnecessarily coy. Dr Lloyd, of course, is a man. We women must be more practical.'

The immediate look of haughty distaste on Miss Challis's face showed that she disagreed, but she said nothing. Thrift lowered her bottom, wincing as the rubber pants shifted. Both pairs encased her hips, the black snug, the pink loose, but the black ended a few inches down her thighs while the pink extended to immediately above her knees, where a frilly edge had squeezed tight to her flesh. A thick pad covered her cunt, making self-abuse impossible, and she could feel the low metal cones digging into her flesh.

Mrs Brodie went on. 'I trust she is regular?'

'Impeccably so, I am pleased to say,' Miss Challis answered. 'Mornings at eight sharp.'

'Ideal,' Mrs Brodie said. 'Stand up, girl, and turn about.'

Thrift stood facing the table to present to them her rubber-clad bottom. She closed her eyes as Mrs Brodie's hand took one plump cheek, squeezing gently. A finger touched at the point where the slit of her bottom merged with her back, pressed, again and a third time. The sides of her pants peeled open and she felt cool air on her buttocks.

'The code,' Mrs Brodie remarked, 'may be found at the rear of the instruction booklet. Should she need to be bared for punishment, you may pass it on to the appropriate person. Take care that it is not written down, as should she learn it she will be able to get at herself and just possibly commit an act of abuse, despite the thickness and stability of the frontal plaque. You are recommended to burn the slip on which the number is written once it has been memorised.'

'I shall certainly do so,' Miss Challis agreed, 'and also pass it on as required.'

'Press the same code in to close the pants,' Mrs Brodie instructed, but did not do so, instead asking a question. 'She is beaten regularly at her school?'

'Hardly,' Miss Challis replied. 'It is a progressive establishment intended for the daughters of senior Diplomatic staff. Inevitably when dealing with foreigners there is bound to be a certain laxity.'

'A great shame,' Mrs Brodie sighed. 'Regular beatings are important, I feel.'

'I concur entirely, Mrs Brodie,' Miss Challis answered and both women went silent.

Thrift waited, acutely conscious of the way her bare bottom was sticking out of the hole in the rear of her pants. After a while Miss Challis spoke again, softly and without her normal confidence.

'It is . . . feasible. Here?'

'Certainly,' Mrs Brodie replied and the next instant Thrift had been forced down over the table, her bottom squeezing fully from the open incontinence pants, to be thrust, fat and round, out to the room.

She squealed in shock, only to be told to shut up as the two women began to spank her, a buttock each, slapping hard and in time to set her cheeks bouncing and spreading. Already crying, she burst into fresh tears of abject misery, with the image of how she was, held down, nude but for the horrible pink and black pants, her breasts squashed out on the table, her bottom flaunted, her anus showing.

For all the pain, for all the indignity, she almost immediately felt her cunt respond, pressing hard to the thick rubber plaque that would prevent her ever from abusing her body. It hurt, the metal studs digging into her soft flesh, and then, as a sudden, burning jolt shot through her groin she realised that she had never even understood what pain meant. She screamed, out loud, as her legs and bottom cheeks went into immediate and ungovernable convulsions and her anus opened in a long fart.

Miss Challis stopped spanking as Thrift collapsed on to the table top, sobbing uncontrollably into her arms. Mrs Brodie continued, pausing only to place a restraining arm around Thrift's waist.

'Do not be alarmed, Miss Challis,' she stated, 'and there is no need to stop. The electrical curb has activated, that is all. It will provide mild electric shocks so long as the sinful flesh remains engorged, thus obliging the wanton to turn her mind from impure thoughts. Naturally, it also tends to activate during punishment, but I understand that Dr Lloyd is working on the problem.'

She had continued to spank as she spoke, and Thrift had continued to jerk in helpless incontinence as shock after shock passed through her cunt. Miss Challis began again, slapping rapidly at Thrift's bottom, quick, stinging slaps, before settling down once more to a firm, even rhythm.

Her cunt twitching to the current, her muscles completely beyond her control, Thrift could do nothing, only gasp and pant out her pain and emotion as the beating went on. The slaps grew ever harder, ever faster, forcing her arousal higher. Her cunt grew puffy and big in response, making the shocks more frequent, and more frequent still, the pain worse, her lewd thoughts worse, of how badly she needed the spanking, of how awful her position was, how complete her humiliation . . .

When the climax came she had no control over it whatever. It simply hit her, the agonies of her burning cunt and buttocks turning to a blinding pleasure itself not far different from pain. Her muscles were already in spasm from the electric shocks, and shocks and climax merged to one with the rhythm of the spanking. She screamed again and again, until her discarded drawers were abruptly pressed to her face to silence her, and with the smell of her own excited cunt suddenly thick in her head a final, unbearable peak hit her and she passed out.

5

London, Autumn 2004

Thrift found herself facing her second year at the Diplomatic School with extreme trepidation, which proved justified. No sooner had the first morning passed than Decency Branksome-Brading accosted her. The conversation was brief, to the point, and one-sided. Thrift was to be Decency's slave as before, or face the consequences. Her reunions with Tatiana and Ana were a great deal more friendly, but not so very different in implication.

Unlike the year senior to them, now departed, the new intake was large, consisting of no less than fourteen girls, which meant that there was very little opportunity for Thrift to be taken into the convenient facilities, either to be tortured by her enemies or made to lick her friends. Despite that, by the halfway point of term, she had licked cunt seven times, bottom five and six pairs of boots.

Each and every time, and many more besides, the swelling of her cunt had triggered the electrical device in the plaque of rubber at her crotch. The current had been adjusted after her beating in Edinburgh, both Miss Challis and Mrs Brodie having mistaken her orgasm for an agony beyond anything that could safely be inflicted on her. Now it simply sent little stinging jolts though her flesh, enough to excite her, but not quite enough to make her climax.

Nor was it her only woe. The thought of Decency discovering that she was both guilty of self-abuse and incontinent was unbearable. One beating and it would come out, in the most shameful possible way, with her corset panel opened to show not the silky folds of her drawers, but the double layer of rubber that now covered her bottom. Miss Challis had passed on the code, and her pants would be opened to expose her, after which she would be beaten. Even at the thought she seemed to hear the other girls' irrepressible giggling.

Her behaviour was immaculate, her studying undertaken with a desperate eagerness to learn. In test after test she achieved top marks, her good memory coming to her aid. Even then it was not easy to conceal her condition. The reservoirs of the incontinence pants were low down, cunningly constructed around her lower thighs so that the bulge made by her piddle was always well concealed by her corset and skirts. They did not show at all, but a further humiliation had been added on the advice of Mrs Brodie, and that did. It was a simple belt of lightweight cotton into which her wrists could be tied, forcing her to keep them by her side. It was used only at certain times, generally outdoors, and more to keep her mind on her shame than for any practical purpose. It proved highly effective, and with Decency frequently in the park her only hope was that its full implications would not be understood.

Occasionally Thrift had seen girls in the same pitiful condition, looking sorry for themselves as they walked with their hands fastened to their sides. Despite fearing the public disgrace, she had always felt their reactions seemed excessive, assuming it to be a punishment for fidgeting. Now she knew the full horror of the treatment, and what it was administered for. Within a few days it had become clear that Decency did not.

Despite Mrs Brodie's assurances, the incontinence pants were painfully tight around her knees. They did at least prevent the piddle escaping, but by the end of a day they would be bulging with it, which resulted in a hideously embarrassing slopping noise unless she walked with exaggerated care and so slowly that it took the best part of a half-hour to get home. The only consolation was that Miss Challis, no less embarrassed by the peculiar noises, made no effort to hurry her along.

Due to her slow speed, more time than ever was spent in the park. This also was intensely embarrassing, as Miss Challis insisted on tying her hands as soon as they had left the school and not untying them until dinner time. The reaction of the women in the park was predictable, sniffs of haughty distaste and carefully averted eyes. Thrift had expected the same reaction from the men, and in many cases it was so, but by no means always. Some, including several of the regular strollers, began to make a point of tipping their hats to Miss Challis, and even addressing her with brief and polite remarks. Miss Challis responded to this with formal restraint, reserving her true feelings for Thrift.

'That I should come to this!' she snapped, after passing a remark on the unseasonably cold weather to the most persistent of the men. 'It is bad enough that I must be Companion to a wilful, wanton, incontinent brat, without being accosted by Frenchmen!'

'The gentleman is French?' Thrift enquired carefully, immediately intrigued as she thought of the nation's reputation for decadence and immorality.

'Yes, French,' Miss Challis answered, spitting out the second word. 'He is Monsieur Alphonse d'Arrignac, a violinist of sorts who is employed by the Royal Orchestral Company, although why we cannot find our own musicians I am at a loss to imagine.'

She walked on, slightly faster, forcing Thrift to follow with her full incontinence pants flopping and slopping around her legs.

Miss Challis realised and slowed once more with a heavy sigh, then began to speak again. 'There is no race more detestable than the French,' she stated with certainty. 'Throughout history they have been jealous of our achievements and, since they were obliged to surrender their colonies in order to pay off their war loans, they have been worse than ever. Why they should even be permitted into the country I cannot imagine.'

She went quiet as another man approached them. He tipped his hat to Miss Challis, but his eyes flicked to Thrift's tied hands, making her blush, a reaction she had found herself unable to overcome.

The Frenchman was in the park the following day, and the day after, on each occasion making a point of passing a remark to Miss Challis. On the fourth day they deliberately took the longer route, as if to pay their respects at the Albert and Victoria Memorial, only to find d'Arrignac already there. He had seen them, and Miss Challis was left with no choice but to respond to his greeting and carefully judged remark.

'A truly remarkable monument it is not, my dear Miss Challis? A truly remarkable monument to a truly remarkable man.'

'Indeed so, Monsieur d'Arrignac,' Miss Challis answered, lifting her eyes reverently to the vast and elaborate memorial with its prancing horses, heroic figures and above all the huge, gilded statute of the first Emperor and his Queen.

Having made conversation once, the introduction was established and the Frenchman became impossible to avoid, or even to pass without a suitable exchange of comments. Within a week he had ventured to pass a remark on Thrift's bonnet, but two days later he took a far bolder step. Meeting them as usual on the path he made an elaborate bow, passed a couple of innocuous comments on the weather as two elderly strollers went past, and then addressed Miss Challis from behind his hand.

'Might I venture a word in private, Miss Challis?'

Miss Challis blushed and was about to make an indignant refusal, but he had already taken her arm and instead she stammered out an acquiescence. He immediately drew her a little way aside. Thrift pretended to take an interest in a flower bed in which a display of late blooms had been planted, but it was still possible to catch at least some of the Frenchman's words, and more of Miss Challis's.

'... No great sum, I imagine?' he asked.

'A sum adequate to my needs,' she answered, barely concealing her outrage, which was shared by Thrift as she realised that d'Arrignac wanted to know how much Miss Challis earned. He went on, too quietly for Thrift to hear, but Miss Challis responded with fresh indignation.

'You are quite wrong, Sir!'

'Ah, but am I?' d'Arrignac replied, louder now and with a touch of triumph. 'I suspect I am not so very far wide of the mark.'

Miss Challis said nothing, but the stony set of her face betrayed her emotions. The Frenchman continued, once more quietly, but said something which turned Miss Challis's frozen mask into blushing outrage.

'Absolutely not!' she gasped. 'The very idea! Now, Sir, I must ask you to leave before I am obliged to call a constable.'

'Consider my proposal,' d'Arrignac responded, coolly tipped his hat and walked on.

'Whatever did he say?' Thrift queried as Miss Challis joined her again.

'Never you mind,' Miss Challis snapped. 'Now come along, and do try not to make that horrible noise!'

The following day d'Arrignac was in the park again, but Miss Challis passed him with her nose in the air. The next it was the same, but on the morning of the third day she paused, made the obligatory exchange of bland remarks and quickly motioned Thrift ahead. This time the conversation was carried out in low, urgent whispers and Thrift caught not a single word. Something had happened between the two, clearly, although Miss Challis refused to be drawn, but her opinion of d'Arrignac had changed sharply.

'Possibly I have been hasty in my appraisal of our friend Monsieur d'Arrignac,' she remarked as they approached the gate of the Diplomatic Enclave. 'After all, he has played before the King himself, and it is quite unthinkable that he should be allowed to dwell within the Quality Enclave were he not suitable.'

'Will he be invited to tea, perhaps?' Thrift ventured.

'That I doubt,' Miss Challis answered. 'Indeed, it would be better were you not to remark about our acquaintance to your parents at all. You know how your father is about Frenchmen.'

Miss Challis stopped to arrange for the gate to be opened and Thrift was left to ponder the curious incident. That afternoon d'Arrignac was not in the park, nor the following morning, although by then the matter had been pushed from her mind. Miss Challis had asked her mother if they might visit the establishment of Madame Moran, a select milliner in Pont Street, on the far side of the Diplomatic Enclave. It had been agreed, and she had spent the rest of the day thinking of new bonnets.

The visit to the milliner's proved disappointing, Miss Challis making a quick selection of a bonnet trimmed with red ribbon, then hustling Thrift out of the shop before she even had a chance to look around. Outside, before they had walked a dozen yards, Thrift noted Monsieur d'Arrignac approaching from the opposite direction.

'How pleasant, it is Monsieur d'Arrignac,' Miss Challis stated to Thrift. 'Good afternoon, Monsieur.'

'Good afternoon, Miss Challis,' he replied, tipping his hat as always. 'Pleasant, indeed, to chance upon an acquaintance, and on such a bracing day, although some might find it a little chill.'

'Not at all, pleasantly fresh I would have said,' Miss Challis replied.

'Fresh, the *mot juste*,' he said. 'Perhaps you and the charming Miss Moncrieff would do me the honour of walking together a little way?'

'We should be delighted.'

Thrift fell into step, slightly taken aback by the warmth of Miss Challis's response to the Frenchman and wondering if the two had not arranged some sort of meeting. It seemed probable, although she could not understand how such a situation could relate to his original enquiry about her income.

They had reached Pavilion Street when d'Arrignac stopped outside a house, the row of gleaming brass buttons beside the door showing that it was divided into flats.

'My residence,' he remarked. 'Perhaps you would care for a cup of tea? It is said, is it not, that no British Lady can survive past the hour of five o'clock without her tea, and we are approaching that very hour.'

Thrift held her face carefully immobile, despite her shock at the thoroughly unsuitable proposal, and waited for Miss Challis's cold refusal.

'How kind of you,' the Companion said. 'Come, Thrift, my dear, tea calls. I trust there will be cake, Monsieur d'Arrignac?'

Amazed, Thrift allowed herself to be led into the house and up two flights of stairs, to a well-appointed flat looking out over the street. A maid had tea ready, adding to her amazement, both at the exact timing and at the idea of a single Gentleman employing a female servant. Used to foreign ways from school, she told herself it was simply an example of French decadence and allowed herself to be poured tea and cut a slice of lemon cake, her astonishment further compounded by d'Arrignac's failure to serve bread and butter first.

Miss Challis seemed agitated, d'Arrignac strangely excited, ebullient even, pacing about the room as he drank his tea, and when he did sit down gesturing from the window at the Empire Tower.

'Ah, the faded glory that is France! In old Paris was a tower to put this metal monster to shame, *La Tour d'Eiffel*, a model in elegance, one thousand metres of glittering steel lattice work, dominating the skyline in –'

'Beg pardon,' Thrift interrupted, 'but the Eiffel Tower was nine hundred and eighty-four feet tall on its completion in eighteen eighty-nine.'

'What impertinent nonsense!' d'Arrignac snorted, only for his tone to soften abruptly as he went on. 'Hmm, just possibly I have confused my measurements. Regardless, it was a magnificent monument and a great loss to France when the Germans demolished it during the second occupation of Paris, out of pure spite, I might add. In any case, do you know what such towers are modelled upon?'

'I do not,' Thrift admitted.

'They are modelled on the pride of man,' he replied. 'Something I might be pleased to demonstrate.'

'You must excuse me,' Miss Challis said abruptly. 'Thrift, you are to be courteous to Monsieur d'Arrignac. Remember that we are in his house, that he is French, and that it behoves us to respect his personal wishes.'

She rose, to walk from the room, leaving Thrift staring after at the door she had left through, her astonishment now complete.

Monsieur d'Arrignac chuckled and spoke again. 'Doubtless your charming Companion has her needs, just as I have mine, and you, I suspect, have yours.'

'I beg your pardon, Sir?' Thrift answered, scarcely able to believe what she had heard.

Monsieur d'Arrignac went on without flinching. 'Now, my dear girl, she informs me that you are notably obedient, yet I notice that you take the air in the park with your hands fixed to your sides.'

'Sir!' Thrift gasped. 'This is not a suitable topic of conversation ... at all, much less between a Gentleman and a Lady. I understand, Sir, that you are French and therefore a degree of latitude must be allowed, yet still –'

'My apologies,' he broke in. 'I assure you I meant no offence. 'Please allow me to phrase my intended question another way. What if, shall we say, a Gentleman of consequence were to ask you to perform a certain task?'

'Naturally I would endeavour to assist, Monsieur d'Arrignac, so long as the task in question lay within my power and was suitable to my station.'

'It is within your power, my dear, eminently so. As to whether it is appropriate for your station –'

He nodded and rose, then crossed to a sideboard on which several decanters stood.

'I shall show you how the French take tea,' he stated, 'or rather, what we drink in the late afternoon, for tea as such is a rarity *chez nous*.'

He had taken up one of the decanters, to pour out a liquid of a vivid and luminous green into two tiny glasses. 'Absinthe, the green fairy,' he said, extending one of the glasses to Thrift, 'a favourite tipple throughout France and, indeed, among your own artistic classes.'

Somewhat doubtful, Thrift took the glass and sniffed at the contents. The drink smelled strongly of aniseed, and she realised that it was nothing more than a refined version of a cordial. Monsieur d'Arrignac had tossed his back at a gulp, and she did the same, intent on following his custom. It proved strong, leaving a burning trail down her throat and seeming to immediately fill her head with fumes. With her eyes watering slightly she turned to him.

'Thank you, most pleasant.'

He was looking at her intently, disturbingly so, and as she lowered her eyes demurely she realised why. A large bulge showed in his trousers, indicating quite clearly that his pego was hard, for her. She swallowed, shocked at the realisation of what his interest really was, and that it was not directed at Miss Challis. Her next thought was of how pleasing it would be to tell Ana that she had a lover, an artist and a Frenchman at that. Unsure what to say in the circumstances, she gave him an encouraging smile.

The next instant he had grabbed her feet and tipped her back into the chair. She squealed in surprise as her skirts flew up, then in pain as she was turned roughly over on to her face. Her skirts were already high, and a moment later her bustle had been flipped up and he was fumbling one handed with the gudgeons of her corset panel as he used the other to hold her down.

'I must have you!' he grunted. 'I must have you now, you saucy little whore!'

'No!' Thrift gasped, even as the first gudgeon popped. 'You must not . . . I – I am –'

'Do not stall me, I have waited too long for you,' he puffed, tearing at the second gudgeon. 'I must have you now. Death of my life, how does one get into these infernal contraptions!'

The gudgeon came loose at that instant, and despite her wailing protests Thrift's corset panel was hauled up, exposing the taut rubber seat of her incontinence pants.

'Sacred blue!' he exclaimed. 'What is this? You are a rubberist? Never would I have guessed at such perversions among the British! Come, Thrift, I must fuck you or burst. How do they open? Do not deny me!'

'They do not!' Thrift wailed, tears of shame welling in her eyes. 'Only Miss Challis can open them.'

'Miss Challis? Bizarre!'

'Please?' Thrift begged. 'Cover me . . . this is too shameful . . . I cannot bear it! Cover me and you may use my mouth. I have been taught how to suck on a man's pego.'

'Taught?' he demanded, letting go of her back. 'By whom? Am I not the first?'

'My friend, a girl,' Thrift gasped, and shut up abruptly as his stiff pego was pushed into her mouth.

He sighed in ecstasy as she took it, then again as she began to work her tongue on the fleshy underside of his rod. Remembering what Ana had said, she took control, cupping his balls in her hand as she mouthed at his shaft, kissing and nibbling. He made no complaint, simply holding her gently by the head and mumbling in French as she worked on her erection.

Thrift's own reactions were rising, and she was wishing she could get at her cunt to masturbate, even to let him burst her hymen although she knew it was the one thing she could not possibly allow. Her cunt begun to jerk to the mild electric shocks, but she knew full well the stimulation would not be sufficient, and kept concentrating on her sucking. Then he had reached climax, suddenly, his pego jerking to spurt hot, salty seed into her mouth as he groaned and gasped in ecstasy. She kept sucking, draining him, then swallowed dutifully, grimacing at the slimy texture of his load but managing to hold it down.

Monsieur d'Arrignac stepped away as Thrift released his cock from her mouth, and a moment later had made himself proper and turned to the window as she adjusted her own clothing. By the time Miss Challis returned to the room, both were sipping tea while d'Arrignac held forth on the merits of the French composers.

Thrift had expected her first experience of a man's pego to be either tender and a little frightening or brutal and extremely frightening, but in either case to be overwhelmingly emotional. Instead it had been brief and somewhat awkward, while if it had made her cunt wet then it was no more so than after licking one of her friends.

The disappointment did not prevent her from wanting to repeat the experience. With Ana still regularly indulging herself with Mr Sullivan-Jones and Tatiana with various men at the Soviet Embassy, she felt entitled to a secret lover, while not having one made her feel unwanted and inferior. Miss Challis handled the assignations in her normal taciturn manner, never once openly admitting what was going on and remaining unfailingly aloof and formal. Nevertheless, on one or two afternoons each week, Thrift would be taken to the house in Pavilion Street, served a glass of absinthe and left alone with Monsieur d'Arrignac just long enough for her to suck his penis.

That was as far as it went, despite a couple of brief conversations held in acrimonious whispers between him and Miss Challis. Thrift was not privy to them, but could guess that he was demanding access to her cunt and she refusing it. It also became plain that Miss Challis was receiving money for her services, something Thrift found hard to understand when her parents were providing the Companion with everything that a woman of her station in life could possibly have wanted. Putting it down to common greed, she pretended that she had not noticed.

Her associated with Monsieur d'Arrignac also improved her knowledge of sexual matters, and words. She learned that 'cunt' was not a polite term, and indeed within the Empire was in general use only among the very lowest sectors of the commonality. He suggested 'quim' as a relatively polite alternative, but pointed out that respectable women simple never mentioned that area of their bodies at all. He considered 'pego' amusing, finding it archaic, but no less so than Thrift did the suggested alternative of 'cock'.

With the Christmas festival break approaching, respectable invitations became more frequent and her liaisons less so. It made little difference to her frustration, as without a single chance to climax since the day she had been fitted with the rubber pants she was finding that the smallest things could trigger her wantonness, even more so than before. Not only that, but, once her quim had swollen sufficiently to trigger the electrical device, the shocks simply served to maintain her excitement, often for hours at a time, and when her piddle was drained each morning and evening it would be milky with juice.

Despite sharing her secret with Ana and Tatiana, she managed to keep it from the others, or at least the truth of it, as she discovered after lunch one day. It being Tuesday, the junior girls had art in the afternoon, and they had been taken to the river to make a study of the Prince George Bridge and were to lunch on the boat. The school seemed strangely empty without them, and Thrift was already expecting to be taken into the convenient facilities to be tortured as both Ana and Tatiana were indisposed.

Sure enough, Decency, Francesca and Xiuying came to sit with her at lunch, and afterwards took her by the arms and led her to the room. Only there did the routine change. Instead of putting her on her knees for a session of boot and bottom licking, Decency held her while the others tied her wrists firmly into her waist-belt, to leave her helpless. She was then pulled hard against a wall by Francesca and Xiuying as Decency stepped up in front of her.

'What – what are you going to do with me?' she asked.

'Nothing,' Decency replied, 'well, nothing unusual, that is so long as you tell me what I want to know.'

'What is that?'

'Who is that man I see your Companion talking to in the park so often? Miss Buckleigh thinks he is French, and an artist of some sort. Now why would a wanton little brat like you court such company? I would not put it beyond you to have been playing dirty games with him. Well, have you?'

'No!' Thrift squeaked.

'I suspect otherwise,' Decency answered. 'Hold her well, girls, and we'll soon have the truth.'

'What –' Thrift began and stopped as Decency began to work on the buttons of her gown. 'No – Decency! What are you doing?'

'Baring your bosom,' Decency answered, 'not because I have any interest in your grossly common body, but because I have invented a method of getting the truth out of recalcitrant little brats.'

'There is nothing to say!' Thrift squealed desperately. 'He is Monsieur Alphonse d'Arrignac, a violinist with the Royal Orchestral Company. He is French, yes, but he is a very respectable – Decency, no! I beg you!'

She began to struggle as the front of her gown was pulled wide and down around her shoulders, further trapping her arms. Decency immediately started on the underdress.

'The truth, Brat.'

'I have told the truth!' Thrift squeaked. 'He speaks with Miss Challis. Perhaps he intends a proposal? That is all, Decency – that is all! Would I dare tell you a lie?'

'Possibly not,' Decency answered, 'but I wish to be sure and, besides, I also wish to try out my new torture.'

Thrift jerked in her captors' arms as her underdress was pulled open, exposing the silky white breast of her corset. Francesca's grip gave, but immediately Xiuying had twisted Thrift's wrist hard up into the small of her back, wrenching the restraint belt around.

'Stay still, pig-dirt!' Xiuying snapped as Thrift cried out in pain.

'Well put, Xiuying, if a touch unladylike,' Decency said as Francesca once more tightened her grip. 'Now –'

She had taken a grip on the neck of Thrift's corset, and strained to pull the sides together.

'Ow! You are hurting me!' Thrift gasped as the hard whalebone dug into her neck and chest. 'Ow! Decency, please, I beg you –'

Decency didn't answer, her face red with effort, then the top catch of Thrift's corset had come open, and the second, the others following more easily as Decency got a better grip. The two halves were peeled wide, allowing Thrift's breasts to swell out to their natural size within her chemise.

'Pig is certainly accurate,' Decency remarked eyeing the bulging front of Thrift's chemise where the opened corset was pushing her breasts together. 'Certainly she is fat enough for a pig. How common! Now, let us see a little more –'

Thrift began to sob as Decency's fingers found the opening of her chemise, and the first tears of helpless frustration were welling in her eyes as one by one her buttons were popped wide. Decency did six, deliberately slowly, then peeled the two halves apart with a single dainty motion, exposing Thrift's breasts.

'Yes, quite as fat as a pig,' Decency said happily, tucking the open chemise in to leave Thrift's breasts fully exposed.

'Enormous!' Xiuying declared. 'You Europeans, you have no delicacy.'

'Mind what you say, Xiuying,' Decency answered the Chinese girl, 'or I shall make you lick the Brat's sit-upon. How would that be?'

Xiuying abruptly hung her head in submission and twisted Thrift's arm a little more tightly. Again Thrift squeaked in pain, while the motion forced her to thrust her chest out, leaving her naked breasts bulging from her open clothes and quivering gently to the agitation of her breathing. Her cleavage was deep and pink between them, her nipples half-stiff. Decency was smiling, cruel and confident, as she reached into the recesses of her dress to pull out a long yellow candle of the sort used on church altars, along with a box of matches.

'On Sunday,' she said casually as she lit the candle directly above Thrift's heaving chest, 'I chanced to spill a little wax, only on my glove, but even through the lace there was a noticeable sting. How, I wonder, does it feel on bare flesh?'

Thrift found out an instant later as Decency tipped the burning candle to dislodge the very first drip of molten wax on to the smooth skin of one plump breast. It stung furiously, making her squeal and jerk in her captors' arms. The motion made her breasts wobble, knocking Decency's arm and dislodging more wax, which spattered across both fat breasts. Thrift screamed in pain, lurching back from the flame by instinct, only to scream again as Xiuying twisted her arm yet tighter.

'Stop, please, I beg you . . . anything –' she gasped, but no notice was taken, Decency grinning wickedly as she once more tipped the candle, to lay a trail of hot droplets across Thrift's twitching skin.

Again Thrift screamed, then bit her lip at the thought of what would happen if they were caught. Her tormentors would be beaten, without question, bare bottomed and in public, yet the idea seemed weirdly inappropriate. She would also be beaten herself, she was sure, both for participating in such an act, willingly or not, and when Decency confessed. Yet when another load of molten wax was dumped into her cleavage she screamed again, as loudly as before.

'Do be quiet, Brat!' Decency snapped. 'You know what will happen if you are heard, do you not?'

Thrift nodded her head, unable to speak for her panting. Her chest was rising and falling, her breasts thrust out, the pink surfaces quivering like blancmange, the little spots of yellow-white wax bright with reflected light. Both her nipples had come fully out, straining to erection, and she could feel her quim responding, her lips pressed to the conductive studs, and she knew that at any moment would come the sting of electric shock.

'Hold her jaw, Francesca,' Decency ordered, and

Thrift's mouth was clamped shut even as fresh wax was poured out across her breasts.

Again she screamed, the sound no more than slightly muffled by Francesca's hand, and with the scream the first electric shock came, making her body jerk and once more bouncing her breasts against Decency's arm. Wax splashed over her again, catching the hard, protuberant bud of a nipple and she screamed afresh. Decency pulled the candle back.

'Noisy little she-cat, aren't you? Can't you hold your tongue for an instant?'

Thrift shook her head.

'Pathetic,' Decency spat. 'How can you call yourself a British Lady? You are a disgrace, Thrift, a miserable, common little guttersnipe. You're not fit to lick my boots, or Xiuying's sit-upon either!'

Thrift nodded in miserable acquiescence.

Decency went on. 'So, this Monsieur d'Arrignac? What of him? The truth.'

'I – I have told you everything,' Thrift gasped. 'He pays court to Miss Challis, that is all – I promise, Decency, I do!'

'Should I believe you?' Decency queried. 'Perhaps I should. Certainly you have no stomach for pain. Then maybe I shall continue anyway. I enjoy this, but it is a shame you are so noisy –'

'Gag her,' Xiuying suggested. 'Wax her cunt . . . wax her dirt hole!'

'No,' Decency answered. 'She would scream the place down. A little more on these fat, common bosoms and we're done, for now. So, Brat, if you want to avoid this, confess.'

'No . . . please . . . please . . .' Thrift whimpered as the candle was brought forward. 'There is nothing . . . I have told the truth, Decency, I have!'

A big pool of molten wax had formed on top of the candle as she spoke. Thrift stared at it, her muscles jumping in fear, her breasts shaking like jellies as it was brought closer, then tipped. Then she was screaming into Francesca's hand as hot wax cascaded down the slope of her breast and over her nipple, to drip from the tip and fly out on to her disarranged clothes as she jerked in their grip. More followed, on the other nipple, even as a second impulse discharged through her quim, to leave her screaming and gabbling inanities, her vision hazy with pain. Once more Decency stood back.

'She must be telling the truth,' Decency sighed. 'A pity, I had hoped she was letting him kiss her at the very least.'

'She is pig dirt,' Xiuying put in, shaking her head. 'She does it, like she does me. Any man could make her.'

'Well then, none have tried,' Decency replied.

'Well, pig dirt?' Xiuying demanded of Thrift. 'You tell truth, or I make you eat dirt pie, fresh and hot. Paper from facility and –'

'Do not be repulsive, Xiuying,' Decency chided. 'Besides, I have a horrible suspicion she would do it. There is a better way. So, Brat, perhaps you should know that a close friend of Miss Buckleigh happened to see you going into a certain house. You were in company with Miss Challis and Monsieur d'Arrignac, a most improper thing to do when I am sure you have not been formally introduced by your parents. Now, next week your mother has invited my family to dine, rather bumptious of her perhaps, but be that as it may, I do wonder how your father would react if –'

'Stop,' Thrift gasped. 'It is true. Monsieur d'Arrignac is my lover, but do not tell my parents, please, I beg you! And – and, if you knew, why – why torture me?' Thrift gasped, then jerked to another electric shock.

'For fun, stupid,' Decency answered. 'Besides, I was lying. I had no idea you actually visited the man. I was assuming some sordid liaison in a back alley. You really are remarkably stupid, are you not? So what happens? Tell the truth, or there will be trouble.'

Thrift hung her head in defeat, her voice coming in a broken mumbling as she spoke.

'I – I take him in my mouth – to – to suck.'

'Take him in your mouth? What are you talking about, you stupid girl!'

'His – his pego,' Thrift admitted. 'I suck it.'

'You suck, his – his –' Decency spluttered, and stopped, unable to say the word. 'His thing? You suck it!?'

Thrift nodded miserably.

'Oh my goodness, I think I'm going to be sick!' Decency said and rushed to a cubicle.

The door slammed and an unpleasant gagging noise was heard, but nothing more. After a moment Decency came back out, her face pale but once more composed as she spoke to Thrift. 'This time you have gone too far in your repulsive behaviour. I find myself obliged to report you to Lady Newgate. Come.'

'No!' Thrift answered. 'Please, Decency, have mercy! Am I not your slave? Do I not do whatever you wish? Come, let me lick your boots for you, it was muddy this morning and I am sure there will be plenty of dirt to make me eat, or –'

'Be quiet, Brat,' Decency answered. 'You truly disgust me, Thrift. I could never have imagined any woman to be so wanton and so low, let alone a member of the British Quality. Where is your pride, girl?'

Thrift didn't answer, knowing she could not even attempt to explain the feelings that grovelling at her tormentor's feet, sucking on cock or licking another girl's bottom brought her.

'So be it,' Decency went on, 'as you seem determined to be my slave, I shall permit it, and, yes, you may lick my boots clean, while I think up some other amusing things to do with you. Also, from now on, save when in general company, you will address me as Miss Branksome-Brading. After all, it would hardly do to be on first-name terms with a creature like you.'

'Thank you, D – Miss Branksome-Brading,' Thrift answered as she sank slowly to her knees.

Decency extended one mud-smeared boot from beneath her skirts.

Despite Decency's threats, Thrift's service as slave became only a little worse. There simply was not the opportunity for elaborate torture sessions, while Thrift's screams under the combination of wax and electric shock had made the last session too risky for Decency's liking. So it was back to boot and bottom licking, with the occasional added cruelty, mainly from Xiuying, and after another week Decency's frustration had begun to show.

On the last morning of term before they broke for Christmas they gathered as usual, and both Thrift and Decency reached the classroom before Miss Evans, who had remained their teacher. To Thrift's surprise, Decency made no threats or unpleasant remarks, but simply went to her desk and arranged the papers she needed for the morning's test. It was to be general knowledge, a series of questions on various topics requiring brief, precise answers, and the final contribution towards their class places. Thrift felt confident, sure that her memory would serve her well and that with little or no requirement for opinion she would be among the best if not top.

All six girls were seated expectantly by the time Miss Evans arrived with the test papers, also her tawse, something Thrift had never once seen her without. The papers were quickly handed out and the teacher retired behind her desk to peruse a novel about whaling in the Antarctic. Thrift turned her attention to the test. The first question combined geology and geography, requiring a list of the strata of the Dorset coast with illustrative examples of fossils for each. She began to write, commencing with chalk and a species of echinoderm.

Shortly before the bell went to announce lunch she was finished, all ten questions completed to the appropriate length in her neatly rounded handwriting. Only one had proved difficult, and she had felt that unfair, a history question asking for the names of the leading traitors in some tiny and rapidly suppressed revolt among the North American colonies. Xiuying collected the papers and managed to drop them under Francesca's desk, much to Thrift's private amusement, and the test was complete.

Lunch passed quietly, with Thrift, Ana and Tatiana discussing the test. Both girls had stumbled on several of the questions, leaving Thrift sure that her only possible rival for the top place would be Francesca, and that was unlikely. It was also impossible for Decency to get at her, while lunch was turkey and stuffing followed by Christmas pudding, with a glass of wine permitted for each course. Afterwards they continued to discuss the test and, when the time for afternoon lessons came, Thrift was feeling distinctly smug, despite having filled her incontinence pants with a copious amount of piddle.

Back in the classroom Miss Evans was seated at her desk, still marking the papers, with her harsh face set in an angry frown. Feeling more smug than ever, and hoping that Decency had made some elementary mistakes, she sat herself down to wait for the results. Half-an-hour passed, all six girls trying not to fidget as Miss Evans's expression grew gradually more irritable. Finally the Mistress put the papers down and addressed the class.

'A reasonable performance, girls, with one notable exception. In order then ... top, Xiuying. Very good, my dear. You have a clear grasp of the facts and also their presentation. Indeed, with seventy-two per cent you have overtaken Ana to reach third place in class overall.'

Thrift glanced to Xiuying, who had responded to the praise with an exactly measured bow of her head. If not top, she was sure she would be second, or third at the very least, while it now seemed impossible for Francesca to catch her. That meant first place in class overall. Feeling smugger than ever, she allowed herself a small smile.

Miss Evans continued. 'Second, Francesca. It is good work, my dear, but when I say the answers are to be brief I still require more than a mere annotated list. Nevertheless, I cannot fault your accuracy. You have scored sixty-eight, which confirms your second place in class.'

Now certain that she was top, Thrift allowed her smile to grow a little broader as she waited for Miss Evans to announce her third place in the test.

'Third,' Miss Evans said, 'is Ana. A commendable effort, my dear, but your weak subjects are letting you down. Fifty-seven, which allows Xiuying to overtake you, and yet I shall certainly be commending your efforts to your parents.'

Thrift felt a pang of vexation. It was scarcely possible that she had scored less than fifty-seven, unless Miss Evans was making an example of her to prevent her from getting above herself. That, she was sure, would be it, and her first place would stand regardless.

Miss Evans continued. 'Fourth, Tatiana. My dear girl, your intelligence is not at fault, nor your memory, yet you must learn to be objective, detached, girl! I am prepared to accept that you wish to focus your remarks on nineteenth-century cloth production in Manchester on the working conditions of the commonality, yet to compare the fossiliferous strata of the Dorset coast with more impressive examples from Soviet beds is simply foolish. You errors are of commission rather than omission, yet they are still errors. I have marked you at fifty-two, which I considered generous and makes no difference to your fifth place in class.'

Tatiana accepted the criticism in the silence taught her by the application of the tawse to her bottom. Thrift bit back another stab of vexation, sure that she was being made an example of.

'Fifth, with a respectable forty-four,' Miss Evans went on, 'we have Decency. Well tried, my dear. As the Welsh bard so aptly wrote, "when all is done, and the evening shadows grow long on pitch or yard or battle-field, there is no nobler thing a man may say, but this – I did my best". You place bottom in class, I fear, but I shall certainly be commending you to your parents for effort.'

The teacher was smiling as she laid Decency's paper down, but her brows furrowed and her mouth set into an angry slit as she turned to the last. Thrift's stomach tightened, fear rising up at the realisation that it was she who had done badly, also consternation from the absolute certainty that she had not.

'And bottom,' Miss Evans said sternly, 'we have Miss Thrift Moncrieff, and a paper that I can only assume is a joke. I am well aware, Miss Moncrieff, that you have come top this term, and that your position was unassail-able even before this test, yet this behaviour smacks not only of excessive pride, but is also flagrantly insolent. Your mark is zero, which will be brought to the attention of your parents. What do you have to say for yourself?'

'I – I do not understand, Miss Evans,' Thrift managed, already on the verge of tears.

Miss Evans raised an eyebrow.

'Well then, if you do not understand, perhaps you would care to explain one of two of your remarkable answers. I quote – "The uppermost stratum of the

Dorset system is bread pudding, in which may be found the fossilised remains of the Great Welsh Windbag, or *Evanus monstros*." Then there are your remarks on the causes of the Great War – "... British cowardice in failing to offer support to those threatened by French expansionism ... " I could go on, but I doubt it is necessary. Well?'

'I – I didn't write that!' Thrift protested.

'No?' Miss Evans answered. 'Thrift, to have played such a foolish, arrogant and insolent joke upon me is one thing, but to then seek to deny it is your work is both stupid and untruthful. Plainly it is your work. It is in your handwriting, and how else, pray, might it have been produced? Nobody but I knew the questions before this morning.'

'I – I – don't know, Miss Evans! Thrift wailed. 'I didn't write those things ... I swear ... on the Bible!'

'You wish to add blasphemy to your crimes?' Miss Evans snapped, her face suddenly reddening. 'So be it, if you are determined to be provocative, you may take the consequences. Six strokes for your poor performance, six for arrogance, six for insolence, twelve for lying and twenty-four for blasphemy. Which makes, Decency, my dear?'

'Fifty-two, Miss Evans,' Decency said promptly.

'Forty-eight, dear,' Miss Evans answered with patience. 'Still, let us split the difference and make it a round fifty. Miss Moncrieff, you will bend across my desk.'

Thrift listened to the sentence in numb horror. Fifty strokes was an impossible amount, far more than any other punishment given, even to Tatiana, who was far, far tougher than she, and yet always ended in tears. They were going to see her incontinence pants, too, and, if the pain and bruising of the beating would eventually fade, then the shame of being revealed as both wanton and incontinent would never die.

Slowly, hardly able to control her own muscles, she got to her feet. A dozen leaden steps took her to the table, where Miss Evans already waited, her brawny arms folded across her massive chest, the horrible tawse gripped firmly in one great fist. Thrift's tears started, hot and thick, running down her cheeks as she bent herself down over the table, her bottom lifted in the regulation position, to strain the rubber pants tight over her cheeks.

Miss Evans came behind her. Thrift shut her eyes are her skirts were caught up and lifted, to be piled on her back. The petticoats followed, her distress growing as each was raised, her face screwed up in misery, her throat so tight she could barely breathe, her tears spurting from under her eyelids. Then the last petticoat was up, her bustle was being inverted over the rear of her corset and it was happening.

Her finger nails were scratching at the desktop in her anguish as one gudgeon, then the second was released. Her corset panel went limp, she let out a last choking sob and it had been hauled high, exposing her shameful secret to the entire class, her bottom cheeks bulging in rubber, the black tight, the pink sagging to the weight of the piddle in the legs. Decency gasped in shock; Xiuying giggled.

Miss Evans gave a cluck of distaste and paused as the full horror of her situation sank into Thrift's mind. Then the big fingers were pressing on the panel above her bottom split and she was blubbering miserably as her incontinence pants spread wide to expose the fat globe of her bottom. Her quim was hidden, she knew, the plaque of thick black rubber still pressed to her flesh, the electrical studs still digging in. Yet the thought of it showing, with the thin pink pee-pee tube protruding from the centre, was worse by far than making a show of bare cunt. Besides, her position and the way the flaps of her incontinence pants had opened meant that her buttocks were spread, with the lewd brown star of her anus on full and blatant show.

'Fifty strokes,' Miss Evans stated calmly.

Thrift gritted her teeth and dug her nails into the surface of the desk, her brain whirling in an agony of emotion as she waited for her beating; utter shame, misery, fear and a biting sense of injustice. She had been tricked, she knew, her paper substituted for another, one written by the all too clever Francesca. Now she was to be beaten in front of the whole class for it, beaten with her skirts up, beaten with her incontinence pants wide, beaten with her naked bottom on show . . .

Everything but pain was blasted from her mind as the tawse came down, and landed plumb across her bottom with a loud, meaty smack. The tip had caught her corset, yet still she screamed, a wail of agony breaking to sobbing, then again, louder as the second stroke came in immediately. The third followed, and the fourth, sending her into a maddened, unbridled dance of hysterical pain and grief, kicking her legs up, wiggling her bottom from side to side, shaking her head and thumping her fists on the table. Only at the sound of cruel, high-pitched laughter from behind did it stop. Miss Evans spoke.

'Xiuying, how ever comical Miss Moncrieff's position and antics may appear to you, be so good as to remember that this is a punishment, and not a matter for levity.'

'Yes, Miss Evans,' Xiuying replied, her voice barely a whisper but still with a hint of mischief.

Thrift lay gasping over the table. Her bottom was a ball of fire, the cheeks hot and swollen, her skin prickly with sweat. She had lost all count of how many strokes she had been given, the pain simply too much for her to concentrate. Still she held her position, too limp to resist, too defeated.

Miss Evans moved directly behind Thrift, and it began once more, the edge of her corset and pants no longer protecting her from the tip of the tawse. One stroke came in, a second, a third, each harder and faster than the last, until once more she had begun to buck and scream, to writhe and wriggle, to puff and fart, tears streaming from her eyes, snot from her nose. So fast were the strokes falling that her screams had merged to a bubbling gurgle as she fought for air, only to ring out afresh as a pulse of electricity jarred her swollen cunt.

Still Miss Evans brought the tawse down, smack after smack, belabouring Thrift's bottom with all the force of her arm, each hit now bringing a fresh electric shock. Thrift's senses had gone, her muscles no longer under her control, so that her body merely jerked and quivered under the impacts like so much meat. Vaguely she was aware of the heavy smacks of the tawse on girlish flesh, again and again as her body jerked and shook to both the beating and the current.

Even when her first climax came it barely registered in her dazed brain, her body and mind taken beyond the point of self-awareness. The second came a moment later, just penetrating to her addled senses, but with pain and pleasure merged into one indistinguishable whole. The third was sharper, making her cry out as she was filled with an overwhelming urge to be subjected to every torment and arousal she had experienced, or heard of. Suddenly she was flaunting her buttocks, the fat hemispheres thrust high, her anus pulsing in the deep slit between, her mouth wide, drool running out over her lower lip as she babbled meaningless inanities, then sense.

'... harder, again ... thrash me ... hurt me ... use me ... break me ... stick the tawse up my bottom and make me lick your dirt, you fat Welsh cow!'

Her words broke to a fresh scream as the tawse hit her with all the power of Miss Evans's massive arm. Her fourth climax followed on the instant, catching the rubber pad to jam it hard against her cunt and send a violent electric shock right through her at the highest peak of climax. Then everything had gone black as her senses left her.

Thrift came to in the school medical room. She was face down on a bed, her incontinence pants still open at the rear, her bottom still bare, also throbbing with the dull pain of bruising and cool with some slippery substance that smelled of antiseptic. There was a thermometer up her bottom. The school nurse was standing over her, concentrating on the level of liquid in a syringe. Seeing that Thrift was awake, she turned her eyes down to the bed.

'I trust you have learned your lesson?'

Thrift could only nod meekly, the events of her beating and the cause of it still hazy as she slowly gathered her wits. The memory of how she had been tricked came back and she gave a sob of angry frustration.

'We'll have none of that, young Lady,' the nurse said brusquely. 'You should be grateful for the time and trouble Miss Evans takes to correct your sins. Now hold still.'

'What –' Thrift began and broke off in a cry of pain as the needle was plunged into the meat of one bottom cheek. 'What – what is the injection for, please, Nurse?'

'No business of yours,' the nurse answered.

Thrift winced as an alcohol-laden swab was applied to her punctured bottom. Quickly the nurse piled her equipment on to a trolley before walking away without a word for Thrift, save a muttered complaint about her time being wasted. Thrift lay still, her bottom bare but not daring to cover it. Laying her chin in her hands, she settled into a prolonged sulk, thinking of how she had served Decency's every whim, and also those of Francesca and Xiuying, yet had still been tricked into taking a public beating. Yet for all her chagrin, she knew that it had mainly been her own fault. Had she admitted to the original offence and apologised, then she would have been given twelve or even just six well-spaced tawse strokes. As it was, she had opened her mouth and earned herself fifty, so she really had only herself to blame for the sorry state she was in now.

She put her face in her hands as she remembered what she had called Miss Evans as her climax went through her – a fat Welsh cow. Worse, she had begged to be made to lick her tormentor's bottom. The consequences were all too easy to imagine. She was sure to be beaten again, probably stripped naked in front of the assembled school, something that had not been done to a girl in years. That would be in the Hilary term, giving her the entire holiday to let her bottom recover and to dwell on what was coming.

There was also likely to be a letter to her parents. That would mean another visit to a doctor, some self-abuse specialist who would presumably put her on a regime even stricter, more painful and more humiliating than Dr Lloyd's Improved. What it might involve she did not dare to think. Then there would be the jibes of her classmates. Most would not see her until the following term, but she was due to attend several of the same functions as Decency, who could be counted on to ensure that Thrift's condition was as widely publicised as possible, also the details of the beating. She was due to see Ana too, who would at least be sympathetic, but amused too.

All in all it made the near future a hard prospect to bear, and the long-term future not much better. With summer would come the end of term and her entry into society proper, overskirts, Gentleman callers, and proposals. Only she was certain that there would be no proposals for her. No respectable Gentleman was going to want a known wanton, and an incontinent one to boot. As Decency had two elder brothers it was absolutely certain to be known. Nothing spread so fast as scandal.

She wanted to cry, but there seemed to be no tears left, and as she lay staring at the dull white paint of the wall beyond her bedstead she found herself filled with a reckless, wild defiance and, against all common sense, pride. There was no reason for the feeling, just the opposite, but it was there nonetheless.

An hour had passed by the clock above the medical room door before she began to wonder if she had been abandoned. Tea time was approaching, and with it the end of term. Down in the afternoon room Dundee cake would be being served, a particular favourite of hers, yet she had no desire to go down. She was also sure the nurse would come back the moment she shifted position, but it was hard to imagine consequences worse than those she was already facing. Finally, with the clock at ten minutes beyond the hour at which she would normally have left the school, she rolled herself carefully out of bed.

Without the code it was impossible to cover her bottom, and she was sure her tender cheeks would feel a lot better bare under the corset in any case. So she merely fastened her corset panel, let her skirts drop and spent a moment restoring her ruined make-up in front of the nurse's mirror. As she worked there was the constant threat of discovery at the back of her mind, but it was a weak thing, her fear of punishment exhausted.

When she finally left the medical room it was to find the school strangely quiet. Footsteps echoed up from the floor below as she reached the bottom of the stairs. She hesitated, knowing Miss Challis would be somewhere about, but not wanting to meet anybody else, then she peered cautiously down over the banister. It was Miss Challis herself, standing in the hall and tapping her foot irritably on the tiled floor. Thrift hurried down the stairs as fast as her corset would permit, her Companion turning as she reached the bottom.

'There you are,' Miss Challis snapped. 'Wherever have you been?'

'In the medical room,' Thrift admitted. 'I –'

'Never mind,' Miss Challis broke in, 'so long as it is nothing serious. We are late already, and must hurry.'

'Late?' Thrift queried and she was hustled out of the building. 'For what, Miss Challis?'

'For your violin lesson,' Miss Challis hissed, using the euphemism they had adopted for visits to Monsieur d'Arrignac.

'I have been beaten!' Thrift protested. 'Very hard as it happens, fifty strokes of Miss Evans's tawse.'

'Well, no doubt it was well earned. Now do come along.'

Thrift hurried to keep up, her full pants wobbling around her legs and slapping together, making her very glad indeed that there were very few people about.

'I need to be emptied,' she whispered as they reached a deserted Cadogan Place, 'and also fastened.'

'Fastened?' Miss Challis whispered back. 'Your pants are still open?'

'Yes,' Thrift answered, 'I fainted, and nurse had to cream me and give me an injection . . . in my bottom.'

'Well, I can't do it now!' Miss Challis hissed and went abruptly quiet as a swarthy man in a white suit and a Panama hat stepped from one of the buildings they were passing.

They had reached Pont Street before the man had drawn sufficiently far ahead of them to be definitely out of earshot, and they maintained a tense silence as they crossed Sloane Street and turned into Pavilion Road. Only at the door to Monsieur d'Arrignac's flats did Miss Challis have a chance to speak again.

'You must simply not allow him to be unduly importunate today. Inform him that you are indisposed.'

'I did so the week before last,' Thrift hissed. 'When he wished to try and fondle my quim.'

'Thrift Moncrieff, your language!' Miss Challis snapped. 'Simply behave, and be sure to satisfy him rapidly.'

Thrift nodded as the door swung open to emit an enormously fat Gentleman in a plum-coloured suit who favoured them with a knowing leer as he passed. They moved into the flats.

'Foreigners,' Miss Challis complained as the door closed behind them. 'An Italian, I imagine, the most detestable of races.'

They ascended the stair, to find Monsieur d'Arrignac waiting at his door. Both were ushered inside, and Miss Challis faded into the parlour as Thrift went to the sofa on which they invariable conducted their trysts.

'A touch of the fairy?' d'Arrignac offered, indicting the decanter of absinthe.

'Thank you, yes,' Thrift answered, the mere mention of the drink triggering a sudden yearning for its effect.

She watched as he poured two measures of the vivid green liquid. Even on the plush cushions of the settee her bottom smarted badly, with each whalebone strut of her corset panel laying a line of dull pain across her hurt skin. He passed her the glass and she drained the absinthe in one, the burning liquid now filling her with a soothing sensation in moments.

'Might I beg another measure?' she asked, welcoming the numbing effect of the absinthe and the sense of unreality it invariably brought.

'By all means,' d'Arrignac replied.

He poured again and Thrift took the glass, wincing as she reached out and a piece of whalebone dug into an exceptionally tender spot on her bottom.

'Are you quite comfortable, my dear?' he asked.

'Not entirely, I confess,' Thrift admitted. 'I have been beaten this afternoon, most cruelly.'

It had come out suddenly, her words breaking into a

sob as she finished, her confession made in the knowledge that, whatever their relationship, d'Arrignac was one of the few people who would be genuinely sympathetic to her plight. He might also be aroused, she realised from occasional probing questions about her spankings, but there would sympathy.

'You British, so stern in your correction,' he said, shaking his head. 'In France the application of a well-meaning hand to a young Lady's bottom is usually deemed sufficient to set her on the correct path. A switch or belt might be used in severe cases, it is true, but we have none of these terrible implements designed purely for chastisement.'

He had come to sit beside her, close enough to allow her to smell the mixture of absinthe and garlic on his breath.

'You were bare?' he asked.

She nodded, wondering why he troubled to ask.

'So British, once more,' he went on, 'to strip you of your modesty as well as your clothes.'

'In France, girls are permitted to retain their clothing?' Thrift asked in surprised.

'But no,' he said with a shrug. 'In France, when a girl must be spanked, her bottom is bared, but this is not to humble her, merely for convenience. Besides, we French are not so very ashamed of that which God has given us.'

'God's gift is not lightly to be revealed,' Thrift quoted.

He merely shrugged and swallowed what remained of his absinthe. Thrift followed suit and allowed her tongue to flick out to retrieve the last drop of the hot liquid from her lower lip. Monsieur d'Arrignac chuckled.

'Ah ha, but your flogging has made you eager, has it not?'

Thrift nodded, already bold with the effects of the absinthe. Her quim now felt a touch swollen, and she knew that not long after his cock was introduced to her mouth her flesh would be twitching to the shocks. The prospect was far from unappealing. He had already begun to unbutton his fly, and as she leaned forwards he flopped his large, flaccid penis out of the slit in his longjohns and into his lap.

'Come across,' he instructed, 'and I shall soothe your poor bottom through those infernal rubber pants.'

'I am bare,' Thrift admitted without really thinking. 'The – the pants were opened for my beating, and so they stay.'

'Ah ha, saucy today!' he declared. 'Come then, I shall stroke you, perhaps apply a little cream?'

'I am already creamed,' Thrift answered as she went down on his cock.

A soothing, content sensation came over her as soon as the big cock was in her mouth. Cock sucking had become a routine, the trepidation it had brought at first now gone, to leave only feelings of arousal and of being needed. She took his balls in hand as he began to stiffen in her mouth, stroking the soft, furry sac. His hand closed on her bottom, and she shifted position, letting him feel, and not even objecting as his fingers began to ease up her gown. A last doubt dissolved at the thought of the thick rubber plaque still protecting her quim. Her virginity was safe, and as she began to tug his shaft into her mouth she was sticking her bottom out to his groping fingers.

Her skirts and petticoats came up as she sucked, his cock growing swiftly harder, until with the rear of her corset on show there was a rigid rod of male flesh in her mouth. She slowed down, now wanting her beaten bottom caressed and made a fuss of, and mindful of what Ana had said about making men climax too quickly. Her panels came open; her bustle was inverted and her bottom was once more nude to the air in a froth of silk and satin and lace.

'My poor dear!' d'Arrignac exclaimed. 'How they have used you! Your poor flesh! The bruises!'

He had begun to touch, his fingertips moving gently over her bruised skin. Thrift pushed her bottom out a little more, letting her cheeks come apart, now eager and wanton. The motion also pressed her cunt more firmly to the studs, and the first tingle of electricity hit her. She gasped, swallowing on his cock and he gave a moan of pleasure.

'Are you to be resisted?' he sighed, more to himself than her, and suddenly his fingers were between her thighs, pushing at the plaque.

Thrift stuck her bottom out, too far gone to care for anything but pleasure and her fantasies of being rudely deflowered. Again he pushed at the plaque, and cursed as it held fast. Thrift continued to work on his cock, now licking lovingly at the thick stem as she tickled beneath his balls.

'I must have you!' he hissed, and jammed a finger firmly up into Thrift's greasy bottom hole.

She gasped, coming up off his pego in shock at the sudden and unexpected penetration of her anus. Then she was sighing as he began to rummage about inside her and bugger her with his finger.

'I must!' he grunted. 'You are too lovely to resist, and if it cannot be your quim, let it be your arse.'

He rose suddenly, pushing Thrift off to let her sprawl on the sofa, then grabbing her hips to haul her around. She gave a mute squeak of protest as she was positioned for buggery, her plump bottom thrust out over the edge of the sofa, her thighs spread in his grip as his erect cock settled into her slit.

For a moment he rubbed, his rod hot and solid between her buttocks, stinging the abrasions to make her cry out in blended pain and pleasure, and also as another jolt of electricity hit her. Then his cock was between her cheeks, the fat, rounded head pressing to the well-greased hole of her anus. He grunted as he pushed, and Thrift cried out again at the stabbing pain as her virgin anus pushed in to the pressure. She gritted her teeth and clutched at the sofa, wanting him inside her, her fantasies running wild in her head. Again he pushed, and again she cried out in pain, a sound that ended in a choking sob as her anus popped to admit him.

He pulled back, pushed again, and moaned as a good half the length of his bloated penis was forced into her back passage. She gasped as she felt her gut swell to his cock and her cunt press hard to the plaque, immediately triggering the electric current. D'Arrignac grunted again as he jammed the remainder of his cock into her straining bottom hole, then settled down to bugger her.

Thrift, impaled on cock, her cunt jumping to the repeated electric shocks, could only gasp out her ecstasy as her bottom was used. It felt glorious, beyond anything she had experienced before, an exquisite pain close to that of when she had climaxed during beatings. Then his stomach had begun to slap against her bruises and it was better still: her cunt started to jerk in response to the electric shocks; her bottom hole began to pulse on the intruding penis and she was at climax.

A long scream of ecstasy burst from Thrift's mouth as the whole of her body went into uncontrollable climactic spasms, her legs kicking up and down, her fingers locking and unlocking in the fabric of the sofa, her cunt squirming against the studded plaque, her anus and gut in spasm on the load up her bottom. Then he too was at climax and she screamed again as the full load of his seed was deposited deep up her rectum.

6

London, December 2004

The expected blow never came. Thrift's end-of-term report arrived a week into the holidays, by which time she had worked herself into a state of exhaustion, imagining being disinherited, diminished to the commonality, even put in a labour factory for the workshy. As it was, the report simply recorded that she had received fifty strokes of the tawse, with details of her individual sins and the number pertaining to each. She was sent to see the Very Reverend Judgement Huxtable for her blasphemy and ended up having to polish the church silver and spend a week in a dress of plain blue wool, but that was all. The report also listed her as top of the class, to her father's delight. She had long suspected that he would have preferred a son to follow him into the Diplomatic Service, something that was close to impossible for women save in roles well beneath her station. With her marks it became at least a worthwhile target. On the day after the report arrived she was called into his study and given a long lecture on doing her best for the remainder of the year.

The Christmas festivities passed in their usual style. There was beef and jam pudding on Christmas Eve, washed down with enough Shiraz and Liqueur Muscat to make her very glad for her incontinence pants during the subsequent six-hour-long evening service. Christmas

Day opened with the ritual exchange of gifts, including Thrift's first overskirt, a magnificent affair of brocaded green silk complete with discreet straps into which her wrists could be tied. Lunch followed in the traditional style, smoked salmon from her uncle's estates, roast goose with appropriate trimmings and Christmas pudding, again washed down with enough wine to leave Thrift feeling dizzy as she handed out pennies to the deserving poor afterwards. Service followed, with Thrift singing a solo rendering of 'Jerusalem' as the pink rubber bags around her knees grew gradually heavier. Boxing day saw yet another lengthy service and also a fast, for which she was extremely grateful as the bones of her corset had begun to dig into her bloated tummy rather painfully.

The remainder of the holiday passed in much the same way. The sprinkling of snow provided on Christmas Day was washed away by a heavy night's rain also designed to prevent the commonality from become overexcited at the New Year's festivities. There were various functions, at which Thrift saw Decency Branksome-Brading several times, and Ana. Monsieur d'Arrignac had returned to France, but came back early in the New Year, although Thrift managed only a single visit and once more was only able to suck his cock.

To Thrift's surprise, Decency kept her secret to herself, providing relief but also trepidation. One thing she was sure she could rely on was that Decency would do nothing so kind without some reason, and that reason would undoubtedly prove both painful and degrading for Thrift.

She also went unspanked for almost the entire holiday, allowing her bottom to return slowly to its normal pristine pink colour and smooth texture. Only on the final day, after her mother had returned to her charitable duties, did Miss Challis exert her authority. Another fall of snow had been allowed, and the park was a sheet of perfect white with every branch and twig outline in sharp black and white contrast against a sky of perfect blue. Miss Challis had suggested a walk, and they had gone as far as the bandstand in St James's Park. It had been crowded, with the band of the Devil's Own playing to a large audience and many strollers.

They had listened to the music for a while, before Miss Challis had accused Thrift of being disrespectful by making a group of pigeons fly up during an anthem. Thrift's automatic protest at the completely unjust charge had met with further admonishments, and ended with her skirts being hauled up and her incontinence pants put on show to the entire crowd, then split to allow her to be bare-bottom spanked. She had screamed and blubbered her way through the punishment, several people remarking on how undignified a display she was making and how ungraciously she accepted chastisement.

It was brief, Thrift left red bottomed and snivelling over Miss Challis's lap after perhaps a hundred smacks to each cheek, and the Companion finished by rolling a large snowball and pushing it between her victim's spread buttocks. Many in the crowd laughed, what would normally have been a completely inappropriate act accepted as nothing worse than comic as it was the festive season.

For Thrift it was far from comic. It had been light hearted, as spankings went, but no less humiliating for that. Nor was the indignity over once her bottom was covered. The slowly melting snowball in her incontinence pants not only left Thrift with a numb quim, but triggered the electrical apparatus, sending her down the path in a series of little pained hops she was quite unable to control, to the carefully concealed amusement of the onlookers.

Hilary term began the next day, Thrift arriving back at the Diplomatic School in an even greater state of apprehension than on previous occasions. As she had feared, Decency wasted very little time in reasserting her power, and had thought of several new and ingenious ways to torture Thrift.

The first Thrift found out about was a way to get around the problem of avoiding official attention. On the Friday after the start of term, Decency, Xiuying and Francesca managed to drag Thrift into the convenient facilities while the majority of the girls were at the windows watching the new and colossal airship, *Majesty*, dock on the Empire Tower. All of them knew that there was little time, and Thrift expected a brief session of dirt eating at Decency's feet. She got it, but afterwards they opened her clothes in front and put a handful of dry and prickly burrs down her cleavage. For the rest of the afternoon every tiny motion brought an agonising prickling sensation between and below her breasts, getting her into such a state that by tea time her quim was swollen enough to trigger the electrical device.

The second was less painful but a great deal more humiliating. Again in a brief moment alone in the convenient facilities, she was caught and held tight by Decency and Francesca. With her skirts lifted, Thrift's corset panel unfastened by Xiuying, who used two ribbons from her hair to fasten her victim's incontinence pants around the very tops of her thighs. Then Thrift was held down and forced to drink from the bowl until she was bloated with the mixture of piddle and water. Her catheter ran all afternoon, so that by the end of the day her incontinence pants were bulging with piddle, her quim and bottom soaked with it, to leave her sore and sorry for herself even after she had managed to untie her legs and the pants had been drained.

The third combined both extreme pain and extreme humiliation. It was also more leisurely, and took place in an empty school room which had been left unlocked. Once again Thrift was caught and held. Her hands were tied to her sides and her bosom exposed. A hair clip was attached to each of her nipples, leaving the little buds taut and swollen. She was then waxed, all over both breasts and her nipples too, leaving the clips caked hard and her tender flesh stinging with pain. By then all three girls were laughing in cruel glee, while Thrift's cunt had begun to jump to shocks. She was then made to boot lick, still with her tortured breasts bare, and to lick Xiuying's anus. Finally her bosom was covered, and she was forced to endure the pain of the clips and wax for the entire afternoon.

By good fortune there proved to be a change in the afternoon programme. Miss Evans was indisposed and they were to be taken by Miss Peel, with the class delayed by twenty minutes. Thrift immediately excused herself, whispering to Ana to join her for the sake of protection. Tatiana also came, and in the seclusion of a cubicle Thrift once more exposed her chest, this time for the wax to be picked off and the clips removed. It hurt more than it had at first, and left her sobbing and shaking, both breasts bright pink, her nipples agonisingly tight and sore and her cunt twitching to the current. Tatiana and Ana held her until she had calmed down, stroking her hair and dabbing away the tears that were trickling down both cheeks, and not bringing up what had happened until Thrift was herself again.

'Why do you allow them to torture you so?' Tatiana demanded.

'It is her nature,' Ana answered as Thrift blushed and shrugged. 'I suspect it brings her deeper pleasures than licking us.'

'No, not really, no,' Thrift said in a tiny voice.

'As deep then,' Ana replied with certainty.

'Perhaps,' Tatiana stated, 'but I do not think we should allow it to go unpunished. How do I look if I let Decency Branksome-Brading torture my friend and I do nothing?'

'Poor,' Ana agreed. 'We should do something.'

'No, please,' Thrift put it. 'Do not trouble yourselves on my account. I hated it, yes, at first. In a way I still do, but I crave it also. Also, I would feel wrong if you were to take some awful revenge on them, Decency especially.'

'I wasn't thinking so much as revenge for your sake,' Tatiana replied, 'as of redeeming my own honour. What do you think, Ana?'

'I would like to take them down to the basement of my father's house and have them fucked by the kitchen staff,' Ana replied. 'That would be amusing.'

'It is hardly practical, and would cause a major incident if it came out, not that they'd admit it,' Tatiana answered. 'Yes, we need something they would be too ashamed to confess to, as Thrift is to what they do to her, but I would bet that all three get their cunts inspected now and then.'

'Decency would, certainly,' Thrift agreed. 'I think Francesca also.'

'Xiuying too,' Tatiana added. 'The Chinese are as obsessed with virginity as any of you.'

'Xiuying is more wanton than Thrift,' Ana pointed out. 'Yes, we could humble her, but she would soon come to like it.'

'All the better,' Tatiana answered. 'As they have done to Thrift, we should turn a proud and haughty Lady into a grovelling wanton. Francesca is sensitive and demure. She will feel any humiliation we inflict on her very keenly indeed. As to Decency herself, we will have to think of something special.'

Ana nodded thoughtfully.

The first to taste Tatiana and Ana's vengeance was Xiuying. They had planned carefully, as had Thrift despite her misgivings, working out a cunning scheme to get their victim alone. During morning lessons, Thrift slipped a note to Xiuying, suggesting that she would be willing to lick, and that it might be more enjoyable without Decency and Francesca present. Xiuying knew that Thrift took pleasure in what they did, and that it was done for Tatiana and Ana too, so accepted without hesitation. The agreement was to meet in the facilities directly after lessons, and to explain their absence from lunch as one having felt sick if questions were raised. It was a risk, but a small one, each Mistress likely to assume that the four girls had been called to task by some other. After all, who would willingly miss the joys of bangers and mash with boiled cabbage followed by roly-poly pudding and custard?

It worked perfectly. Thrift went first, as agreed. Tatiana and Ana were already concealed in cubicles, and when Xiuying arrived they simply grabbed her. They had her helpless in moments, held tight as her pretty red silk dress was hauled up over her head to reveal her naked body beneath, tiny breasts and meaty little buttocks jiggling to the motion of her struggles. She had no chance, but fought hard, and cursed them as she did so, in Mandarin, reverting to English only when it became obvious that she was captured.

'What are you doing? Get off me, daughters of pigs!'

'Temper, temper,' Tatiana replied. 'We want you to lick our cunts, that's all, maybe our bottoms, if you're feeling dirty.'

'Never! I am a Lady!' Xiuying squealed. 'If you want your fat, dirty cunts licked, make pig-dirt wanton Thrift. She is your friend. She will lick!'

'She often does,' Tatiana assured her. 'We thought a change might be pleasant.'

'Not me!' Xiuying screeched. 'Do each other! Make Francesca! Make Decency!'

'No,' Ana answered firmly. 'We want you. Do you know why?'

'Obvious. I am small and pretty, not like you grossly overweight western ox-heifers!'

She broke off in a squeal of pain as her arms were twisted harder into her back.

'No,' Tatiana answered her. 'It is not because we find you especially attractive. It is because you will hate it the most.'

'Not true!' Xiuying squealed. 'Francesca and Decency, they are European, very shy, very prudish.'

'True,' Tatiana admitted, 'but then they aren't as wanton as you. They wouldn't break down and lose control halfway through. They wouldn't end up fingering their cunts with their tongues stuck up our bottom holes. You will.'

Xiuying immediately went into a stream of hysterical denials, half in English, half in Mandarin. Both Tatiana and Ana laughed at her response, and even Thrift found herself giggling. The little Chinese girl was also struggling frantically, kicking her legs about and even trying to bite her captors. It made no difference whatsoever. Tatiana and Ana, both bigger and stronger by far than their victim, simply held her as they used the silk sash from her dress to bind her hands tight behind her back. Still kicking and snapping with her teeth, she was dragged into a cubicle and forced down into a kneeling position, her face towards the bowl, as she would have to be to lick her captors.

'So, will you do it?' Ana demanded. 'Or do you need a wash first?'

'Wash, what wash is this!?' Xiuying spat. 'Let me go, you pig-dirt bitches! I will never lick you! Never!'

'Wash her,' Tatiana advised. 'She needs it.'

'Certainly her mouth does,' Thrift agreed.

'Good idea,' Tatiana answered her and reached out to take a bar of soap from one of the sinks. 'Ana, stick this in her mouth first.'

Tatiana had grabbed Xiuying by the hair as she spoke, and used her other hand to hold the Chinese girl's nose. Xiuying fought back, her mouth tight shut, trying to shake her head to loosen the Soviet girl's grip as her face went gradually red, then purple. Finally her mouth came open in a great, urgent gasp, only for the thick soap bar to be stuffed well in. Laughing, Tatiana clamped her hand firmly over Xiuying's mouth to hold the soap in.

'In she goes!' Ana declared happily and they began to force Xiuying's head down into the china bowl of the facility.

The hapless Chinese girl's pleas grew from muffled whimpers to a high-pitched, hysterical squealing as she was pushed roughly down, already with soap bubbles coming out of her nose. Both girls ignored the outcries, Tatiana holding Xiuying's head well into the bowl as Ana cocked one long leg over it, trapping the Chinese girl in place, cunt to head. Still Xiuying fought, kicking up her bound legs in a futile and comical attempt to get at Ana. The black girl sat down a little more firmly, the flesh of her big buttocks squashing out over Xiuying's back. With a hiss of urine she begun to pee down the back of Xiuying's neck and the squeals of protest became more hysterical still. Thrift watched, her hand to her mouth as Ana's piddle squirted out into Xiuying's hair, soaking the fine black strands to leave them hanging down in sodden rat's tails. Soon there was a forth of piddle and soap bubbles hanging down around Tatiana's hand, and from the Chinese girl's nose, while her protests had become a weird gurgling sound, completely incoherent yet still furious. Ana reached out, pushed the button above the facility and the sound of Xiuying's rage was drowned out in a rush of water.

'She'll lick now,' Ana predicted as Xiuying finally stopped kicking her legs up and down. 'Pull her up.'

Tatiana hauled on Xiuying's head as Ana dismounted. The Chinese girl came up, her hair plastered around her face, a beard of yellowish soap bubbles hanging down from her chin. She immediately spat out the soap, and more bubbles blew from her nose and around her lips as she struggled for breath.

'Well?' Ana demanded. 'Time to lick cunt?'

'No! Never, pig-dirt bitch, stinking n –' Xiuying screeched, only for her furious protests to turn to a grotesque burbling as her face was thrust under the water of the facility.

The Chinese girl was held under, Tatiana ignoring the frantic drumming of her bound legs. Casually, Ana reached down, slipping her hand under Xiuying's bottom, to manipulate both cunt and anus. Xiuying's buttocks went tight, and a new flood of bubbles erupted up from around her head a moment before the water level fell to leave her gasping and spitting into the bowl.

'No,' she gasped. 'You must not . . . you cannot –'

Ana just laughed, her fingers working expertly in the helpless Chinese girl's cunt, her thumb teasing the well-splayed anus. Xiuying moaned, as much in despair as ecstasy.

'Wanton, no question,' Ana stated as her thumb punctured Xiuying's anus and a finger slid up into the well-lubricated cunt hole. 'She would be ready for an elephant!'

Xiuying gave a defeated sob and suddenly she was rubbing her cunt and bottom on Ana's hand with a desperate, animal urgency. Both Ana and Tatiana laughed aloud, Thrift giggling in delight as well. Ana snatched her hand away and Xiuying moaned in disappointment as she was once more pulled up from the facility bowl, this time to have her head pushed close to the black girl's crotch. Ana quickly pulled up her skirts, along with the lace at the front of her abbreviated corset, to reveal a thickly furred, black cunt in a froth of white lace and bows of multicoloured ribbons.

'Now will you do it?' Ana demanded.

Xiuying nodded weakly and put her tongue to the black girl's cunt. Ana laughed.

With Xiuying suitably humbled, there was no difficulty in persuading her to help them catch Francesca. Indeed, if anything, Xiuying was keener than they for the Liechtensteiner girl to suffer, and even suggested a torture designed to exact the maximum of humiliation from such a sensitive and prudish victim. She was to be figged.

It was obvious that the trap which had worked so well to catch Xiuying would not work for Francesca, while the chances to use the convenient facilities were few and far between. A better choice was the school library, where Francesca spent much of her spare time and in the darker corners of which it would be easy enough to inflict a punishment. The only problem was the possibility of Francesca screaming and by ill luck a Mistress being within hearing range.

That Tatiana overcame, and one day late in the term Francesca was caught in a quiet corner of library after lunch and the Soviet girl's abbreviated drawers forced into her mouth and tied off with Xiuying's sash. Knowing full well that she was in serious trouble, Francesca fought, struggling and kicking as she was hauled over the table at which she had been reading. So determined was she that in the end it took both Tatiana and Ana to hold her down, leaving Thrift and Xiuying to inflict revenge. Thrift held back, uncertain, but Xiuying had no such qualms. Making sure the helpless, squirming Francesca could see, she produced something from within the tightly coiled mass of her hair, a neatly carved piece of ginger root, with two big, rounded ends and a narrow middle.

'This is for you, Francesca,' she said happily, 'for you to get the same as me. It is so shaped for insertion and retention in the anus, and maybe, after an afternoon with it in yours, you will be a bit less tight and stuffy.'

She finished with a laugh as the fear in Francesca's eyes turned to outright horror, and Tatiana and Ana were forced to use all their strength to hold the blonde girl down as Xiuying went behind her.

As she lifted Francesca's gown, the Chinese girl went on. 'This is very popular in China, not as punishment, but as sport. Sometimes we would have our servants catch a peasant girl and tie her hands, and put the ginger root in her arsehole. It was so funny to see them hop and squeal and, to get it out, sometimes they would foul themselves! So much fun!'

She ended in a peal of high-pitched mirth, even as Francesca went into new and even more frantic struggles, kicking her legs out behind and waggling her bottom furiously from side to side. Xiuying nimbly avoided the kicking legs and hauled their victim's underskirt and petticoats high as one, throwing them up on to Francesca's back. The response was a muffled sobbing and, with no bustle or corset, the movement left Francesca's drawers on show, big panel-backed ones embroidered with pink roses and fastened with over a dozen buttons.

'Hold the pig, or she'll kick me,' Xiuying instructed as Francesca burst into tears.

Thrift came reluctantly forwards, to catch one leg, then the other. It was a lot easier to hold Francesca's legs than she imagined, the little blonde pretty well helpless in her grip. She also had a prime view, her face just a foot or so from Francesca's frantically jiggling bottom as the buttons were undone. Xiuying wasted no time, using both hands to pop the buttons as Francesca's wiggling became ever more urgent and her sobbing ever more distressed.

The panel fell away and Francesca's neat, cheeky bottom was exposed, the flesh quivering as she fought, the lips of her cunt pouting out from between her thighs, plump and wet between. Xiuying laughed again.

'See her cunt! She is wet! For all her airs she has a wet cunt, no different from any other pig-dirt whore!'

'Be quick, Xiuying!' Tatiana insisted. 'And do try and be a little less noisy!'

Xiuying merely giggled as she bent down. Francesca's legs were kicking hard in Thrift's grip, and a weird gulping noise had been added to the miserable sobbing, then there came a muffled wail expressing a truly agonised humiliation as her tight little buttocks were hauled apart to show off her neat pink anus.

'Too dry,' Xiuying declared. 'Lick it, Brat.'

Thrift hesitated only an instant, and then her tongue was wedged firmly into Francesca's bottom hole. Her mouth filled with the acrid, pungent taste as it hit her how low she must be to be licking the anus of the girl undergoing torture, yet it felt right. She kept licking, her passion rising as her tongue probed up into the muscular little bottom hole, barely hearing the miserable sobs issuing from Francesca in response. Then Xiuying was pulling at her shoulder.

'Enough, pig-dirt Brat! You want to lick arse, lick mine, later.'

Even as she had spoken, Xiuying had pushed the plug of ginger root to Francesca's now well-moistened anus. The little pink ring spread, the star shape changing to a taut circle, as Francesca squealed in pain through her gag. Then it was in, the tiny bottom hole well plugged, with the muscle closed on the neck of the ginger root. Francesca let out a hopeless, broken wail as Xiuying let go of her bottom cheeks and they closed on the plug.

'Now dress her, quickly,' Tatiana ordered.

Thrift and Xiuying hastened to obey. Francesca had given up, and lay limp and defeated over the table as her drawers were buttoned up and her skirts dropped. They untied and pulled out the gag, letting her stand, with the muscles in her cheeks twitching from the effect of the ginger and her puffy red-rimmed eyes full of mute accusation and pain, also deep, deep humiliation.

'Time to lick, yes?' Xiuying demanded.

'Here?' Thrift queried.

'Safe enough,' Ana stated, her voice thick with passion. 'I for one would enjoy it.'

Tatiana nodded, then spoke.

'Quickly then. Thrift, get your tongue up Ana. Xiuying, make Francesca do me, then I'll help you if she won't behave.'

Xiuying nodded as Tatiana grappled for her trousers. They came down, exposing her bare bottom, even as Thrift kneeled meekly for Ana. Francesca didn't move, but stood still, staring in numbed shock at Tatiana's bottom as it was pushed out for her attention. Xiuying gripped her head, pushing down.

'Lick it, pig-dirt! I have been made to, so must you! Lick it! Lick it!'

Her voice had risen to a screech, and both Tatiana and Ana put their fingers to their lips in alarm. Xiuying went silent. Francesca was still standing, too big for the minute Xiuying to handle for all her own small size. For a moment they listened, but there was no noise whatever, then Ana sighed, caught hold of Francesca by the scruff of the neck, forced her to her knees and stuffed her face between Tatiana's out-thrust bottom.

'Thank you, Ana,' Tatiana said, reaching back to take a firm grip on Francesca's head. 'Now lick it, Francesca, get your tongue well up and don't stop until I'm finished.'

Francesca's response was a series of muffled squeals from between Tatiana's buttocks.

'Lick it!' Tatiana hissed. 'What, do you think you are better than Thrift, better than Xiuying?'

'I cannot!' Francesca wailed, pulling back. 'The ginger hurts too much. It is burning!'

'Don't be so pathetic,' Tatiana snapped and thrust Francesca's face firmly back between her bottom cheeks. 'Now lick my anus, or I swear I'll pop your precious cunt for y –'

She broke off with a sigh of pleasure as a wet slurping noise started from between her bottom cheeks. Thrift took a last glance at Francesca, pretty face buried between Tatiana's hard, muscular bottom cheeks, eyes shut in humiliation as her tongue worked up another girl's bottom hole for the first time in her life, and with her own bottom hole figged into the bargain. Then Ana was lifting her gown and petticoats and she was faced with her own bottom to lick, full and meaty and black, the anus a pouting knot of yet darker flesh, the cunt showing rich pink between fleshy lips.

'Bottom hole first, then my cunt,' Ana instructed.

Thrift rocked forwards on her heels, not needing to be forced but knowing her place. Her tongue came out, to briefly lap at Ana's anus, cleaning around it and in the hole, then burrowing in with her lips pressed to the puckered black flesh in an urgent, wanton kiss. Ana moaned in pleasure as Thrift set to work, licking bottom with both experience and a sense that she was in her place. Now that she had put her tongue in Francesca's anus, that made four out of her five classmates. As she licked and probed at Ana's musky little hole and her cunt began to twitch with electricity, she was thinking of how it would feel to be made to complete the class, and do Decency, in front of the others.

Unlike Xiuying, Francesca immediately told Decency what had happened, although Thrift suspected not all of it, and as predicted she was far too ashamed to go to authority. Xiuying's story also came out and Decency became extremely cautious, not even trusting her friends, but sticking as close as possible to Miss Evans and the other teachers, while never, ever visiting the convenient facilities unless it was crowded with junior girls.

Tatiana and Ana waited their chance, but it never came. Term finished, and the next began, but still Decency never once allowed herself to be caught offguard. Thrift's feelings were mixed, her sense that it was inappropriate for Decency to be punished undercut by a desire for revenge. She also found herself longing for her own torture and, to the open disgust of both Tatiana and Ana, she began to make up to Decency, flattering her and doing little helpful tasks whenever she could. It made little difference and, with Tatiana and Ana watching Decency's every move, Thrift went month after month without the humiliation she now craved. Instead she had to content herself with the occasional session of bottom licking, but with the element of coercion removed it was simply not the same.

What did continue as before was her relationship with Alphonse d'Arrignac. At least once every week she would find herself kneeling at his feet, or on the sofa with her head laid on to his lap, or in some less conventional position, but always with his penis in her mouth as she sucked him to climax. Often he would fondle her rubber-clad bottom, with her skirts up and her corset panel open at the back, or her breasts, with the front of her clothing disarranged. He also liked to talk about the pleasure of sodomising her, especially as he approached his climax.

Miss Challis had become complacent, taking little care about being seen on the way to Pavilion Street, and also showing purchases she had made with her extra income, a fur muff on one occasion, a pair of sapphire earrings on another. Concerned at first, Thrift soon fell into the same habit, assuming that, if her liaison had been noticed, then it was another of those things that were simply never spoken about.

At last her final day at the Diplomatic School came. Even walking across the park she was struck by a deep sense of nostalgia, and for all that she had suffered she knew that she would miss it keenly. When she arrived there was a sense of change, as if she no longer belonged, and this grew stronger as, instead of starting the normal morning lesson, she and Miss Challis were ushered up to a large, panelled room at the end of a corridor on the second floor.

Her unease was immediate. For one thing heavy blinds covered the windows and the sole illumination was electric. For another, ranks of chairs had been arranged, and these were filling up, not only with her immediate colleagues, but with the junior girls, Companions, Mistresses and other staff. Most sinister of all, a peculiar apparatus had been erected on the low stage that occupied one end of the room. It was a frame, made of dark wood and rough brown leather, both stained in places. A trestle of sorts, the four thick legs stuck out at right angles to one another and at some 45 degrees to the floor. Struts joined them, making the object rigid, while each leg was bolted to the floor, fittings that clearly went far beyond the need for mere stability. The top was not flat, but rounded, a padded bar some three feet long and perhaps a foot thick. Below it hung a thick leather strap. Each leg also had straps, two per leg, a good two inches wide and also thick. Each strap was fitted with a heavy-duty brass buckle. Without a shadow of a doubt it was designed for securing girls so that they could be whipped, presumably harder than it was possible to bear unrestrained and quite clearly in front of an audience. Turning to Miss Challis, she found her Companion wearing a knowing, wicked smile.

With her heart hammering in her chest she took a seat beside Ejura, Ana's stepmother and Companion. Ana was beyond and the two girls shared a nervous smile before turning their attention to the front as Lady Newgate came in. The Headmistress was in full academic robes, embroidered black silk with the hood trimmed with red to indicate her status. She also carried a cane, a long, brownish-black implement with a crooked handle on which Thrift's eyes remained fixed. Taking the stage, Lady Newgate eyed her audience, her expression cold, disapproving and faintly irritable. A pair of late-comers sat down hastily and the Headmistress began.

'Ladies, staff of the Diplomatic School, as you know, it is not our usual custom to call you all together in assembly. We prefer quiet and orderly method, and those girls who upon leaving require some special attention are seen singly. Today, however, I find it necessary to set an example. It is with great reluctance that I do this, but after considerable thought I have decided that the moral considerations are overwhelming. I regret to say that the personal records of our senior girls this year have not been without blemish. There have, indeed, been some serious misdemeanours but, allowing for diplomatic considerations, these will bring no more than the usual consequences. However, there is one notable exception, which cries out for immediate and severe retribution.'

Thrift's heart sank into her boots. Decency had done something, arranged some trick. Thrift was about to be accused of some terrible crime, something for which her denials would only make it worse. She would be stripped, thrashed, utterly humiliated, and with the entire junior year watching in giggling amusement . . .

'Miss Branksome-Brading,' Lady Newgate stated in a voice like the crack of doom. 'If you would please stand.'

Thrift had hung her head in defection, but looked sharply up, amazed. Yet her amazement was nothing to that of Decency, who was staring open mouthed, her expression flickering between outrage, disbelief and fear. Finally she got to her feet but, rather than approaching the front, she spoke, her voice loud but quavering.

'I do beg your pardon, Lady Newgate, but, although I realise that my academic record is not perfect, I am certain Miss Evans will vouch for my diligence. Also, I believe my personal record to be spotless.'

'Your academic record is not at issue,' Lady Newgate replied coldly. 'Your personal record is.'

She touched a switch. Immediately a section of the panelling slid up to reveal a white cinema screen. A picture appeared, the interior of the girls' convenient facilities viewed as if from some point on the high ceiling. Decency, Francesca and Xiuying were visible, checking that the cubicles were empty. Thrift stood beside them, looking scared and miserable. Decency was seen to select the middle cubicle and pull Thrift quickly inside, leaving the door open, then her voice sounded, addressing Francesca and Xiuying.

'You two must watch, the Brat will hate it so much more that way, but be quick with the door should anyone come.'

'Yes, Decency,' Francesca answered, quickly taking hold of the door.

'On the floor, Brat,' Decency ordered, pointing to the tiles in front of the facility. 'Kneel to me.'

Thrift's face was burning with blushes as the implications of what she was seeing sank in. It had been taped, probably all of it, her every humiliation, boot licking, bottom licking, cunt licking, having her breasts waxed . . .

Now it was boot licking. On the screen she dropped slowly to her knees. Decency sat back on the seat of the facility, crossing one knee over the over, making the richly layered lace trim of her gown and petticoats rise just far enough to expose the lower part of her dirty boot. Thrift hesitated.

'Come, come,' Decency chided. 'You wouldn't be being disobedient now, would you, Brat?'

Thrift shook her head, but still she hesitated.

'Lick it up, Brat!' Decency snapped. 'I will count to three, and –'

She stopped, laughing as Thrift immediately bent forward to poke her tongue out on to the dirty boot sole and the screen went blank. All six girls were now staring dumbstruck at the screen where the image had been, Decency white faced and shaking.

Lady Newgate continued. 'The recording is continuous, and thus you may all be assured that your sins have been exactly detailed. All your sins. There has been some discussion with the appropriate embassies, who, I am pleased to say, have responded in a fine spirit of co-operation. Miss Francesca Scaan, Miss Xiuying Shi, Miss Ana Lakoussan, Miss Tatiana Zhukov, you are to be spanked. Kindly form a line. Thrift, you also have sinned, but we have decided your suffering has more than atoned for your behaviour, while your wantonness is a matter for others better qualified to deal with such things. Miss Branksome-Brading, stand by the apparatus.'

The four girls due for spanking stood up, moving reluctantly into a line as Lady Newgate, Miss Evans, Miss Peel and Mrs Leary took their places at a line of chairs. Lady Newgate signalled to Tatiana, who was first in line, and the Soviet girl stepped forwards, poised yet trembling as she undid her trousers with her mouth set in a hard line. Lady Newgate ignored the implied defiance and took Tatiana's arm, pulling her forwards. Tatiana's trousers fell down as she bent, exposing bare buttocks divided by a line of white cotton lace pulled deep into her slit. To Thrift's surprise the little drawers were left up, Lady Newgate contenting herself with twisting Tatiana's arm up as Miss Peel beckoned to Ana.

The black girl came forwards, no less poised and defiant than her friend, unresisting as she laid herself across the gaunt woman's lap. Her skirts were pulled up, one by one, exposing the rear of her corset, Miss Peel frowning in disapproval at the cutaway rear as she turned up the abundant folds of lace to expose Ana's drawers. Like Lady Newgate, she did not make the final exposure.

Xiuying was next, stepping forward in an attempt to hold her poise but failing miserably, her stony expression suddenly breaking into a miserable, self-pitying scowl as she began to lay herself down over Mrs Leary's huge knees. A moment later and Xiuying's dress had been tugged up over her little bottom, the fat Irishwoman giving a grunt of disgust to discover it already bare.

Francesca came last and took it worst, first hesitating to come forwards, then refusing to bend over, and howling wildly and beating her fists on Miss Evans's legs as she was forced down into spanking position. One brawny arm encircled her waist the moment she was down, and she was held, still kicking and sobbing as her clothes were disarranged and the bulging seat of her drawers put on show.

With all four girls over the laps of the women due to punish them, the girls' bottoms were stripped methodically, save for Xiuying, who hung limp across Mrs Leary's lap as the others were dealt with. For Tatiana it was simple, the tiny, boyish pants were whipped straight down to her knees and she was bare. Ana's offered little more difficulty, Miss Peel spending a moment groping for the hems before peeling the voluminous split drawers wide to show off the full black bottom within. Only Francesca was awkward, pleading tearfully to be let off the indignity of exposure as the buttons of her fancy panelled drawers were opened one by one, and going into a brief fit of hysterics as the flap was lowered to show off her nudity.

At last a line of four bare bottoms was presented to the room, with four neat young cunts pouting out from between four pairs of girlish thighs. Only then did the spanking begin. All four Mistresses laid in as one, applying firm, regular swats to the soft female bottoms, making the cheeks bounce and jiggle, showing off the tight brown or pink bottom holes hidden between and drawing out squeals and gasps of shock and pain.

Tatiana took it well, stolid and uncomplaining despite Lady Newgate's best efforts. After a moment she even managed to get her toes to the floor, thus raising her belly in a deliberate and provocative show of the hammer and sickle emblem tattooed on her cunt mound. Lady Newgate's response was to snatch up the cane from beside her chair, hook a foot around one of Tatiana's legs to spread her fully, and as the tip of the stick was applied to the swollen cunt lips, the Soviet girl began to kick and scream with the rest.

Ana also tried to hold back, suffering Miss Peel's furious assault on her big black rear end in stoic silence, apparently indifferent to the display of her naked bottom, and kicking only a little. Perhaps a hundred smacks had been delivered when she suddenly broke, for no obvious reason, bursting into tears and abandoning her efforts at self-control, her legs starting to kick in earnest, and to scissor, showing off both cunt and anus in a thoroughly indecent display.

Xiuying showed no reserve whatsoever, kicking her legs about with the first few slaps and clearly in too much pain to even try and hide herself. She squealed crazily too, her pain very evident, and within a couple of dozen spanks she had burst into tears, wailing and babbling apologies and pleas for it to stop. The big Irishwoman took no notice whatever, merely continuing to belabour the little round bottom, her fat face set in an expression of determined self-righteousness.

Francesca made as big a fuss over her spanking as she had her exposure. She was in tears before the first smack fell, and screaming hysterically even before her bottom cheeks had bounced back to their normally rounded shape. From then on she went wild, forcing Miss Evans to tuck one brawny arm around her waist and hold her bodily as the spanking was administered to screams and thrashing and tears. With Francesca's bottom a plump red ball of angry flesh, her control snapped completely and she wet herself, urine spraying out from her well-splayed cunt, over the floor, her clothes and Miss Evans's leg, thus bringing her punishment to a premature halt.

As the tear-stained and exhausted Francesca was dumped on the floor, Miss Evans stood, and slapped irritably at the small wet patch where the piddle had soaked through. Francesca didn't even stop, but stayed squatting down on the floor, bottom bare behind her, piddle still squirting from between her open thighs to form a broad pool on the floor. By the time she finally covered herself her stream had already died to a trickle. Lady Newgate stopped beating Tatiana.

'You will clean that disgusting mess up yourself, Miss Scaan. Very well, you may rise, and I trust you feel suitably chastened?'

'Yes, Lady Newgate,' Tatiana answered, panting as she rose, and grimacing as she slipped a hand between her thighs to clutch at her whipped cunt.

'None of that,' Lady Newgate snapped. 'Cover yourself immediately. Have you no shame?'

Tatiana didn't answer, but limped back to her chair. Miss Peel had stopped and Ana was climbing unsteadily to her feet, while Mrs Leary still had Xiuying in a firm grip and was dishing out a last few smacks to the wriggling little bottom.

'That will do, I think, Mrs Leary, thank you,' Lady Newgate stated.

The big Irishwoman stopped with ill-concealed reluctance and Xiuying was allowed to stand. A school servant had a mop and bucket ready at the back, and Francesca was left to clean up her piddle as the others sat down. Lady Newgate stood, once more taking up her cane as her gaze came to rest on Decency, who had gone to the apparatus as ordered, and watched the spanking with an increasingly red face. All too obviously she was due to be fixed to it, then caned.

Thrift was biting her lip, and trying to fight down the feeling that what was happening was utterly, impossibly inappropriate. It seemed insane that the proud, superior Decency Branksome-Brading should have her bare bottom thrashed as if she were some pouty, sulky brat, but it was going to happen, without question. Lady Newgate had already mounted the stage, also Miss Evans and Miss Peel. The Headmistress spoke, addressing Decency.

'The only thing I have to say in your favour, Miss Branksome-Brading, is that you are not wanton. You have, however, shown remarkable cruelty, lied and generally behaved in a manner most unbecoming for a Lady of the British Empire. Do you have anything to say for yourself before receiving correction and justice? Perhaps an apology to Miss Moncrieff and those you led astray might be in order?'

Decency opened her mouth, but no sound came out.

'No?' Lady Newgate enquired. 'Very well, and be assured that I shall take your obduracy into account. Kindly lie across the whipping frame.'

Decency immediately found her voice.

'No! You cannot do this! You cannot! I am the daughter of a Baron, a peer of the realm! I am a Lady!'

'Miss Evans, Miss Peel, if you would be so kind?' Lady Newgate stated.

The two big women came forwards without hesitation. Decency tried to walk away, still protesting, but was too slow, her corset hobbling her. She was caught, turned about and dragged to the whipping frame, struggling and bleating every inch of the way, protests, threats, denunciations, anything and everything that might possibly have allowed her to escape punishment.

It made no difference. Neither Miss Evans nor Miss Peel reacted to the outcries, but forced Decency down over the frame, head first, leaving her bottom up, her face set in an agony of consternation, her limbs thrashing, her hair already spilled loose from its restraining net.

With Decency bent down, Miss Evans took a firm grip on her waist. Miss Peel attempted to grapple one kicking leg, but Decency's shoe caught her shoulder. Mrs Leary mounted the stage, and together they managed to force the furiously struggling, screaming girl down properly, her booted ankle held tight to the leg of the frame as the strap was applied, crushing Decency's immaculate white ladyspat. The second leg, trapped by Decency's tight corset, was left to jerk about within the confines of satin, whalebone and lace. Now to all intents and purposes helpless, Decency continued to struggle, and the look of furious consternation on her face grew stronger and stronger still as her arms were taken by the two Mistresses. Miss Evans released Decency's waist to turn her attention to the wrist straps, fastening each tightly into place to complete their victim's bondage, Decency still screaming and struggling even with three limbs secured fast to the frame. Lady Newgate spoke as she stepped close.

'Well, I would have expected a little more decorum from the daughter of a Baron, but we often do find that it is those who deserve retribution the most who are the least willing to accept it.'

'I do not accept it!' Decency howled. 'I do not accept it at all! You cannot do this, not to me. All I did was put a brat in her proper place! I must not be beaten! I will not be beaten! I will not! I will not!'

Her voice had risen to a hysterical scream, what was about to be done to her clearly something she simply could not take in. Lady Newgate waited calmly for the tantrum to subside, then answered. 'I beg to differ. You will be beaten, and well. As to your remarks concerning your father, rest assured that I have already discussed the matter with him. He is eager that you expiate your sins in full.'

'No,' Decency answered, but suddenly her rage was gone and the word came out in a sob.

'Yes,' Lady Newgate answered. 'Indeed, what other reaction could you possibly expect?'

'None, I admit,' Decency answered, suddenly contrite. 'I apologise, Lady Newgate, for my unseemly behaviour. Pray dispense justice as you see fit. I ask only that I remained clothed, as befits the modesty of a Lady.'

'As you know full well,' Lady Newgate answered, 'a woman who must be punished forfeits all right to modesty until the chastisement in complete. Miss Evans, kindly proceed.'

'No!' Decency squealed, all her fire returning in an instant. 'Not bare! Not bare! Not bare!'

She was screaming, her voice high pitched and again tinged with hysteria. She was thrashing violently on the frame too, her foot jerking against the strap, her fingers clenching and unclenching in her torment. Yet she could barely move, save to wiggle her upturned bottom in the most comical fashion, drawing giggles from more than a few of the watching girls. Then Miss Evans had taken hold of the rear of her gown and her struggles had become more desperate still, her bottom bucking up and down in a futile, pathetic attempt to stop her exposure. Her face was red with rage, and she was already crying, tears of frustration streaming from her eyes and her lower lip shaking with emotion.

Up came the gown, lifted high and turned down across her back. She let out a long, miserable wail as the stripping began, holding the note even as her underdress joined the gown on her back, to break off into hysterical sobbing. Miss Evans continued, as calm and placid as if she had been arranging linen on a table, not over a young woman's back in preparation for caning. Decency's outer petticoat was lifted and turned up, the rich silk rustling as it moved. The second followed, heavy flannel that allowed the contours of her bustle to show, up and over. With the third Decency went suddenly quiet, just shaking her head from side to side, as if no longer able to take in what was being done of her. The heavy strap that hung beneath the trestle top was pulled up and fastened across Decency's back, fixing her in place and ensuring that her clothes would stay up and out of the way, however much she struggled during the beating.

Decency's bustle was showing, a high, whaleboned scallop, deeply cleft in the centre, projecting up over the swell of the rear of her corset. Miss Evans turned it up, making sure Decency's bottom would present an unobstructed target, and bent to unfasten the twin gudgeons that held the corset panel closed. Both came loose, to the sound of Decency's laboured breathing and urgent sobs, but the panel was not lifted. Instead, Miss Evans moved to tug loose the thick bow of lacing that held the lower part of the corset closed, then squatted down to pull the catches free.

As Decency realised that her legs were to be spread her struggles began anew, if anything more urgent than before. The instant her leg came free she kicked out at Miss Evans's face, but her ankle was caught and she was hauled wide, her corset opening to show off the silky underside of her voluminous panel-backed drawers. A moment later, for all her violent kicking and hysterical screams, her foot had been fastened into the strap and she was spread out fully on the frame.

Miss Evans rose, a little red in the face, and with some irritation began to twitch open the buttons which held Decency's drawers closed at the back. Decency's struggles grew wilder and wilder as the buttons were undone, her screaming protests now incoherent, the prospect of having her bottom bared in public simply too strong for her to keep control. Then it had been done, the drawers peeled open and the full, cheeky orb of her bottom was showing at the centre of her inverted clothes, like some bizarre flower of cotton, silk and lace, white around a centre of bulbous pink flesh. She was split wide too, showing off a meaty, golden-furred cunt and the pink star of her anus. Her skin was very pale and her shape rather plump, her bottom deeply cleft and hairy between her cheeks, making her anus especially prominent. It was a thoroughly indecent sight, and as Thrift took in the lewd details something deep within her seemed to snap.

She'd been wrong. Decency was nobody to be looked up to, no untouchable paragon of virtue whose boots she was privileged to lick clean. Decency was just one more snotty-nosed, fat-bottomed little brat, as deserving of stripping and whipping as any other. Somewhere, perhaps, there was somebody she could worship, but it was not Decency Branksome-Brading. Suddenly what was about to happen no longer seemed inappropriate, but the exact opposite, clear and simple justice, and, as Miss Evans made a few final adjustments to leave the full, fat globe of Decency's bottom available for caning, Thrift was thoroughly looking forward to watching.

With her bottom bare, Decency had broken down completely, wailing hysterically in between broken, choking sobs that shook her whole body. Long strands of mucus were hanging from her nose and a forth of spit bubbles fringed her mouth. Sweat had started on her skin, giving her naked buttocks a glossy appearance, while her hair hung limp and bedraggled around her face. Her cunt was as shamefully wet as Thrift's had ever been, while her anus was dilating and contracting to a slow, lewd rhythm.

Lady Newgate flexed the cane above the quivering buttocks and spoke. 'You may take a moment to contemplate the indignity of your position and those sins which have brought you to it. Then I shall cane you. There will be a dozen strokes for lying, a dozen strokes for behaviour inappropriate to your station, a dozen for lewd behaviour and failing to report the lewd behaviour of others.'

Thrift felt a stab of disappointment at the thought of Decency receiving fewer strokes than when she herself had been tawsed by Miss Evans.

Lady Newgate went on. 'In view of the frequent recurrence of these sins and your lack of contrition, the punishment will be doubled. Seventy-two strokes.'

Decency let out a long, wordless wail of fear and self-pity at the news, then went back to blubbering. Lady Newgate, her face expressionless, extended the cane and tapped it to the pale, soft flesh of Decency's bottom. Thrift watched as the cane came up, and down, to smack hard into the fat, female flesh, drawing a scream of pain from Decency and leaving a thin white line where it had struck. Exaltation filled Thrift, and she found herself biting her lip in excitement. Decency was being caned, and it was wonderful, simply the happiest moment she could remember, and also immensely arousing. She realised she had been in thrall, but she had broken free, and now wanted nothing more than to see her rival reduced to the same state of grovelling submission she herself had known so often.

It was going to happen too. Lady Newgate was caning with a steady, merciless rhythm, laying in stroke after stroke, indifferent to Decency's now demented struggling, indifferent to the pitiful screams and tears of broken misery. Nor was Thrift the only one enjoying the view. Tatiana, Ana and Xiuying, even Francesca, all so recently spanked to tears themselves, were watching in rapt delight, and not one of the juniors, nor the staff, nor the Companions, showed anything other than the reserved approval that passed for enjoyment. Even

Decency's own Companion, Miss Buckleigh, had allowed herself a quiet smile.

The hysterical screaming never stopped, Decency totally unable to control herself and clearly overwhelmed by her own emotional reaction. Thrift could imagine it, all too easily, the burning, horrible shame, the awful sensation of exposure, the hideous knowledge of just how wet her cunt was and just how blatantly it showed, and then the pain, the helpless frustration of being strapped up, the agonising consternation and self-pity and misery. Decency, she knew, would have it all, and probably stronger than Thrift had ever had.

On around twenty strokes Decency added to her own humiliation by wetting herself. With one stroke a little spurt of piddle came out of her spread cunt and with the next a second, larger spurt. With a third stroke the whole lot erupted, gushing backwards from her peehole, all over the floor and the inside of her drawers, soaking her corset and petticoats and gown. Nor did it stop, the full contents of Decency's bladder ejected into her clothes in a series of gushes, with each impact of the cane drawing a fresh squirt of piddle. By thirty or so strokes she was empty, with the inverted flower of her petticoats dripping piddle and a ragged pool on the stage behind her.

Lady Newgate continued without a pause. At around forty strokes Decency's anus opened to emit a long, rasping fart, a humiliation of punishment Thrift remembered only too well. It seemed to break Decency in some way because, while her screams of pain never stopped, her struggles did, save for the spasmodic jerking of her legs each time the cane slashed down on to her new badly welted buttocks.

At fifty Lady Newgate took mercy on the now purple bottom and switched her attention to the slice of creamy thigh showing where the panel of Decency's drawers hung down between her legs. Again welts sprang up on fresh skin, and Decency's screams took on a new intensity, true, helpless hysteria, and on some sixty strokes it all finally became too much. Deceny's bucking and jerking stopped abruptly; she went limp, and the final dozen strokes were delivered to her inert body.

The caning done, Lady Newgate stood back, as serene as ever, leaving the school servants to clean up the mess. The nurse came forwards from the audience, clucking in disapproval at the extra work made for her by Decency's weakness as she gave the girl a brief but thorough check over. By the time she had finished, the straps had been undone, and two servants supported Decency from the room to have her bottom creamed and injected.

Thrift, her cunt tingling with need, and with electricity, sat in a daze, her head spinning with wanton lust and a dozen other emotions, many conflicting. It had been wonderful to see Decency beaten, yet part of herself wanted the same treatment, reacting with an instinctive jealousy that seemed superficially absurd. Beaten or not, she needed to climax. As Lady Newgate went into a long speech on the responsibilities of life and the high moral standards girls of the school were expected to maintain, she was thinking hard of how to do it and cursing her rubber pants.

For a full forty minutes Lady Newgate droned on, and when she did finish it was with a list of girls who were to come to her study in the afternoon, including Thrift, at four-thirty. With that they broke up for lunch, Thrift praying the other girls would drag her into the facilities for a long and cruel revenge. It was impossible, with all the Companions present, and she was left more frustrated than ever, only to discover that there were no calls on her time for the whole afternoon before her appointment. For a moment she considered evading Miss Challis's attention and seeking out Ana, but the black girl was nowhere to be seen.

At last they left the school, Miss Challis speaking as soon as they were on the pavement. 'A just punishment, despite all, but a disgraceful exhibition on the part of Miss Branksome-Brading.'

'I entirely concur, my dear Miss Challis,' Thrift responded, catching the slight tremor in her Companion's voice that betrayed extreme emotion.

'Quite disgusting too,' Miss Challis went on, 'hardly, I think, the behaviour of a Lady to lose control of herself in that way.'

'Not the behaviour of a Lady at all,' Thrift agreed, 'and the way she screamed, very common, I thought.'

'Very common indeed,' Miss Challis said and went quiet as they passed a pair of black-suited Liechtensteiners, only to speak again the moment they were out of earshot.

'We have some three hours,' she remarked. 'Possibly the time might be pleasantly passed in the company of Monsieur d'Arrignac?'

'Indeed it might,' Thrift answered, then hesitated, wondering if she was more in need of Monsieur d'Arrignac's cock in her mouth or a thorough spanking from Miss Challis. The ideal was both, but it hardly seemed possible, and after a moment of reflection she realised that the spanking was what she truly needed, and more likely to bring her to climax. Past experience told her she dare not ask, for all Miss Challis's mood. Yet something had to be said and, taking her heart in her mouth, she uttered a few carefully chosen words.

'Pleasant indeed, Miss Challis, and yet I do feel that this morning Lady Newgate was perhaps unduly merciful in my case. If absolute justice were to be done, I too should have been punished, at least with the others.'

'No doubt,' Miss Challis answered immediately. 'No doubt whatever.'

Miss Challis did not elaborate, but as they walked on Thrift realised that she had made an important discovery, or at least she thought she had. To actually say that she needed regular spanking was unthinkable, at least, it was unthinkable to admit that it was for purposes of mere physical gratification. On the other hand, it seemed that to suggest that justice demanded she be punished was entirely acceptable, even laudable. The end result would be the same, a smacked bottom and a wet cunt, but there would be no suggestion of impropriety. If Miss Challis spanked her, it would prove her right, and she was sure that was exactly what was going to happen as the Companion took her arm and led her across the road to the gardens.

As they entered the garden her heart jumped. There, in casual conversation were two men, one in the perfectly cut uniform of a high Soviet official, the other immaculately suited. One was Tatiana's father, the other her own. Immediately her castle of erotic expectation collapsed. To be spanked was wonderful, to have it done in front of strangers more wonderful still, but for her father to see was very different. Yet it was going to happen, the niceties of her personal feelings immaterial, her unspoken agreement with Miss Challis good only in so far as it allowed the Companion to express her cruelty.

Her face had gone a rich purple with embarrassment and her skin was crawling with fear. There was a bench nearby, empty and in full view of her father, a bench perfect for her to be placed across Miss Challis's knee, bared and soundly spanked. She tried to make herself react, thinking of how Francesca had fought to preserve her dignity, and in fighting retained at least some of it. Yet she was not Francesca. There was no fight in her, and as they reached the bench she knew she would go down, meek and pathetic, for all her raging feelings.

It didn't happen. Miss Challis simply steered her past the bench and gave a polite curtsey to Thrift's father. After a moment of bemusement, Thrift did the same, her greeting coming out in a thin, reedy whisper.

'Good afternoon, Papa, how pleasant to chance upon you.'

'Good afternoon, Thrift, Miss Challis,' her father replied. 'You know Ambassador Zhukov, of course.'

Thrift managed a curtsey for Tatiana's father.

Her own father went on. 'Yes, I shall be taking tea with Lady Newgate presently. For the moment you must excuse me.'

Dismissed, Thrift walked on, completely bemused. If her judgement of Miss Challis's hidden feelings had been at all correct, then nothing should have given the Companion greater pleasure than to dish out a bare-bottom spanking with Thrift's father watching. Certainly, on the rare occasions it had been done in front of her mother when Miss Challis was Governess, it had seemed to provide a special pleasure, which Thrift had always taken for satisfaction in the full dispensation of moral justice. It was possible she had misjudged the whole thing after all.

She was more confused than ever as they walked on, across the square and into Pont Street. Clearly they were still going to visit Monsieur d'Arrignac, and she walked in rising trepidation and excitement as they crossed Sloane Street and turned into Pavilion Road. Thrift glanced back as they reached the door of the Frenchman's flats, half-expecting to see her father despite the sure knowledge that he was busy and highly unlikely to leave the Diplomatic Enclave in any case.

He wasn't there, but she was feeling more guilty and secretive than usual as they climbed the stairs once d'Arrignac had caused the door to open. The Frenchman was as ever, his dress as perfect as it was eccentric, a suit of dark-green velvet and a patterned cravat in paler shades of the same colour. Smiling broadly, he went straight to his sideboard, where he took up the decanter of green liquid. Miss Challis made to retire, but he held up a finger.

'Not, my dear Miss Challis, today,' he stated. 'Today you may do more than merely watch. Today you may participate.'

Miss Challis had frozen, her face a mask, but with strong emotion showing in her eyes. Her mouth came open, then closed as Thrift turned to her in astonishment. Monsieur d'Arrignac continued as he began to pour out a glass of absinthe.

'Ah yes, Thrift, my little innocent. Miss Challis watches us, through the eyes of the great Emperor.'

He indicated a print of Napoleon the First, a picture to which Thrift had never given more than cursory attention, but which she now realised hung on the wall beyond which lay the room where Miss Challis and d'Arrignac's maid waited while she performed her duty. Not knowing whether to be outraged, delighted or what, she simply stood silent, accepting the glass of absinthe with numb fingers. Miss Challis did the same, but d'Arrignac carried on imperturbably.

'You are surprised?' he asked Thrift. 'You should be. Such knowledge is quite improper for a young Lady of your breeding, yet in this case I think we may make an exception.'

'That would be far from appropriate!' Miss Challis snapped, finally finding her voice.

'I think not,' d'Arrignac continued. 'I, after all, am French, and frankly I tire of being obliged to conform to your absurd and hypocritical British morals. Yes, Thrift, Miss Challis watches. Indeed, she was most disturbed by my sodomising you and would have come to your rescue had your quim not been quite so well guarded. She has also spanked little Elise, my maid, on occasion, and I suspect they apply their tongues to each other's quims.'

'I –' Miss Challis began, her face now beetroot coloured, only to stop as d'Arrignac wagged a finger at her.

'Denial is useless,' he went on, 'and in any case I only make these remarks as a prelude to my proposition. A touch more of the fairy, Thrift? By all means.'

As Thrift accepted her second glass of absinthe all had begun to come together in her head. Just as the pleasure of spanking was never admitted to, so it was with outright wantonness. Clearly Miss Challis and the whole commercial class indulged themselves in the same way, never once confessing to their real feelings but finding every excuse nonetheless. The incident with the chauffeur, her spanking with Mrs Brodie, it was all part of the same pattern.

'What proposition did you have in mind, Monsieur d'Arrignac?' Miss Challis asked weakly. 'If we really must speak openly.'

'We must,' d'Arrignac informed her, 'and pray do not concern yourself. Rather, comfort yourself in the knowledge that I am a decadent Frenchman and know no better.'

'This is certainly the truth,' Miss Challis answered frostily.

D'Arrignac laughed and went on. 'My proposition is this, that first you should pull up Thrift's clothes and take off her absurd rubber pants –'

'Take off her pants?' Miss Challis demanded. 'No, Sir. Many things you may do, but never shall I permit a Lady of the British Empire to be so basely deflowered, never shall –'

'Pray reserve your speech for a more suitable moment,' d'Arrignac interrupted. 'I have no design on Thrift's precious virginity, rest assured. I merely desire to sodomise her and, if it is so important to you, you may merely open her pants at the back to let me at her arsehole.'

Thrift was blushing crimson at the casual and lewd discussion of her body, and reeling with the revelations made by her lover, yet at the suggestion that she be buggered her quim twinged at a jolt of electricity.

Miss Challis raised her chin in defiance and spoke. 'Why pray should I do so much? You have committed a gross breach of trust, Monsieur d'Arrignac, and while I would seem to have little choice in –'

'Please, compose yourself,' d'Arrignac interrupted once more. 'Perhaps my choice of words was wrong. Proposition, after all, implies that you might reasonably choose to refuse. You will not refuse.'

'Why, pray, should you imagine that?'

'Because, Miss Challis, you and I are conspirators, both as responsible as the other, but while were the story to come out I would merely be sent back to France, where this story would merely amuse my associates, you, Miss Challis, would certainly lose your position, along with any prospect of finding another.'

'You would not dare!'

'I would, but no matter. There is the additional matter of your spanking Thrift.'

Miss Challis didn't answer, her face set in consternation. Thrift glanced from one to the other in puzzlement.

'I have been doing a little research into your bizarre British customs, you see,' d'Arrignac went on, 'and I discover that it is highly inappropriate for a Companion to give physical chastisement to her Lady. The good British public would naturally never dream of interfering in such a matter. Certainly none would so much as allow the idea of informing the young Lady's parents to enter their heads. A Frenchman on the other hand, unaware of the social niceties, a trifle crass perhaps –'

'I fully understand you, Monsieur d'Arrignac,' Miss Challis, 'but you are wrong. Rest assured that I would allow the whole of your scandalous behaviour to become known rather –'

'Rather than allow me to sodomise your precious Lady?' he cut in. 'Come, come, my dear Miss Challis! Is it really so important! I have had her once, her virginity

– in so far as the term may apply to a girl's bottom hole – is gone, poof, a fart in the wind! Besides, she is eager, note the twitching of her body as that horrible electrical device with which she is fitted discharges into her quim. Is that not so, Thrift?'

Thrift nodded, her emotions too heated to think of making a denial, then said what was really on her mind, to Miss Challis. 'All this time, and you were not permitted to spank me?'

'I did what I thought best,' Miss Challis answered primly.

'Ah but no,' d'Arrignac declared. 'You did what amused you, as you well know, yet which your absurd British hypocrisy prevents you from admitting.'

Miss Challis went silent, her mouth pursed in consternation, her eyes blazing. She swallowed her absinthe at a gulp then spoke again, her voice harsh with frustration. 'Oh very well then, Monsieur d'Arrignac, but you are no Gentleman, rather a cad and a blackmailer.'

'I am French,' he answered, 'is it not what you British expect of us?'

She didn't answer, but made an impatient gesture to Thrift, signalling her to bend over the back of the sofa. Thrift obeyed, her senses flooding with the most exquisite humiliation as the Companion pushed her upper body roughly down. Miss Challis began to flip up Thrift's clothes, not troubling to prolong the agony of exposure, but hauling up the full mass in one go and inverting the bustle with the petticoats. Two quick twists loosened the gudgeons on Thrift's corset panel; it came up and her incontinence pants were showing. Miss Challis punched in the code and the pants rolled back over Thrift's bottom, exposing her and leaving her panting at the suddenness with which she had been prepared for sodomy.

'There,' Miss Challis announced, gesturing to Thrift's naked bottom, 'is that what you want, Monsieur d'Arrignac?'

'Absolutely,' he agreed, 'and, believe me, I well appreciate why you enjoy spanking her so much. She is divine. Indeed, I feel a little spanking might be appropriate now, don't you?'

'If you must,' Miss Challis answered. 'Shall I, or do you wish to do it yourself?'

'Neither,' d'Arrignac answered, replacing his glass on the sideboard. 'It is not Thrift I wish to spank, Miss Challis, but you.'

'Me? Why – why me?' Miss Challis demanded, backing hastily away. 'Come, Monsieur d'Arrignac, this is foolish. Better surely to spank Thrift. Is it not true that the higher the Lady the greater the pleasure in her chastisement?'

'I have heard this phrase,' he answered, advancing on her, 'and I can understand why you British might find it so. In France we are not so ridden by class, having introduced so many of our aristocrats to *Madame Guillotine*. But, yes, in the same sense it gives more pleasure to spank a haughty woman than a meek one, which is why I intend to do you, and in front of Thrift.'

'No!' Miss Challis squeaked as he suddenly lunged forwards across the table she had hidden behind, to catch her sleeve.

Thrift raised herself a little to watch, knowing that another of those she had set up as icons of superiority was about to be belittled but unable to tear her eyes away. Miss Challis was fighting, but d'Arrignac was already proving stronger and, despite a few scratches and a bite to his hand, soon had Miss Challis's arm twisted hard behind her back. The Companion continued to struggle, and to demand to be released, but it did her no good. She was dragged down across d'Arrignac's lap as he sat himself into a chair, her arm twisted hard as her skirts were hauled high with no more ceremony than Thrift's had been, petticoats and all, to expose a pair of split-seam stained drawers and the lace fringe of a short corset.

'In France,' d'Arrignac remarked as he casually hauled Miss Challis's drawers apart to expose a plump white bottom with two hairy cunt lips peeping out from between soft thighs, 'such short corsets are worn only by cabaret girls, striptease artistes, the cigarette girls in theatres and so forth.'

Miss Challis gave an angry grunt in response, but she had given up struggling, accepting her fate. D'Arrignac chuckled and began to spank, still holding her arm safely up in the small of her back. It was not hard, just taps with the tips of his fingers, and Thrift was immediately surprised by the low, miserable wailing her Companion at once set up.

'She is distressed, my dear Thrift,' d'Arrignac explained, 'because she thought I was going to punish her. Watch closely, this is no crude beating such as you British dish out, but an erotic spanking, French style, where the bottom is slowly warmed as the cunt grows wetter, bringing the girl to a peak of uncontrollable wantonness, as I suspect Miss Challis knows very well.'

Miss Challis's answer was a sob. D'Arrignac went on spanking unhurriedly, slowly turning the Companion's bottom from white to a blushing pink. Thrift watched, her own bottom bare, her cunt twitching to the occasional jolt of electricity, to keep her warm and ready. After a while she reached back, giving in to her wanton feelings, and stroked and slapped her bottom as she watched the slow, steady spanking.

Before long Miss Challis's cunt was a sopping, juicy hole. Her sobs had turned to moans and she was sticking her bottom up, making the cheeks spread to show off the rude dimple of her anus. At the sight Thrift reached between her cheeks, finding her own bottom hole, moist with sweat. She slid the tip of one finger in, thinking of the big cock that would shortly be invading her as she masturbated herself, and watched her Companion spanked.

Monsieur d'Arrignac was in no hurry, but had begun to use the full scope of his hand, cupping Miss Challis's bouncing bottom cheeks with every smack, save for the occasional one delivered across the rear of her pouted cunt. Her moans were growing louder, more urgent, and when he finally let go of her arm she made no effort to get up. He kept on spanking, harder now, and he slipped his spare hand under her belly to her cunt.

Miss Challis gave a last, despairing moan as d'Arrignac started to masturbate her, still spanking as he rubbed at her cunt, his face set in mischievous glee. Then she had given in completely and was wiggling herself against his hand and pushing her bottom up to meet the spanks, lost in wanton ecstasy as she started to come, her cunt hole tightening, her anus winking, and crying out in abandoned ecstasy. She came to climax in a welter of splashing cunt juice and wobbling buttocks, d'Arrignac never once pausing until she was done, and only then pushing her to the ground.

A moment later his cock was out and she was sucking on him, on her knees at his feet, his already stiff erection in her mouth, sucking his cock with no more reserve than Thrift had ever shown. Thrift stared, her cunt jumping to the electric shocks, her finger working in and out of her now slippery bottom hole. Miss Challis's aura had gone, utterly, more or less from the moment she had stopped struggling and let herself be exposed, but there was still arousal, and a burning need for her own climax.

D'Arrignac stood and gently detached himself from Miss Challis's head. He smiled to Thrift and came towards her, holding his erection, and popped it into her mouth. She began to suck, revelling in the taste and feel of cock, her cunt now so swollen she was twitching steadily to the electric shocks.

After a moment he pulled out of her mouth and walked around the sofa. Thrift stuck up her bottom and reached back to spread her cheeks, blatantly offering her bottom hole for penetration. He chuckled and put his cock between, rutting in her crease with his hairy balls tickling the soft tuck of her bottom. Miss Challis stood, her face slack with pleasure, yet still with a glint in her eye. She came close, turned, and, as d'Arrignac's cock head was put to Thrift's bottom hole, so Miss Challis's bottom hole was offered to her mouth.

She licked without hesitation, burying her face between the soft, warm cheeks in delight at the prospect of being made to lick bottom for a woman who had herself just been spanked. Then her own anus was spreading to the pressure of d'Arrignac's cock and for a moment she was forced to concentrate on letting him in, her teeth gritted in pain as her hole was forced. She gasped as her ring popped, then sighed as her rectum began to fill with cock, the pain fading to a dull ache, then submerged in the pleasure of sodomy. Turning her attention back to her Companion, she once more began to lick Miss Challis's bottom hole, delighting in what was being done to her, used at both ends, her anus for a man and her mouth for a woman.

Almost immediately she knew she was going to climax. Her cunt was covered, the shocks were not too strong, yet each push of d'Arrignac's' balls was squashing the rubber plaque to her bump, bringing her slowly up and up. She took hold of Miss Challis's hips and pulled her face in, her tongue as far up the open, juicy bottom hole as it would go, her mind drifting to all that had happened to her, the way she had slowly been brought low, and to enjoy it, the spankings, the humiliations, being put in incontinence pants, boot licking, bottom licking . . .

Then she was there, her bottom ring squeezing over and over on his erection, to make him climax too, with a loud gasp, and suddenly she was pumping his sperm into her own bottom, ramming her tongue up Miss

Challis's bottom, her feet kicking clear of the ground, her cunt twitching violently to the electric shocks, her breasts agonisingly sensitive within their cage of whalebone and satin, the rubber tight around her hips and waist, the lace tickling her thighs, everything in sharp intensity as she went through a climax far, far beyond anything she had experience before.

Thrift kept her appointment with Lady Newgate, arriving back at the Diplomatic School in time for a cup of tea, a slice of brown bread and butter and a little Dundee cake before she went up. Miss Challis had washed her bottom and generally tidied her up, making her comfortable and presentable. There was no trepidation as she knocked on the door to the Headmistress's study. If Lady Newgate had meant to punish her it would have been done in front of the assembled school, as it had to Decency, who had been at tea, silent, crestfallen and waddling.

The door swung open and Thrift entered, leaving Miss Challis outside. Lady Newgate was alone, and with her tight mouth curved up into what might possibly have been described as a smile. Thrift curtseyed and took the backless chair that was evidently meant for her to sit on.

Lady Newgate steepled her fingers and spoke. 'I wish to see you, Thrift, in order to discuss your future. First, however, a few points. You are not a particularly gifted girl, either academically, or in the arts, and yet you have managed to achieve first place in your class, in competition with at least two girls of exceptional intelligence. Your diligence is to be commended.'

'Thank you, Lady Newgate.'

'It is no more than your due, and by stark contrast your personal record is deplorable. Not that I in any way condone the behaviour of Miss Branksome-Brading, nor your other tormentors, but I have been in teaching too long to imagine that the same would have happened had they not had so appropriate a victim.'

Thrift hung her head, unable to deny the truth of the assertion. Lady Newgate spoke again, surprisingly gently.

'What of the coming season? Do you wish to participate, perhaps hope to catch the eye of a suitable Gentleman?'

'No, Lady Newgate,' Thrift answered.

'That is probably just as well, although it grieves me to say it. What of the charities, or seclusion?'

'No, Lady Newgate,' Thrift answered, for once in her life determined to be strong, 'I do not feel either vocation would suit me.'

'Nor I,' Lady Newgate agreed without hesitation, 'yet it is difficult to see where else you might fit in, save for one fortuitous possibility. Your father has made a request that you be considered for the Diplomatic Service. I need hardly say that this is scarcely a suitable occupation for a young Lady, and yet there are times when one must place Empire first. Besides, you are eminently well qualified.'

'I am?' Thrift queried.

'Indeed,' Lady Newgate replied calmly. 'You possess an excellent memory, impressive loyalty both personal and Imperial, have a remarkable tolerance for suffering, are quite without hope of a suitable marriage and, above all, you are an irredeemable wanton.'

Nexus

NEXUS NEW BOOKS

To be published in January

KNICKERS AND BOOTS
Penny Birch

When Stephen Stanbrook consults therapist Gabrielle Salinger about his yearnings towards sexual dominance, her girlfriend, Poppy, is intrigued. Determined to find out more, she traces his exploits on the net as he seduces two young submissives, Nicola and June, known in the SM community as Knickers and Boots. Before long she's put through her paces by him, together with them, and all in uniform. Meanwhile, Gabrielle's old playmate Jeff Bellbird is stalking them in the hope of something even more perverse.

£6.99   ISBN 0 352 33853 9

THE PUNISHMENT CLUB
Jacqueline Masterson

Twenty-year-old Fudge and her mistress, Clarissa, join a club devoted to traditional discipline and the 'training' of attractive young women. They discover a whole network of quintessentially English societies dedicated to bondage, domination and spanking. The fun becomes ever more competitive and arduous, however, and Fudge finds that she must help the club take on its great rival 'The Church of the Birch' at its annual summer fete and sports day.

£6.99   ISBN 0 352 33862 8

CONFESSION OF AN ENGLISH SLAVE
Yolanda Celbridge

Introduced to the joys of bare-bottom discipline by lustful ladies, naval cadet Philip Demesne, posted to the far east, painfully learns true submission from the voluptuous dominatrix Galena, aboard her private carriage on the Trans-Siberian Express. Escaping from her lash, he is kidnapped to serve in an English school of female domination, transplanted to the emptiness of Siberia to escape do-gooding restrictions on corporal punishment. His male arrogance utterly crushed, Philip gladly submits to total enslavement by women with unlimited flagellant discipline.

£6.99   ISBN 0 352 33861 X

To be published in February

PRINCESS
Aishling Morgan

Princess follows the (mis)fortunes of Aeisla, her compatriot Iriel, and their ad hoc band of nubile, amazonian warrior women as they are forced to flee their native Aegmund or face bizarre and public erotic punisment. Their passages worked copiously, they arrive by ship at the kindom of Oretea. Political scheming, slavery and perverse punishments ensue in this, the fabulously inventive final part of Aishling Morgan's *Maiden* saga.

£6.99   ISBN 0 352 33871 7

THE SMARTING OF SELINA
Yolanda Celbridge

Blonde journalist Selina Rawe eagerly infiltrates Her Majesty's Prison at Auchterhuish, where corporal punishment is mandatory for wayward girls, along with more specialist treatments from a gorgeous resident nurse, while the lustful Hebridean mariners provide little – or perhaps too much – relief. Sapphic governess Miss Gurdell worships the bottom beautiful, and Selina is horrified to learn that hers is the tastiest of all. A novel of craven submission from the author of *The English Vice*.

£6.99   ISBN 0 352 33872 5

THE INSTITUTE
Maria del Rey

When Lucy is sentenced to be rehabilitate in a bizarre institute for the treatment of delinquent girls, she finds that the disciplinary methods used are not what she has been led to expect. They are, in fact, decidedly perverse. By the author of *Dark Desires*, *Dark Delights* and *Obsession* – 'The Queen of SM' *Caress*. A Nexus Classic.

£6.99   ISBN 0 352 33352 9

If you would like more information about Nexus titles, please visit our website at www.nexus-books.co.uk, or send a stamped addressed envelope to:
  Nexus, Thames Wharf Studios,
  Rainville Road, London W6 9HA

Nexus

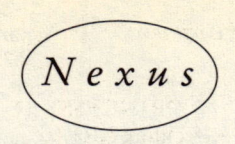

NEXUS BACKLIST

This information is correct at time of printing. For up-to-date information, please visit our website at www.nexus-books.co.uk

All books are priced at £6.99 unless another price is given.

THE ACADEMY	Arabella Knight 0 352 33806 7	☐
AMANDA IN THE PRIVATE HOUSE	Esme Ombreux 0 352 33705 2	☐
ANGEL £5.99	Lindsay Gordon 0 352 33590 4	☐
BAD PENNY £5.99	Penny Birch 0 352 33661 7	☐
BARE BEHIND	Penny Birch 0 352 33721 4	☐
BEAST £5.99	Wendy Swanscombe 0 352 33649 8	☐
BELLE SUBMISSION	Yolanda Celbridge 0 352 33728 1	☐
BENCH-MARKS	Tara Black 0 352 33797 4	☐
BRAT	Penny Birch 0 352 33674 9	☐
BROUGHT TO HEEL £5.99	Arabella Knight 0 352 33508 4	☐
CAGED! £5.99	Yolanda Celbridge 0 352 33650 1	☐
CAPTIVE £5.99	Aishling Morgan 0 352 33585 8	☐
CAPTIVES OF THE PRIVATE HOUSE £5.99	Esme Ombreux 0 352 33619 6	☐
CHALLENGED TO SERVE	Jacqueline Bellevois 0 352 33748 6	☐

CHERRI CHASTISED	Yolanda Celbridge	0 352 33707 9	☐
CORPORATION OF CANES	Lindsay Gordon	0 352 33745 1	☐
THE CORRECTION OF AN ESSEX MAID	Yolanda Celbridge	0 352 33780 X	☐
CREAM TEASE	Aishling Morgan	0 352 33811 3	☐
CRUEL TRIUMPH	William Doughty	0 352 33759 1	☐
DANCE OF SUBMISSION £5.99	Lisette Ashton	0 352 33450 9	☐
DARK DESIRES £5.99	Maria del Rey	0 352 33648 X	☐
DEMONIC CONGRESS	Aishling Morgan	0 352 33762 1	☐
DIRTY LAUNDRY	Penny Birch	0 352 33680 3	☐
DISCIPLINE OF THE PRIVATE HOUSE	Esme Ombreux	0 352 33709 5	☐
DISCIPLINED SKIN £5.99	Wendy Swanscombe	0 352 33541 6	☐
DISPLAYS OF EXPERIENCE £5.99	Lucy Golden	0 352 33505 X	☐
DISPLAYS OF PENITENTS £5.99	Lucy Golden	0 352 33646 3	☐
DRAWN TO DISCIPLINE £5.99	Tara Black	0 352 33626 9	☐
AN EDUCATION IN THE PRIVATE HOUSE £5.99	Esme Ombreux	0 352 33525 4	☐
THE ENGLISH VICE	Yolanda Celbridge	0 352 33805 9	☐
EROTICON 1 £5.99	Various	0 352 33593 9	☐
EROTICON 4 £5.99	Various	0 352 33602 1	☐
THE GOVERNESS ABROAD	Yolanda Celbridge	0 352 33735 4	☐

THE GOVERNESS AT ST AGATHA'S	Yolanda Celbridge 0 352 33729 X	☐
GROOMING LUCY £5.99	Yvonne Marshall 0 352 33529 7	☐
HEART OF DESIRE £5.99	Maria del Rey 0 352 32900 9	☐
THE HOUSE OF MALDONA	Yolanda Celbridge 0 352 33740 0	☐
IN FOR A PENNY £5.99	Penny Birch 0 352 33449 5	☐
THE INDIGNITIES OF ISABELLE	Penny Birch writing as Cruella 0 352 33696 X	☐
INNOCENT	Aishling Morgan 0 352 33699 4	☐
THE ISLAND OF MALDONA	Yolanda Celbridge 0 352 33746 X	☐
JODHPURS AND JEANS	Penny Birch 0 352 33778 8	☐
THE LAST STRAW	Christina Shelly 0 352 33643 9	☐
NON-FICTION: LESBIAN SEX SECRETS FOR MEN	Jamie Goddard and Kurt Brungard 0 352 33724 9	☐
LETTERS TO CHLOE £5.99	Stephan Gerrard 0 352 33632 3	☐
LOVE-CHATTEL OF TORMUNIL	Aran Ashe 0 352 33779 6	☐
THE MASTER OF CASTLELEIGH £5.99	Jacqueline Bellevois 0 352 33644 7	☐
MEMOIRS OF A CORNISH GOVERNESS	Yolanda Celbridge 0 352 33722 2	☐
MISS RATTAN'S LESSON	Yolanda Celbridge 0 352 33791 5	☐
NON-FICTION: MY SECRET GARDEN SHED £7.99	Ed. Paul Scott 0 352 33725 7	☐
NEW EROTICA 5 £5.99	Various 0 352 33540 8	☐
NEW EROTICA 6	Various 0 352 33751 6	☐

THE NEXUS LETTERS £5.99	Various 0 352 33621 8	☐
NURSES ENSLAVED £5.99	Yolanda Celbridge 0 352 33601 3	☐
NURSE'S ORDERS	Penny Birch 0 352 33739 7	☐
NYMPHS OF DIONYSUS £4.99	Susan Tinoff 0 352 33150 X	☐
THE OBEDIENT ALICE	Adriana Arden 0 352 33826 1	☐
ONE WEEK IN THE PRIVATE HOUSE	Esme Ombreux 0 352 33706 0	☐
ORIGINAL SINS	Lisette Ashton 0 352 33804 0	☐
THE PALACE OF EROS £4.99	Delver Maddingley 0 352 32921 1	☐
THE PALACE OF PLEASURES	Christobel Coleridge 0 352 33801 6	☐
PALE PLEASURES	Wendy Swanscombe 0 352 33702 8	☐
PARADISE BAY £5.99	Maria del Rey 0 352 33645 5	☐
PEACH	Penny Birch 0 352 33790 7	☐
PEACHES AND CREAM	Aishling Morgan 0 352 33672 2	☐
PENNY IN HARNESS £5.99	Penny Birch 0 352 33651 X	☐
PENNY PIECES £5.99	Penny Birch 0 352 33631 5	☐
PET TRAINING IN THE PRIVATE HOUSE £5.99	Esme Ombreux 0 352 33655 2	☐
PLAYTHINGS OF THE PRIVATE HOUSE £6.99	Esme Ombreux 0 352 33761 3	☐
PLEASURE ISLAND £5.99	Aran Ashe 0 352 33628 5	☐
THE PLEASURE PRINCIPLE	Maria del Rey 0 352 33482 7	☐

PLEASURE TOY £5.99	Aishling Morgan 0 352 33634 X	☐
PRIVATE MEMOIRS OF A KENTISH HEADMISTRESS	Yolanda Celbridge 0 352 33763 X	☐
PROPERTY	Lisette Ashton 0 352 33744 3	☐
PURITY £5.99	Aishling Morgan 0 352 33510 6	☐
REGIME	Penny Birch 0 352 33666 8	☐
RITUAL STRIPES	Tara Black 0 352 33701 X	☐
SATURNALIA £7.99	Ed. Paul Scott 0 352 33717 6	☐
SATAN'S SLUT	Penny Birch 0 352 33720 6	☐
THE SCHOOLING OF STELLA	Yolanda Celbridge 0 352 33803 2	☐
SEE-THROUGH £5.99	Lindsay Gordon 0 352 33656 0	☐
SILKEN SLAVERY	Christina Shelley 0 352 33708 7	☐
SISTERS OF SEVERCY £5.99	Jean Aveline 0 352 33620 X	☐
SIX OF THE BEST	Wendy Swanscombe 0 352 33796 6	☐
SKIN SLAVE £5.99	Yolanda Celbridge 0 352 33507 6	☐
SLAVE ACTS	Jennifer Jane Pope 0 352 33665 X	☐
SLAVE GENESIS £5.99	Jennifer Jane Pope 0 352 33503 3	☐
SLAVE-MINES OF TORMUNIL	Aran Ashe 0 352 33695 1	☐
SLAVE REVELATIONS £5.99	Jennifer Jane Pope 0 352 33627 7	☐
SOLDIER GIRLS £5.99	Yolanda Celbridge 0 352 33586 6	☐
STRAPPING SUZETTE £5.99	Yolanda Celbridge 0 352 33783 4	☐

THE SUBMISSION GALLERY £5.99	Lindsay Gordon	0 352 33370 7 ☐
TAKING PAINS TO PLEASE	Arabella Knight	0 352 33785 0 ☐
THE TAMING OF TRUDI	Yolanda Celbridge	0 352 33673 0 ☐
A TASTE OF AMBER £5.99	Penny Birch	0 352 33654 4 ☐
TEASING CHARLOTTE	Yvonne Marshall	0 352 33681 1 ☐
TEMPER TANTRUMS £5.99	Penny Birch	0 352 33647 1 ☐
THE TRAINING GROUNDS	Sarah Veitch	0 352 33526 2 ☐
UNIFORM DOLL	Penny Birch	0 352 33698 6 ☐
VELVET SKIN £5.99	Aishling Morgan	0 352 33660 9 ☐
WENCHES, WITCHES AND STRUMPETS	Aishling Morgan	0 352 33733 8 ☐
WHIP HAND	G. C. Scott	0 352 33694 3 ☐
WHIPPING GIRL	Aishling Morgan	0 352 33789 3 ☐
THE YOUNG WIFE £5.99	Stephanie Calvin	0 352 33502 5 ☐

------ ✂ -----------------------

Please send me the books I have ticked above.

Name ....

Address ....

....

....

.... Post code ....

Send to: Cash Sales, Nexus Books, Thames Wharf Studios, Rainville Road, London W6 9HA

US customers: for prices and details of how to order books for delivery by mail, call 1-800-343-4499.

Please enclose a cheque or postal order, made payable to **Nexus Books Ltd**, to the value of the books you have ordered plus postage and packing costs as follows:
 UK and BFPO – £1.00 for the first book, 50p for each subsequent book.
 Overseas (including Republic of Ireland) – £2.00 for the first book, £1.00 for each subsequent book.

If you would prefer to pay by VISA, ACCESS/MASTERCARD, AMEX, DINERS CLUB or SWITCH, please write your card number and expiry date here:

....

Please allow up to 28 days for delivery.

Signature ....

Our privacy policy

We will not disclose information you supply us to any other parties. We will not disclose any information which identifies you personally to any person without your express consent.

From time to time we may send out information about Nexus books and special offers. Please tick here if you do *not* wish to receive Nexus information. ☐

------ ✂ -----------------------